And on the
Surface Die

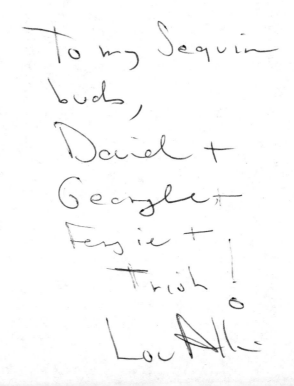

To my Sequin
buds,
David +
George +
Fergie +
Trish !

Lou Alli

And on the Surface Die

A Holly Martin Mystery

by Lou Allin

RendezVous Crime

Cover design by Vasiliki Lenis/Emma Dolan

LE CONSEIL DES ARTS
DU CANADA
DEPUIS 1957

THE CANADA COUNCIL
FOR THE ARTS
SINCE 1957

We acknowledge the support of the Canada Council for the Arts for our publishing program.

We acknowledge the financial support of the Government of Canada through the Book Publishing Industry Development Program for our publishing activities.

RendezVous Crime
An imprint of Napoleon & Company
Toronto, Ontario, Canada
www.napoleonandcompany.com

Printed in Canada on FSC standard recycled stock.

12 11 10 09 08   5 4 3 2 1

Library and Archives Canada Cataloguing in Publication

Allin, Lou, date-
        And on the surface die / Lou Allin.

ISBN 978-1-894917-74-2

        I. Title.
PS8551.L5564A64 2008   C813'.6   C2008-905620-5

To Nikon, who saw his women safely to Vancouver Island before joining Freya at Rainbow Bridge. He was a prince among dogs, and his sense of ethics amazed us.

The Kraken

Below the thunders of the upper deep;
Far, far beneath in the abysmal sea,
His ancient, dreamless, uninvaded sleep
The Kraken sleepeth: faintest sunlights flee
About his shadowy sides; above him swell
Huge sponges of millennial growth and height;
And far away into the sickly light;
From many a wondrous grot and secret cell
Unnumber'd and enormous polypi
Winnow with giant arms the slumbering green.
There hath he lain for ages and will lie
Battening upon huge seaworms in his sleep,
Until the latter fire shall heat the deep;
Then once by man and angels to be seen,
In roaring he shall rise and on the surface die.

-Alfred Tennyson

Prologue

The sea spread satiny glass across the sheltered bay. Amid lazy undulations, a blue heron rode his kelp-bed carpet and peered for minnows. White meringue clouds watched their reflections, overweighted galleons on a cerulean mirror floating towards the Olympic Mountains of Washington State. Up poked the mustachioed face of an acrobatic seal, which flipped in a lazy pose to warm its belly in the September sun. Deep below, a red rock crab found something to its liking. Soft tissue gave way as it inched along propelled by large nippers, using smaller chelipads close to the head to urge meaty delicacies into its eager maw. Then a fickle current swept the meal away, and the hapless crab dropped over a shelf to the deeper sea floor, where it was seized by an opportune Dungeness cousin.

Trailing a frothy cloud of bubbles, a snorkeler angled down for a peek at a host of purple sea urchins. Carrying an underwater camera, he feathered his fins through the heavy tendrils of bull kelp, bulbous at one end, fat whips which bobbed on the tides until tossed ashore. The man paused to admire a cluster of whelks and a nervous school of sculpins, then took a few grab shots of a sea cucumber. A forest of leathery brown rockweed, clinging to the slippy basalt with its disc-like holdfasts, drifted into his path, then the dark crimson blades of Turkish towel seaweed. Carefully he pushed it aside, startling a juvenile octopus, which had scuttled from a mollusk-mounded crevice. He checked his watch. Ten o'clock already. He should be getting back to the car. Monica was meeting him for brunch at Point No Point. With his appetite fueled by the cold water and exertion, he could almost taste their luscious cheese scones.

Then something large glided into his peripheral vision, and he turned, moving his legs to stabilize himself. Whales were common around the island, but they didn't usually come so close to shore...unless they were sick or injured. A mane of yellow hair and a chalk-pale face with vacant light-blue eyes searched his like a diffident lover. Hands clutched at him. He coughed out his mouthpiece and surged to the surface with a silent scream, choking as he yanked off his mask and thrashed his fins as if a killer shark rode his tail. When he scrabbled over the rocky shelf, his prize Canon fell onto the coral, cracking the lens.

One

You can't go home again. As a tautology, it was both as true and false as the nostalgic snows of yesteryear. Here in body, here in spirit, but many grains of sand had fallen through the hourglass.

Corporal Holly Martin opened the creaky door of the white clapboard house and saw a head turn at the reception desk and nod in pointed silence. No warm welcome on her first day in charge. Once the ice was broken with Ann Troy, she had confidence that the business of policing the small community would proceed. So far she felt like an interloper. They'd only been introduced a week ago, but how could you offend with a "hello"? Easy enough if that person had expected to have your job.

The RCMP Fossil Bay Detachment, an hour west of Victoria, British Columbia, had seen its leader, Reg Wilkinson, take early retirement. A product of sausage-and-egg breakfasts, the tall, barrel-chested man had earned a triple bypass at fifty-two and was resigned to oatmeal, cholesterol medication, and half-an-hour a day on the treadmill at his cottage in Chemainus. In a cautionary tone during their interview in his office a month ago, he'd told Holly to expect a cool reception from Ann. "She's a good officer. She'll come around." Had they been closer than colleagues? Reg was personable, a courtly charmer. Ann, a decade younger, was a single mother. At Holly's raised eyebrow,

Reg sat large and silent as the Sphinx. "None of my beeswax. You'll find all you need to know in the staff bios."

"Morning, Ann," Holly said, making a point of using the woman's name. She poured a fresh cup from the coffee maker. Half empty already. How early had the woman come in? It was only seven twenty. Holly had imagined herself opening up on her first day, asserting command if only in a minor way. "Next pot's on me. Do you like it strong?" Nothing but a shrug in response. "I brought banana bread. My dad baked it."

She placed the plate on the table and folded back the foil in unspoken invitation. Contrary to the romantic *Rose Marie* notions of red coats, a full-dress mode for special occasions, Holly wore a grey shirt, long-sleeved now in fall, with a dark blue tie, dark blue pants with gold strapping along with ankle boots spit-shined this morning, and a policeman's style cap. Leaving on her protective vest, she hung her Gore-Tex jacket in the narrow closet, tucking her hat onto the shelf and relishing the new freedom of the mild climate. In The Pas, her first post, she had worn a parka eight months of the year. Southern Vancouver Island was Canada's Caribbean. Little if any snow, but deluges of hail, sleet and rain all winter. Three sturdy umbrellas nestled in the corner.

Corporal Ann Troy wore her uniform with pride, but at 5' 4", she carried one hundred and thirty-five pounds on two fewer inches than Holly. A latecomer to the force after raising her son into his teens, Ann had been posted to Fossil Bay, on track to take over. But her intervention at an armed robbery at a convenience store had saved a young clerk's life and changed hers forever. A crazed Victoria man had gone on a one-man crime wave, stealing car after car and crashing them as he sped west on the narrow coastal road. Ann had happened on the scene as he exited the store, waving a shotgun, people screaming

4

behind him. A volleyball player in her youth, she had courted unaware the gradual onset of degenerative disk disease. The skeletal shock of tackling the large man had been the trigger that wore away the final lumbar cushion.

The exams she'd passed with honours the week before the accident gave her the nominal rank of corporal, but after an unsuccessful rehabilitation failed to improve her chronic condition, under the "duty to accommodate" regulations, she was given a desk job consisting of paperwork, phone answering and supervision of the small volunteer staff. Disability offers had been snapped back in the face of the administration. She didn't intend to sit at home and measure her life with coffee spoons. Ann lived for the law, her son Nick and her cat Bump. A framed picture of the apricot devil with its rhinestone collar sat on her desk in reception. Nick's college graduation picture had equal pride of place. He was model material, but his mouth had a kind and innocent smile. Perhaps in her happier pain-free days, Ann had once shared that attractive quality. Minutes ticked by on the wall clock as Holly sipped coffee.

"Seems quiet," Holly said in an implied question, then realized how foolish she sounded. The overture had been made. Why grovel so much that she was annoying even herself? She moved to the front window, looking out on an empty gravel lot. "Where's Chipper?"

"He took the car for servicing at Tri-City," Ann said as Holly startled at the resonant alto voice. She felt so tense from the atmosphere that blood was surfing in her ears.

"We don't have any stoplights, so nothing ever changes but the weather. Even the geese don't leave," Ann said with bitter punctuation, fixated by figures on her computer screen. She wore her lustrous dark brown hair in a short, no-nonsense style, trimmed tight around the ears.

Tiny Fossil Bay, named for the hosts of Oligocene creatures, snails, mussels and clams, which over twenty-five million years ago had become trapped in the sandstone and conglomerate of rocky beaches, consisted of barely five hundred people in a dozen streets. The fateful store where Ann had seen her life change. A Petro-Canada station. To cater to tourists, a number of seasonal B and Bs and a fishing charter. Nan's, a small restaurant, flirted with bankruptcy. The lone grade school was on the brink of closing when new housing developments at nearby Jordan River had made the board in Victoria reconsider. With unusual foresight, the RCMP detachment had been opened at the same time as the fabled Juan de Fuca and West Coast Trails had raised the number of visitors. The trio's job was to take the heat off the larger Sooke post to the east.

Holly watched the unappreciated pile of luscious banana bread. A sore back could make anyone crabby. Maybe the woman was trying to keep her weight down, too. Females could be cruelest to each other. She cursed herself for the unpolitic move. Unable to summon an appetite for a slice, she went into her office, one of four rooms in the former cottage.

On the wall were framed university diplomas and her certificate from police college. At twenty-two, she had been finishing her degree in Botany at UBC when her mother had disappeared. Desperate to help but powerless as the futile search wound down with a whimper, she'd switched to Criminal Justice courses, then joined the RCMP. Initial training took place in Regina. She had passed the exams with nearly perfect scores, been mentored for six months and served at The Pas, Manitoba. When an opening on the north island at Port McNeill arose, she was happy to return west. RCMP members were expected to move to different posts after no more than four or five years, preventing the establishment of close ties to the locals. That made marriage difficult enough for men, but an impossible dream for women.

Her final transfer, along with a bit of luck, brought her home to paradise, where roses sprouted in February. She liked the freedom of the rural and semi-wilderness setting with the amenities of nearby Victoria. Border living was another advantage. Seattle was a quick ferry ride.

British Columbia, known as E Division, encompassing policing at most provincial, federal, and municipal levels, was the largest in Canada, with 126 detachments and over 6,000 employees, about one-third of the total RCMP enlistment. Only twelve municipalities in B.C. had their own forces, and on the island, only Victoria, the capital city. The island itself had only 850 officers spread across its wilderness, many hours away from back-up.

At thirty-two, in a few more years, she could take the exam for sergeant, then staff-sergeant. At that level, she'd command a post with fourteen members, not including civilians, a comfortable number. Holly wanted to stay on the island, but moving any higher up the ranks would mean a transfer to a larger city with noise, crowding and major crimes. Call her unambitious, lover of Lalaland, but Holly had no desire to walk mean streets, even in Nanaimo, though she might entertain the idea if she could join a Canine Unit.

With a proprietorial eye, she considered her new preserve and nosed stale cigarette smoke from the decades before the new laws. A coat of paint wouldn't hurt. That she could do herself. And maybe an area rug. Then a few hardy plants and a picture of her German shepherds, now playing at Rainbow Bridge.

She resigned herself to paperwork, reading the latest crime figures for the province. The Capital Region of Victoria had one of the lowest stats in the country for gun-related incidents, fewer than one per cent. Knives were more popular. Among the bulletins on emerging technologies for law enforcement, one report claimed that soon pistols would be personalized; only the owner could fire it. An officer shot with his or her own gun would be an ugly irony of the past. Another focused on robotic delivery of pepper spray in cases where the suspect couldn't be approached. Every black-leather duty belt held OC, aka pepper spray, along with metal handcuffs, a 9 mm Military and Police Smith and Wesson, a collapsible asp baton, keys, and a radio. Only those who chose to take an orientation carried the controversial Taser. Recent deaths across the country and in the U.S. had raised serious questions about the excessive use of that defensive weapon. The Taser should be used as a last resort before the gun, not merely to subdue without breaking into a sweat.

From the monthly statistics Ann had compiled, Holly pinpointed the petty efforts at crime that dogged the community. Reg had told her what to expect, and she'd had a taste in Port McNeill. Thefts, stolen vehicles, noise complaints, unruly dogs and unrulier drunks. Now and then a police car visited the many beach parks down the coast on open-container violations or to take a report on an auto break-in. French Beach, China, Mystic, Bear, all the way to Botanical, a necklace of rain-forest emeralds beckoned tourists from California to Calcutta.

"Don't discount penny-ante crime," Ben Rogers, her mentor in The Pas, had told her. "Sometimes they're part of a bigger picture, and it usually involves drugs. Why steal a CD player you can sell for only a twenty unless you need another fix?" But Ben had made his own fatal error. Their last month together, checking out a stolen car seen at a trailer park, he hadn't expected the twelve-year-old deaf boy to be holding a

8

rifle instead of an air gun. The frightened child fired, and Reg went down with a hole in his chest where his heart had been. Holly had secured the rifle, turned the boy over to a motherly bystander, then cradled Ben's head in her lap until the ambulance came. When she'd cleaned his office to give personal items to his wife, the *Classic Car* calendar's date read "Ninety-nine days to go!"

Around eight fifteen, a bump of unidentifiable music sounded outside, a cheerful whistle came up the walk, and into the office came Constable Chirakumar "Chipper" Knox Singh. Though both his parents were Sikhs, his father had been raised in a Scottish Presbyterian orphanage in the Punjab and baptized with the name of Knox. Like many immigrants, Gopal Singh had worked menial jobs, living like a pauper, finally able to open a convenience store with an ethnic foods sideline in nearby Colwood. Transferred last year from his first post in the Prairies, twenty-eight-year-old Chipper wore a handsome light-blue turban, designed for the force, with a yellow patch to match the stripe down his pants. A trim light-brown beard set off his café-au-lait face. Earnest black eyebrows capped a handsome brow and fine features. At six-three, he towered over the women.

He saw Holly and saluted. "Welcome, Corporal, or should I call you 'Guv'?" he asked with a grin.

"You've been watching the BBC too much." Her cheeks pinked, and she wondered if Ann had heard the informal exchange.

"Blame my mother. She never misses *Coronation Street*. Anyway, the car's all set. That squeal was the fan belt. No big deal.

Hoping to make an ally, she pointed to the banana bread. "Dig in."

The phone rang, and Ann answered. As she listened, a frown creased her freckled brow, and she wrote rapidly on a pad. "Calm down and tell me what happened. There's no rush *now,* is there?" Her manner reminded Holly of her own mother, who could still troubled waters with a quiet assertiveness. Clearly here was one of Ann's strengths.

Holly and Chipper exchanged glances. His hand paused over a slice, then plunged in as if he might lose the opportunity. Holly felt her heart battery switch to recharge. Another impatient speeder trying to pass on deadly West Coast Road? The logging trucks were making the most of the dry weather. The last few summers had brought increasing drought. She hardly recalled the most recent rain, more the promise of a kiss. Relentless dust made washing her car a never-ending chore.

"We'll be right out. Half an hour, barring traffic." Ann listened, taking a few notes and pausing for confirmation.

"That long? Can't be Bill Purdy beating up on his wife again." An "old hand" after his first year at Fossil Bay, Chipper had memorized the names of the local troublemakers. Finishing the snack, he gave an appreciative "mmmmm" and wiped his handsome mouth with a serviette. His shirt and pants were ironed razor sharp. Mother's work. Chipper still lived at home in the apartment over the store, though his parents had been trying to arrange a marriage for him with a nurse in Sidney. Holly hoped he wouldn't be transferred too soon. He was bright, ethical and personable, a winning combination in any profession. Though she'd only met him when Reg had given her an orientation, she'd studied the personnel files as part of her homework. Yet records often weren't the measure of a person. No one looking at the three of them would realize that the thickset older woman was the hero.

"There's been a drowning at Botanical. A girl...just a teenager." Ann stood and stretched. A casual gesture in some interpretation, but Reg said that she did simple exercises every few hours to ease her back muscles. "She tries to stay off painkillers on the job," he had added. "But don't call her after dinner when she's been into the sauce. That's why she's better at a desk with regular hours in a small detachment with eight-hour shifts instead of ten. Policing's a 24-7-365 job, especially with a skeleton staff."

Holly massaged the bridge of her nose, sad but not surprised at the news. The tides were renowned for their dangerous and quixotic nature. In bad winds, a rogue wave could snatch a storm watcher from the beach, sending the body down the Strait of Juan de Fuca. A boy who'd been lost this year at Tofino had never been found. At least it wasn't a brutal and bloody car wreck. Holly had noticed the new vogue for commemorative descansos along the coastal road: flower tributes, stuffed animals, even a scooter. The concept seemed better adapted to hot, dry climates instead of rain-forest country. "A drowning?"

Ann sighed, the corners of her mouth sad commas. Pale from lack of sun, she wore no make-up, and small wrinkles sucked at the top of her thin upper lip. Old laugh-lines creased the edges of her hazel eyes, but the face was humourless. Was she on medication now? As her commanding officer, Holly should know, but asking would be tricky. And certainly not on Day One.

Ann's fingers flipped a page in her notes. "Apparently. There seemed to be some head injury at first glance. Kids should know better than to dive, but they do. I told them to leave everything in place. You know the likelihood of that, though. Someone already pulled the body from the water."

Chipper shook his head as he looked at a wall map. "I've

been there a couple of times. That beach is very rough. How will we secure the scene? Sand, rock, a nightmare for evidence."

"Evidence." Holly tossed him a skeptical look and tapped his arm. "Come on, Chipper. Let's not jump to conclusions. And we don't know where the victim went in. She could have floated on the currents down the coast for miles."

"No missing person reports," he said, scanning the bulletin board. "But it could be recent, maybe a boating acci—"

"What are you two going on about?" Ann broke in. "We have an ID."

Deciding to ignore the woman's abruptness, Holly shivered. The idea of looking at a floater didn't appeal to her. "How long had she been gone?"

Ann touched a finger to her long sharp nose. "Lucky you. The girl was in camp only last night. Annual high-school senior bonding exercise. Not enough chaperones. Never are. Not all the armies in the world can stop hormones when their time has come."

Holly saw Ann's eyes glance at the graduation picture of her son. Was that what had happened? As Holly's plain-spoken mother reminded her, nothing could screw up a woman's life faster than an early, unplanned pregnancy. Life was an uphill battle after that, not impossible, but tough on everyone. "No-fail protection," Bonnie Martin had said in a wry tone to her bored young daughter in their birds-and-bees talk, crossing her fingers in a telling gesture. "Keep your legs closed."

"Paramedics have the location, but they're tied up for an hour. No need for resuscitation in this case, sadly." As the two headed out, Ann added, "I'll call Boone."

Boone? Hadn't Reg mentioned a coroner? "Oh, right. Thanks." Her mind racing, Holly grimaced. Her first serious situation as a leader, and she wasn't even rolling on four wheels. What did

12

anyone expect from a tiny outpost, one staff member chained to a desk? Suppose something didn't look right? Should a murder investigation ever be necessary, protocol dictated that larger resources would come to her service. Sooke was headed by a staff-sergeant, so an inspector would come from Langford, the West Shore detachment. She gave herself a mental scold as calming logistics kicked in. Why be so dramatic? This is going to be simple but monumentally tearful, as are all senseless young deaths.

After grabbing her pristine notebook, Holly headed for her jacket. "So we're off, and—"

Ann looked up with a slow, deliberate question. "Don't you want to know the girl's name?"

Holly turned away to bite her lip. "Of course. Guess I'm just...never mind." Confessing her weaknesses to this woman was not an option.

Ann said. "Angie Didrickson." Then she spelled it.

Outside, as they approached the five-year-old white Impala, Chipper patted the trunk, frowning. "We should have our own FB decal, not SK." The huge black initials helped helicopters identify each detachment and coordinate efforts.

"We're lucky to get Sooke's castoffs. I was guessing a quad and a couple of bikes," Holly said, belting up. Parked behind their building was a 1985 Suburban with 250,000 Ks, another donation from the big dogs. Still, it would come in handy in winter if they had to go off-road or up the tortuous steep hills north into the San Juan Ridge.

As they headed down West Coast Road with Chipper at the wheel, ugly clear-cuts began skirting the road. "Not even a margin any more," Chipper said. "Is this going to be the next Sun River, with thousands of houses?"

"It's oceanfront or oceanview. Pure gold. Only the zoning gods will hold the balance."

13

Checking the time, Chipper reached for the siren, but she said, "Leave it off. No need to pass on this road. It's too late for her, and it'll only frighten the tourists and attract gawkers. We don't want a parade."

They slowed at Jordan River, no longer a landing site for logs, as in its historic past. Electrical generation from the river had first reached Victoria in 1911, and the massive structure of the old powerhouse upstream had once attracted visitors. More people came to surf now than to ogle ancient buildings, and the storms of fall and winter brought peak conditions. Though there was only a brisk wind today, six or seven hopeful people on boards paddled out to catch the waves. The Chula Coffee and Juice Bar sold exotic fruit drinks and custom coffee, the closest Canada came to Malibu. At the beach, campers and vans lined the shore, some VWs with flower-power paint jobs. Every so often, a free camping spot could be found, but for how long?

Holly owed her job to what loomed ahead, a billboard advertising the first major housing development west of Fossil Bay. To her left and right, great roads were being dozed into the woods or carved across former clear-cut hills. Million-dollar properties, especially on the oceanfront. Recent rulings by the Minister of Forests, with no consultation or conditions, had threatened to allow the timber companies to turn tens of thousands of hectares of lease land into lucrative real estate. Hit hard by a downturn in demand for timber products, the companies claimed that their debts could be settled better from immediate revenue, not wood scheduled to be cut in 2050. Mills were closing everywhere, from Nanaimo to Campbell River. Citizens and environmentalists fought back in public meetings, and surprisingly draconian zoning laws had temporarily halted the deals. Everyone knew that the battle had merely paused for breath. The boomers were on the move, especially from Ontario, and those not able to afford houses in costly Victoria wanted property. Moving vans went west and returned empty. Meanwhile, laid-off timber employees wondered if they should join the building trades.

The farther they drove, the paler Chipper looked. He took a hand off the wheel to rub his cheek. She noticed that he had left the music off. "Anything wrong?" Holly asked.

He shook his head like a wet dog. "Uh, I've never seen a body before." He swallowed back his words as if to master a gag reflex. "Wish I hadn't eaten such a big breakfast. Spicy food and stress don't mix, but I couldn't hurt Mom's feelings."

She smiled to herself. Even a few more years gave her the edge. It was the way of the force to pass on wisdom and experience. Not everyone made a good candidate. Ben Rogers, her old mentor, had been chosen for his intuition, coolness, talent for details and tact. He'd never use tasteless slang or refer to a victim as a "crispy critter" to draw a cheap laugh.

"There's a first time for everyone," Holly said. "Mine was pretty bad. The victim had been lying in a remote bush camp for a week in thirty degree Celsius temperatures. His wife sent us looking when he was days late returning from hunting. A pro told me to put Mentholatum in my nostrils."

He reached into a storage compartment and pulled out a tube. "Cherry Lipsol. Do you think this will work?"

"It made me sneeze, and anyway, this girl...Angie just died." She gave him a quick glance and sent a challenge she knew he couldn't ignore. "You can stand to the side, Constable. No problem." In public, Holly automatically reverted to rank instead of a first name, a tenet of professionalism. And calling civilians "you guys" was equally prohibited. "You're not a waitress in a truck stop," Ben had told her.

"No, Guv, I mean ma'am," he said as his nostrils flared like a young stallion's. "Count on me. I'll be your right-hand man."

A red hawk drifted on the thermals over the cliffs. She closed her eyes for a moment as the car streaked along at eighty kilometres per hour. A campfire last night, headed for a coffin in the morning. How large was the group, and how many other people were in the popular area, enjoying the scenery? Then she sent relaxation messages to her flexed stomach. It was an accident, nothing more. Over and out. Nervous this morning, she had breakfasted on only an apple. Now she felt slightly nauseous from the coffee.

"Careful: Winding Road," the sign read. The island's terrain was like an overlapping series of green, ribbed reptiles. Water flowed off the glaciated hills as quickly as it arrived. With only thirty more kilometres to Port Renfrew, the speed limit slowed to fifty on hairpin turns. Little opportunity to pass unless courting suicide. "Jeez," Chipper said. "These bicycles." They watched as five racers, their heads bent low, legs pumping like young locomotives, sped along in line. Technically they owned the lane, but sometimes they would shift over like a flock of birds if the berm was smooth. Holly wouldn't have risked it. A small pebble under the skinny wheel might skew a rider under a tractor-trailer tire.

"Hit the siren and lights," she said. "Polite isn't cutting it."

He flicked switches with a grin. The teardrop-helmeted crew shot glances over their shoulders and moved aside smartly. Once past, the car moved in silence, Chipper with his strong hands at ten and two on the wheel.

Twenty minutes later, they reached the small town at the end of the line. There were only bush roads north to Fairy Lake, Lizard Lake, and massive Lake Cowichan from that point on. Fewer than two hundred white people lived here, with half as many First Nations members in the immediate area. Originally the Pacheedaht tribe had made their homes on the coast and throughout the San Juan Valley. Earliest contacts had been prickly between the locals and newcomers, starting in 1798, when the crew from HMS *Iphigenia* engaged the residents in a dispute. Though logging had waned and the railroad tracks had been replaced by a road, the old beach camp area was soon converted to houses. By lucky coincidence, Port Renfrew sat at the L-shaped confluence of the northerly West Coast Trail and the easterly Juan de Fuca Marine Trail, which ended at Botanical Beach. The beach had been recognized at the turn of the twentieth century as such a gold mine of tidal life that the University of Minnesota had set up a research station. Though that unit was long defunct, strict regulations applied to the pristine shoreline. PICO meant "pack in and carry out."

Nor was the beach the only attraction. From her younger days camping and exploring, Holly knew that nearby a forest legend spread its roots, sucking up the twelve feet of rain. The largest Douglas fir tree in the world, the Red Creek fir, with a circumference of over forty-one feet, grew on the outskirts of town. Passing the tourist centre, modest restaurants, a motel and a quaint old inn, they took the turn for the beach. Minutes later, they reached the parking lot and pulled through the gate, guided by a man waving his arms. In his early sixties, in a tan park uniform with shorts and knee socks English style, he was probably retired and happy for the extra money in a part-time job. On a boom box in his battered camo-coloured Jeep, an oldies station was playing "Love Me Tender". He sipped from a water bottle and wiped his mouth with the back of his hand as they got out of the car. Splotched cheeks testified to a long life of malt appreciation.

"I didn't hear you guys coming. What happened to the siren?"

Holly shook her head. Expectations already. Around the lot were parked a dozen cars and an assortment of trucks, vans and campers, with visitors from Alberta, Saskatchewan and Washington. The pay-for-parking machine sold daily windshield tickets for three dollars. Sporadic attempts to break into the little coin banks were another reason for regular RCMP patrol, though it was nearly impossible to catch someone in the act.

She made the introductions. "Are the students camping here? It wasn't allowed in my day."

Tim Jones waved a gnarly hand. "No way. Botanical's too fragile and rare for that kind of disturbance. There's an RV park in town. 'Course, you can't always stop it. Shut the gate, they find a way around. Nature of the beast to keep trying. I live nearby and take a final look-see with the wife at nine, then I'm outta here. Come nightfall, some hitchhike, get dropped off, slip into the bush. Kind of a dare. Can't blame them. Harmless enough, romantic even." He gave Chipper a "between us men" look.

Holly opened her notebook, freshly inked and dated. Day One of My New In-Charge Career. Ben had collected what looked like thousands, neatly lined up in cabinets at home, to consult as backup to his court appearances. "Where will we find Angie?" She hoped she'd never become so hardened that bodies lost their identities. It was too late to help the girl, but the least she could do was serve her in the formalities of death.

"Follow that path. Come out on the beach, then go right a couple hundred feet till you come to a big mother chunk of fir with roots halfway to the sky. I call it Butt." As he read their faces, he gave a self-deprecating cough. "No offense. That's a logging term for the bottom of the tree. Kids are always building driftwood shelters off old Butt. Just lay on boards or straight branches. They float out with each high tide. Butt's dug in like a two-ton tick. It would take the mother of all storms to carry him away."

After grabbing a roll of yellow tape from the trunk, Chipper assumed a straight and serious posture which made him even taller. "Should we secure the scene, Corporal?"

"Good idea. Last thing we want is to wade through a bunch of thrill seekers. A girl is dead here." She told Tim to keep an eye out for Mason Boone, the coroner, though from Reg's description, he would be hard to miss. Meanwhile, Tim folded his arms in vigilance as if he were participating in a crime show.

The bright sun and warm temperatures made the beach an ideal destination, especially on a less-crowded weekday. Knotty shore pines bent from the ocean blasts, and swooping cypress shaded the area beneath the massive trunks of Douglas firs spared from the axe. They marched down the path with a "beach" sign, the gravel from the lot quickly turning into sand and duff. Halfway, a nearly new mountain bike lay on its side, unlocked and ready for the taking.

"That's a beauty, but the owner is an idiot," Chipper said. "A camera was stolen from a car here last week."

"We'd better tell Tim. Maybe he can keep the bike safe at the gate until the owner returns. A cheap lesson."

In a cool, wet section heavy with deer fern and shiny, rampaging salal, Holly spotted a banana slug in the middle of the path. Seven inches long, it was a leopard, haute-couture cousin to the traditional army khaki model. She bent down and gently lifted the creature to safety. "I brake for detrivores," she said.

Chipper watched with a nostalgic smile. "In my survival course, we had to eat one of those. The wusses cooked it first. Once the...guts are out, a pinch of curry makes the difference. Everyone laughed. Then they all wanted some."

"You must carry an unusual kit." With a disgusted moue, she inspected the slime on her hands. "I don't know why I do this. Maybe I'm thinking I might be reincarnated as one, not that I'm a Buddhist, or is it Hindu?"

"Whatever, I think the idea is to move *up* the ladder."

"Hey, except for being slow and gummy, they vacuum the earth with only one lung. What more heavenly duties can you ask of a creature?"

They traversed a grove of sumac with wild roses blooming and forming rose hips, faint perfume for a funeral, not a wedding. The deepening sand, holding hardy beach plants such as silverleaf and yellow verbena, was littered with footprints, rough going for their leather boots.

Some island beaches were Hollywood stretches of fine silica, but Botanical had no pleasures for the foot, only tidal pools carved from sandstone and interspersed with ridges of shale, quartz and black basalt. As they hit the rock-shelved shore and turned, she saw why Tim had christened the huge stump "Butt". What great wind had toppled the tree, and what greater tide had ferried it here, she couldn't imagine. A photographer's dream, except for crude initials carved into its bulk, it lay on its side, and from a branched bare root, pieces of driftwood artfully arranged like planks made a whimsical but secure shelter. Sand underneath had been scooped out so that two people could crawl out of the wind. Closer to the water, they picked their way between glistening tidal pools etched by time, wind and creatures like sea anemones, which hollowed out round homes for their delicate filaments.

A small group had gathered behind the berm of logs and twig trash at the high-tide line. American sea rocket and gumweed, hardy survivors, brushed at Holly's pants as she walked. By itself, away down the grey basalt shore, was a small bundle. Blinking in the bright light, Holly tipped back her cap and swore softly.

"Covered with a blanket. And twenty feet from the edge. These rocks could have given her fresh abrasions."

Chipper shielded his face from the sun. "But the medical examiner can tell. No bleeding post mortem, right?"

"Perhaps if a bone is broken with no bruising, that would be the case." The winds had been high last night, she recalled. Unable to sleep, she had heard waves crashing onto the shore at midnight.

The tide was still going out, but the turn would come. The wind had risen, and a small chop rode the waves. Plumes of spray crashed over the rocks and soaked her boots. She turned to the crowd and managed a friendly but serious smile. "I'm Corporal Martin, investigating the accident. In a few minutes, after we've looked around, I'd like to speak to some of you about what you might have seen, starting with the person who found Angie. If you have any information, please wait at the picnic table over there. And could the rest of you clear the beach until we're finished? It would make our job easier." She saw three or four children carrying foam snakes and plastic beach pails. "We'd appreciate your taking the young ones a long distance away."

She heard a few mutterings, but her politeness seemed to work. Except for five or six people, the crowd dispersed. A man of about thirty in swim trunks checked his watch pointedly, then came forward. Lean, with knotty muscles, he sported a colourful tattoo of a dragon, its fiery tongue licking around one shoulder. His hairy legs were slightly bowed. A few knee scrapes testified to the unforgiving rocky shelves. A trickle of blood still flowed. "I saw her in the water. Bob Johnson. It's getting late for me, so could we—"

Taking a deep breath, Holly met his eyes until he lowered them. "Did you move this girl, Mr. Johnson?"

His voice wavered, and he swiped a hand through his thinning blond hair. "Jesus. It...she was floating in the bay, trapped in the kelp bed. You know these riptides. Another minute, and she could have been dragged out to sea. Thought I was helping out, lady...officer."

Holly glanced around. Chipper had roped off his fourth tree, hand on his slim hips, and was admiring his work. "I understand. As I said, we need to check the scene first. You'll be first in line when we're ready. That's a promise, sir."

He grunted and moved off, moving his arms in a "what can you do" expression.

After slipping on latex gloves, Chipper and Holly walked forward. Wind, waves, people running about. Already the scene was a circus. Whatever happened to death in a quiet room? Then she chastised herself, reaffirming the sobriety of the moment. She knelt by the form and gently withdrew the blanket, an old army-surplus model. Probably gathering every sort of material in a car trunk since Mulroney left office. The girl's eyes stared up at her, revealing the milky sheen of death. The effect wasn't as shocking as she'd thought, poignant instead. It reminded her of the bright red starfish she'd once brought home from French Beach and left outside to dry on the steps. Slowly it had faded to white, the elusive spark of life gone. Over weeks it disintegrated into calcifications, then blew away as if it had never existed.

Holly blinked, pulling herself back. No major damage was evident on Angie's face, but scrapes and cuts from the rocks and the marine life would make the coroner's job trickier. Crows passed raucous approval from the trees. Ever vigilant for food, a host of motley juvenile seagulls floated on the waves, scavenging sea creatures. One on shore pecked at a blue-black mussel shell. One creature's bier was another's smorgasbord.

"God, look at that."

TWO

Chipper pointed to an area half an inch long on one of the girl's forearms, where tiny predators had been chewing in furtherance of future generations. He put his hand over his mouth and stumbled away, one foot tripping in the cracks that fractured the basalt.

"Who's in charge here? I passed a few villages missing their idiots, or isn't that phrase acceptable these days?" a jovial voice called, panting for breath around the stem of a corncob pipe. Mason Boone ambled forward, lugging a large black satchel that might have done duty at 22 Baker Street. His rice-sack gut pooched under suspendered grey work pants. Hush Puppies slurping on the wet rock, he urged his bulk toward them with surprising grace.

The B.C. Coroners Service was a unique animal, setting fast and tangled roots in one of Canada's younger provinces, much of which was still wilderness outside of the sushi bars of Vancouver and the tea rooms of Victoria. The province employed twenty-one full-time coroners, but the approximately one hundred and twenty community coroners dispersed throughout the territory worked on an as-needed basis. Some thought that anyone of good character could qualify as a community coroner, but the preferred background was in the legal, investigative and medical fields. Retired nurses and lawyers made good choices. They did not perform autopsies, but should circumstances warrant, they authorized pathologists to take charge. They were responsible for assembling the facts in a death: identifying the deceased and how, when, where and by what means the person died. Complicated forensics were left to the medical examiner, if one were needed. Fault or blame was not the coroner's bailiwick, though no one should be incurious.

Boone Mason had been a private investigator in Vancouver before a knee had blown on him during a handball game and compromised his mobility. At sixty-five, he lived quietly off a disability pension supplemented by his occasional coroner assignment and Texas hold'em poker winnings at the legion. His relationship with the RCMP in the Western Communities wasn't smooth. A stubborn nature often made him a gadfly. "He's a good man with a beak for the truth," Reg had told her. "Pain in the ass or not, don't underestimate him."

"Poets are goddamn liars. Death is never pretty," he said after introductions as he put down his satchel and snapped on a pair of latex gloves. He tucked the pipe, apparently empty, into his shirt pocket. "I can see why that poor slob pulled her on shore. Natural reaction. But if anything's hinky, Christ on a cupcake."

Holly felt her chest tighten. She looked for Chipper, but he was still parked on the other side of a Sitka spruce. A white handkerchief had come from his pocket, as if he had given up the battle. "But how could you—"

Boone turned his grizzled face to hers. He had assumed the retired male's habit of shaving only when necessary, but stopped short of wearing a beard like a hundred local Santas. She could also see why Reg had mentioned his nose for the truth. Large and craggy, it gave him the look of a friendly vulture. "Ninety-nine per cent of drownings are accidents. It's up to me to make recommendations to prevent future harm.

25

Relax. Just making small talk. Reg told me you were taking over. Figured you needed some fatherly guidance."

He pulled away the rest of the blanket. Holly's throat felt like she was trying to devour a four-headed balloon animal. Boone gave her a sidelong glance. "First body?"

"No, but first day in charge. Some timing."

"Shoulda stood in bed." He chuckled to himself and narrowed his eyes in assessment. "Craziest saying. Don't know what the hell it signifies."

With straightened shoulders, Chipper had returned to the periphery and was studiously avoiding any connection with the body, his dark glance following a bald eagle high overhead, its feeble peeping cry belying its reputation as king of birds. From far away, Holly could see inquiring heads in the underbrush and hear fragmented comments. Walking over, she directed Chipper to keep away the onlookers, who, now that the coroner had arrived, sensed a melodramatic story to take home to Anacortes or Kamloops. "This looks straightforward enough. Maybe we'll get lucky and avoid complications," she said, back at Boone's side.

"We're already luckier than she was. And besides, complications make life interesting. Doncha like no challenges?" Boone rotated the neck and head, then parted the hair, frowning. "Serious blow to the side of the head. From a dive or a fall. At the edges of the cove where the rocks meet the water." Then taking out a thermometer, he positioned himself to shield the body and turned Angie onto her side with a gentle "Up we go, darlin'." Holly followed an instinct to flinch and turned away as if to keep an eye on the crowd. Squeezing her fists until the nails bit the palm, she knelt next to him. The girl wore a bikini, and wore it well. Not an ounce of fat, and a neat six-pack revealed long-term toning, if not avid body building. An athlete? The shoulders were broad, the hips slim. Her legs and arms had been shaved. A swimmer? Odd that she hadn't worn her hair short, but she'd probably used a cap. On her shoulder was a tasteful blue rose. How many teens didn't have a tattoo?

Boone then placed the thermometer in the water for a short while, retrieving it with a nod. "Nearly water temperature. Not surprising. Plays hell with rigor and time of death. Not as bad as being in an air-conditioned or heated room, though." He looked up, breaking into Holly's thoughts. "You and the rajah could give a gander to the area. We're not going to be able to hold this scene for long. Wind and waves wait for no man." Holly bristled at the unexpected racial jibe, nor did she appreciate the directives. They were more or less equals, each with a job. "How about watching your language, Mr. Boone?"

He grinned and poked her leg. "Just kidding. Lighten up. My late wife of forty years was born in Bombay or Mumbai, whatever. One hell of a cook when it came to pilafs and curries. And it's plain Boone to my friends."

Holly looked down and toed away a string of kelp affixed to her boot. Now she'd alienated the coroner. Things had been so different when Ben Rogers called the shots. "So, does there have to be an autopsy? Is it at the discretion of the parents?"

"Not always, but no to your second question. It's my call. Vic Daso at the Jubilee will probably take this one. He's a crackerjack. Help if we could find some witnesses so we could figure this out," Boone added, rocking back on his bulging haunches. In the distance, a siren was wailing.

Holly had seen a couple of drownings in The Pas, when snowmobilers had gone down crossing the narrows on fickle Cedar Lake. March was the worst month. People got cocky about conditions, especially when alcohol was involved. Men in their twenties were the prime offenders, thought they were invincible and rejected flotation suits and hand picks as sissy gear. She searched her mind for the few training classes on autopsies.

"He'll check for water in the lungs, though there is such a thing as a dry drowning."

"That seems like a conflict in terms."

"Not really. Ever jumped into icy water? Shock makes the throat constrict. So the victim dies from lack of air. Suffocation, to be exact. He'll run a toxicology report. It's fair to believe that there's been drinking at this party, if not drugs. Pot. Cocaine. Meth, I doubt."

In the recesses of the tidal pool flats, a round, pinkish shape shimmered in a half inch of water. Anemone. She touched it with her finger, and it shrank into itself. Odd that it knew exactly where to move and where to stay. Up nearer the tide line, it would find itself dry, if only for a few hours, and die. But then, perhaps some of the fairy-like creatures had done just that and exited the gene pool.

"Penny for 'em. Make that a loonie. Flying higher than the eagle these days." Boone stared at her in some amusement.

"Wool gathering, as my grandmother used to say. What was that about meth?" A rare frown cut the space between her eyebrows.

He stuck out his lower lip in cogitation. There was a slight scar on one end. "In more urban areas, we're starting to assemble a nice mix of stats on meth overdoses, but Notre Dame Catholic Academy? Probably not."

Notre Dame. Ann hadn't passed on such specific information, and why would she? Holly felt the beginnings of an ugly trip down memory lane. Fourteen years ago, she'd said a joyous goodbye to that private school in Sooke and its snobs and cliques. She'd been a maverick and proud of it. The only faculty member she'd respected was the crusty librarian, Sister

28

Dympna. How often she'd hidden out there and buried herself in books on trees, flowers, birds and animals of the island. At that time, the school had been all-girl, a deadly species, gatekeepers to a private hell. Her one friend Valerie, a natural comic and troublemaker, had joined the army and hadn't been in contact since.

"How did you know which school it was?"

He rubbed his chin, making a rasping sound. "Ann said when she called me."

Two paramedics made their way down with a stretcher. "Sorry to take so long. Hydro was taking a leaning tree at the Shirley curve. About time, but traffic was backed up for miles."

"That's all right, boys. She's in no hurry." Boone packed away his kit and motioned for the stretcher. "Good to go. Time of death's not going to be easy. First in the water, then in the sun. Sure hope someone saw her somewhere sometime. Stomach content will be a helpful factor."

Holly stripped off her gloves. "That's what bothers me. Was she here alone? That seems strange." Not for herself, though. She'd spent many quiet evenings on a beach, beside a small driftwood fire, thinking her own young thoughts as she grilled hot dogs.

Chipper had assembled a collection of paper evidence bags as they joined him. "Lots of trash. An open condom foil. Probably means nothing. It's a beach, a place for partying."

"Cleaner than most," Holly said. Volunteers patrolled on a regular basis to polish their world-class jewel.

As Boone walked off and the paramedics knelt to attend to the body, Holly checked the boundaries. Chipper had done well, but if something had been overlooked, now was the time to find it. She passed a clump of Saskatoon berry bushes, generously dangling their luscious, supersweet fruits. A tall bunch of innocuous-looking plants threatened to brush her sleeve, and she pulled away. Stinging nettle. Fine in soup but painful to even the slightest brush. Then under a bush she saw a loose braid of greenery. To anyone else it might have appeared natural, but Holly's trained eye spotted the anomaly. She inhaled its pleasant herbal aroma. Common sweetgrass, used in purification ceremonies among aboriginal North Americans.

At the parking lot, she took a fresh bag from Chipper, then watched Boone drive off in his rusty Land Rover, the tailpipe held in place by wire, nodding fractious acquaintance with the gravel. "What's that?" Chipper asked, searching her eyes in a gesture of uncertainty.

"Sweetgrass."

He considered the bundle, wrinkling his nose. "Like weed?"

She tried not to laugh. "No, First Nations people don't smoke sweetgrass. They burn it like incense."

His face brightened. "My mother loves sandalwood. She has a shrine to Ganesh. So what's your take on this?" he asked.

"A blank slate. Safest that way. Let's go talk to everyone. They've been patient...curious more than rude. If longer statements are warranted, if there's been negligence on the part of the school, we can call them back. There could be conditions for a lawsuit here, and we might need to testify. "

Holly introduced herself to a group at the picnic table. "I'm going to talk to Mr. Johnson here, then Constable Singh and I will get your names and addresses."

One tall and muscular girl with a tongue ring spoke up. "How come? Wasn't it an accident?"

Holly kept her voice low and reasonable, a combination of seriousness and approachability. "Just routine."

When she heard a young man whisper "raghead" to his buddy, she shot him a stern look. A study in neutral, Chipper revealed neither by face or demeanor that he had heard anything.

She and Bob Johnson took seats on a huge log twenty feet from the group. Holly was determined to take her time and do things right from the start. "Mr. Johnson, you're probably not familiar with our procedure for statements, but this is how it works. Tell me what happened in a chronological order. I ask questions and listen. Then you tell me again, and I write it down. I read it back to you to check the accuracy. Nothing too formal at this point." She was trying to cover all the bases but realized how difficult that was with only a staff of two to handle a crowd. Suppose she missed something important? And worse yet, someone might be lying. The basic training scenarios, domestic violence, auto accidents, didn't match. She thought of the tricky bar-fight scenario. How to winnow out those with helpful evidence and ignore the time-wasters, not to mention the confused drunks. With the events leading up to Angie's death possibly taking place after dark, the circumstances called for a thorough investigation, leaving no one out. As Boone had said, certain information might help prevent future tragedies.

Bob told her what he had witnessed and when. He'd arrived at eight and snorkeled for an hour. Natural underwater treasures were one of the island's greatest attractions. Because of its stable temperatures, the Northern Pacific had the greatest number of species compared to the more frigid oceans. Ninety species of starfish against only twenty in the North Atlantic. "One of the year's lowest tides today. One metre. You can get out to the good stuff. Plumrose anemones, red urchins, maybe even a coon-striped shrimp or a sea cucumber if you dive deep enough." He'd come back to the beach to snack on the coffee and muffin he'd brought, then gone back in for another half hour. That's when he'd found Angie.

"And you're by yourself here?" Holly asked. "Where do you live, for the record?"

"Oak Bay. We have a condo."

With that tony address, Holly pegged him as an up-and-coming executive, especially when he added that he worked in Vancouver for Dell Computers. He also said that his pictures had appeared in *B.C. Magazine.*

Then she turned to a man who stepped forward with a mild air of authority. Well-groomed, his dark red hair with half-sideburns, he had a winning smile and soft grey eyes, crinkled at the edges. By his side on a leash was a tiny Yorkie, whimpering petulantly at the commotion. He picked it up and rubbed its silken head. A Harley Davidson bandana circled its neck. "Chucky," he said. "More like the movie. He's a real devil."

An animal lover, Holly reached forward in reflex to pet the dog, but it gave a wicked growl, then a snap, and she pulled back her hand with an involuntary gasp.

"Sorry," he said and gave the dog a mock shake, fastening its leash. "I'm Paul Gable. Vice principal." He gave a gentle smile, then firmed up his lips as he watched her turn a fresh page. "It's hard to believe this is happening. I don't know where to start."

He explained that Notre Dame sponsored a senior trip at the start of the year. The class had raised money through candy sales and car washes. Botanical Beach had been chosen for the hiking, kayaking, swimming and marine life, as well as its convenient distance from Sooke. That the area was rural and isolated was a bonus, since administrators hoped to keep the inevitable substance abuse to a minimum. They couldn't prevent the occasional mickey of rye, but at least driving was already arranged. This year, two teachers had come down with early flu, so they were short on supervision. "I had to fill in myself at the last minute. Camping with teenagers isn't my choice of weekend activities."

Holly looked around. The crowd at the fringes had vanished. A slight headache from the sun began to explore her temples. Her hat felt tight. "So where are your students now?"

He looked wary, then embarrassed. "Um. Hope I didn't make a bad decision, but I loaded up the kayaks and sent them back in the vans."

"Back to?" If the students had already left for home, this was going to be much more difficult.

"To the campsite in Port Renfrew. It was awkward. We got to the beach around ten this morning. Didn't even know Angie was missing. Some thought she had slept in, stayed behind." He stuttered over the next words. "Then the diver found her. They say he moved...the body. Poor guy. I would have done it myself. You can't let..." With a crack, his voice trailed off, and he looked at the sand.

"It was a natural reaction, Mr. Gable." Holly's reassurance seemed to relax his shoulders, and she smiled. "How long will you all be staying?"

"Scheduled for another day, but the trip is over. Preparations will have to be made. The family contacted."

"I see. We'll need to talk to some of the students. While they're together, it's more convenient for everyone."

"Tell me how to help. The girls are all crying, and the guys aren't far from it. They'll probably need some counselling. Father Drew is a great guy in a crisis. A prayer assembly, then individual conferences as necessary. Teenagers don't expect death to come calling. I remember when a boy in my fourth grade fell from a cliff. Harold Bach was his name. Just a quiet little guy, but he crawled out on a dare, and the ledge gave way." He turned to her with naïve wonderment. "Why do I still recall his name? So weird. He wasn't a close friend, and I didn't go to the funeral. None of us did. Wasn't expected in those days."

The way he was rattling on seemed morbid. She needed to learn how to direct an interview, but sympathized. "Do you think about Harold very often?"

He scratched his head. "Once a year on Hallowe'en. That's when it happened."

"Then you're reinforcing the memory, bumping the curve back up each time." She checked her watch. "We'd better get to the camp so that you can start home now. Sooner is better than later for collecting information."

Along the path, she pointed to the bike. "Yes, it's one of ours," he said, inspecting a metal tag welded to the frame. "We brought six trail bikes. They're not allowed on the beach, but they're fine for the park roads."

"Could Angie have ridden it here?"

He shrugged. "I suppose so. Someone is supposed to be in charge of inventory at the end of the day, but maybe they slipped up, and it's been here since we came over yesterday."

"We'll toss it in the car," she said, motioning to Chipper to collect it.

As they returned to the lot, Gable stood awkwardly with Chucky, spreading his arms in a question. "My ride's gone. Can you..."

She opened the rear door. "He's welcome. We've had worse passengers. At least he's sober."

The trunk contained emergency equipment. A shovel, plastic cones, a blanket, rain gear, bottled water, even a stuffed bear in a plastic bag for when a child needed comforting. Chipper secured the bike, then tied the lid with polypropylene rope. He got into the front and started the engine. In the back seat, Gable shuffled around with Chucky in his arms, perhaps uncomfortable in the confines of a vehicle with reinforcements to prevent glass breakage. On one of her favourite shows, *Cops*, a suspect had braced himself and kicked out the rear window of a cruiser.

Holly rolled down the windows to catch the breeze. With its computer equipment, radio and brackets for a shotgun, the vehicle was crowded. Opening the clear slider so that they could talk, she half turned towards Gable. Phrases from psychology and interpersonal communications courses came to mind. "This must be a terrible shock for you, sir."

"Please, Paul is fine." He wiped his freckled forehead. His arms were strong, and knobby, hairy legs protruded from his tan shorts. She recalled that he also wore sandals with white socks. "You can't imagine, or maybe you can in your line of work. It's just impossible that this could have happened to Angie."

In minutes, they turned into Les's RV and Camping, following Gable's directions to the group area at the forested rear section beside the showers and washrooms. Chipper turned off the vehicle and excused himself. Holly led Gable to a picnic table, where Chucky began to nibble on grass.

He told her about the activities the day and night before, leading to the discovery of the body and the steps to contact the authorities. In the second stage of the interview, she began writing.

"And her full name is...please spell it, too." She poised with her pen, listening as he proceeded.

"Angie Didrickson. Our star swimmer. Butterfly champion of the province."

Now the physique made sense. Holly jotted more notes. "A reliable girl then. She'd have to be to undergo that kind of discipline and training." She paused, her memories searching back. "But Notre Dame doesn't have a pool, does it?"

"No," he said, "but we have an arrangement with Seaparc.

Angie and a few other diehards would be there at seven every morning to practice." He wiped at his eye. "She was headed for a full scholarship to the University of London. Her dad was so proud, and so was the school."

"And her mother?" Holly felt herself wanting to understand that this victim was a human being with a life behind her. Was it worse to die at eighteen or to disappear in your forties? Unholy balances.

"Grace Didrickson died in an auto accident a few years ago. Nate did a damn fine job raising her and her little brother."

"And the last time you saw her..."

He gave a sniff, pulled out a handkerchief, and honked his small, beaked nose. "You mean..."

"Of course. Alive." She cautioned herself to show more patience, even though the questions were obvious. This wasn't a race. Slow and sure, Ben would say.

"That would be last night at the campfires. A sing-along. Marshmallows, the traditional thing. Started near dark, around nine. The chaperones and I had our own blaze, but I made the rounds from time to time to keep everybody honest, not that I was counting heads. You have to give kids some degree of trust. And you can't expect them to be tucked in by ten." He smoothed his thick hair, a cowlick raising a stubborn shock. "I'm sure on the perimeters the usual vices were present. Cigarettes, a can of beer, maybe even a joint or two. But not in sight."

"So you saw her as late as..." She kept her pen poised. Reports with initialed changes were frowned on.

On the road, the guttural roar of a motorcycle caught their attention. Whimpering, the dog started running circles, entangling the lead, and Gable kept trying to undo it. "Chucky, stop." He looked at Holly with a plea. "Can I tie him to a tree over there? This is distracting."

"Sure." String him up was more like it. Holly hated ill-behaved, aka ill-trained animals. If any dogs were neglected in obedience matters, the small varieties were. Much easier to scoop up the thing and tuck it under your arm than teach it manners. German shepherds had to be under control, at one with their master, their partner. She missed that bond.

On his return from attending to Chucky, Gable said, "Now where were we? Oh, right. The time. Somewhere near eleven. It was pitch dark. I don't have one of those glow model watches. Anyway, the kids seemed to be heading off to bed without problems." He gave an ironic laugh. "That's how much I knew. Jesus, she was out there and—"

"It must have been difficult in the dark. And you can't put a teacher in every tent. How many students are on this trip?"

"About forty-five. Our graduating class, minus a few who had other things to do. Not all the kids like camping. On the weekends, some head for Victoria for the music scene, whatever that is now. I'm still listening to the Beatles. Sort of retro at my age. At least I'm not into Elvis like my wife's family." A flash of embarrassment crossed his face. "Listen to me going on. Guess I'm nervous."

"Everyone reacts differently to this kind of stress. Take your time. Tell me about your chaperones."

He shook his head as if to clear it. "Me, Kim Bass, who teaches English, and Terry Grove, our coach. I blame myself for the short staff. We should have done more to find someone to help or postpone the trip. Father Drew would have come, but he had to take mass to a shut-in."

She thought of the difficulty of juggling all those teens and their hormones. "Just three, then."

"I know what you're thinking. That's fifteen each to keep track of. But the school has had a fall trip since it was founded in 1950. That's a long tradition. There was a bit of pressure. Established dates for future weekend activities. The kids would have been disappointed."

Holly's idea of camping was to grab a backpack and head into the wilderness with her dog. "So who was in Angie's tent?"

Gable took a list out of his jacket pocket. "Just Janice Mercer. She's very shy. These trips build self-esteem. Students like that I didn't want to disappoint. Having a successful senior year can make all the difference. Rites of passage. Ninety-five per cent of our students go on to university. Edward Milne can't compete with that." He referred to the public secondary school in Sooke.

Holly glanced at her watch. This was taking too much time. Though in charge, she couldn't and she shouldn't do all of the interviews herself. The students might appreciate a younger officer....provided that they held no racial prejudices. And even if they did, Chipper had to face his demons like she'd dealt with *Playboy* centrefolds on her locker during training.

Calling Chipper over, she directed him to sort out those with helpful information. She'd take the two teachers, and if his numbers were high, share the students. "I'll need you to explain the layout," she said to Gable.

At the campsite, a few dozen students sat on logs and stumps, on the ground, at picnic tables or milled in the area with pop cans or bags of chips. Gable pointed out a village of tents in various sizes. He, Coach Grove and Kim Bass each had a small pup tent. The students slept in the other eight, two, three, four, depending on tent size. Gable introduced the teachers to Holly. Chipper, in his usual organized fashion, had lined up the students and was talking to each one privately. She was impressed at the way he'd sorted everyone out without a ruffle. Even in the sombre moment, some of the girls seemed entranced with him, heads together in chatter as they watched him.

Grove, a fit man in his late thirties, hadn't seen Angie after dinner. Muscles corded on his weightlifter's body as he fastened an expensive mountain bike with front and rear shocks onto a carrier. Smelling faintly of herbal soap, he wore denim cutoffs, a polo shirt with Notre Dame Saints and a halo logo, and hi-tech sandals on his large feet. He repeated Gable's praise of the school's star swimmer and ran a hand over his curly black hair, prematurely thinning at the temples.

"With her training, I find it strange that she drowned," Holly said, leaving an implied question.

He bit his lip and looked at the ground, where a line of ants was reaping the crumbs of campers. "A cramp. Alcohol. Kids make bad decisions. Maybe this was her first and last drink. Nate is going to take this hard. She's his princess."

"Paul Gable mentioned his suspicions that someone brought liquor. Do you *know* she was drinking? Did you see or smell anything?"

He bristled at the implied accusation. "If I had, I would have confiscated it. No one on our teams drinks during training, or they're out. But Angie's the last—"

"How about her friends?" At Notre Dame, everyone knew everyone's business.

"She was dating Jeff Pasquin. Went to the junior formal with him last year. As for friends, Lindsey Benish." He paused to think, rubbed his finger pads together. "But they must have had a falling out. These kids and their head games. It's even worse in a small school. Feelings get hurt."

"Point them out to me." Not much had changed at the home of the Saints. A tapestry with knots behind it. How dense and how deep? What looked perfect on the surface was a tangled mess behind.

He nodded toward the group, a few elbowing each other to

take their turns with Chipper. "Jeff's got his head shaved. He's a swimmer, too. Went all the way to the Nationals. And Lindsey..." He craned his head as a girl with extra pounds only a seventeen-year-old could carry well blew her nose on a tissue. "She's the one in cargo pants and the polka-dot bikini top. Nothing shy about her. A few more years, and look out." Then he cleared his throat and smiled, revealing one chipped incisor, which added a touch of vulnerability. "Any other questions? I'm overdue to call my wife. She's eight months pregnant and keeps me on a short leash."

Kim Bass, the English teacher, had an oval face with high cheekbones. About Holly's age, she wore wheat jeans and a faded plaid shirt. Her sleek black hair was razored at the sides. She wore soft, beaded moccasins that looked more comfortable than Holly's hot, stiff boots, which had raised a blister on her heel with the prolonged and irregular beach walking. Kim's voice was husky and low, sweet as lemonade on a July afternoon. "Angie was in my British Lit survey this year. I also had her in tenth grade for Communications. Straight A's."

"When did you see her last night?"

She shuddered, even though the day was warm, sun streaming through the trees. A sheen of sweat broke out on her brow. Doe eyes and a faintly darker complexion made Holly wonder if she had First Nations connections. "Dinner, of course. There was a volleyball game." She pointed to an open area, where a net was set up. A lone, deflated ball sat to one side. "We were all playing. Angie won nearly every serve. A natural athlete."

"And afterwards?"

"I developed a headache and went to my tent for an early bedtime. Smoke from the campfire maybe. Kills my sinuses." She gave a small cough into her hand. "Not that I expected to get much sleep with all these teenagers, but I took a sleeping pill."

Holly's eyebrow rose. "I see."

"My head was throbbing like a jet engine." She levelled her gaze at Holly and gave a weary sigh. The sclera were pink and inflamed. "You remember slumber parties. Girls can yak all night. The boys keep it down."

"Lucky you brought a supply, then." Had the woman been unconscious? Was she on a medication with unusual side effects like sleepwalking?

"Just generic stuff. They were in my personals bag from a trip to England a year ago. I always take a couple on the plane."

* * *

Having been told that Jeff had been Angie's former boyfriend, Chipper directed the young man to a bench under a massive Sitka spruce with its trademark cracked bark. "Do you carry one of those cool daggers?" Jeff asked, unable to take his eyes from Chipper's uniform.

Chipper's soft smile hid an internal eye roll at the naïve question, but he refused to answer directly. "Actually, it's called a sword, though the use is purely ceremonial. It's a very old custom dating back over four hundred years."

"Wicked. I've seen a few. Way better than crucifixes and rosaries." Jeff awarded himself a congratulatory snort on the joke.

Chipper explained the interview process to the young man. "And your relationship to Angie?"

Jeff straightened his broad shoulders and completed a bullish neck roll. "We were dating. *Were.* Not this year."

"What happened between you, if I may ask?" Chipper made a point of writing neatly. It was one of his trademarks.

Jeff blew out a contemptuous breath. "That's no secret. Everyone used to see us arguing."

Chipper's pen poised. The boy seemed more angry than wounded by the death. On instinct alone, he didn't like the teen. Cocky and immature. Interested in immediate gratification. Disciplined about his sport, but accustomed to the accolades as a birthright. Jeff wouldn't have had to fight for anything. Chipper found himself listening to his inner voice instead of his subject and gave an internal shake. "Arguing about what?"

"Hey, man, you know chicks. Teasing you. Gets to be a hassle." He lowered his voice almost to a whisper.

"We need to be clear. Are you saying that she wouldn't... have sex with you?" One ebony eyebrow arched into a question. His stomach rumbled faintly, and he shifted.

"Don't spread it around, man. I had all the guys thinking I'd been into her pants for months." Then his eyes narrowed, and he turned away, miming a cigarette toke at a friend raising a pack. "Almost finished, dude," he called.

"Were you trying to get back together with her last night?" Chipper asked, annoyed that Jeff seemed to have his own agenda. He needed to take back the interview. A small muscle in his neck started aching from tension.

Jeff turned to him with a worldly-wise curl to his full lips. "Just some fun. Why not? Didn't work out, so I blew her off. We were going off to different universities anyway. Who cares? Follow what I'm saying?"

"Oh, I follow completely, sir." Chipper snapped his notebook shut.

*   *   *

Last on Holly's list was Janice Mercer. A short, wide girl with blocky glasses came over. Instead of the revealing shorts that most girls wore, her denim pair hung nearly to her knees, topped by a Save the Rainforest sweatshirt. Her eyes were beady and swollen, and she sniffed at intervals. "I was her tent partner, but honest, I conked right out around nine. Mom says I sleep like a log. I never saw her after dinner at all. She just, like, vanished."

Holly let her talk for a moment. Janice hugged herself and gave a shiver. "Brr. I've been going all hot and cold, but I'm not sick. Do you think it's shock?" She blinked at Holly, an innocent calf-like creature at first glance, but with crafty intelligence behind the pose. She reminded Holly of someone who sought small advantage by talking behind a person's back. A sneak.

"Very likely. If there's a regular soft drink around, try that. Or coffee with sugar."

"Yuck. I never drink caffeine. Just herbal tea. Chai." Her cautious diet hadn't helped a serious case of acne. Having skated clear herself as a teen, Holly could only imagine the humiliation.

"Please tell me what happened. Anything you remember."

"Not that she was my good friend. I'm not very popular. That's 'cause I believe in hard work, not fooling around like some of these...kids." She waved a stubby hand in their general direction. Her nails were short and serviceable, without a hint of polish.

"It's tough. I was kind of independent, too." Holly revised her strategy. Here was a girl on the edge of the crowd, quiet, paint on the wall, but perhaps a conduit for information. On the other hand, sometimes these types sucked up extra attention, embellished their stories or even lied to attract a rare spotlight. She moved closer, locking eyes as if they were confidantes. "What's everyone saying?"

Janice gave a humph. "I don't pay them any mind. They're all so stupid. The boys show off like gorillas, and the girls talk

43

about nothing but clothes and make-up. And they read *Teen* magazine. My parents gave me a subscription to *National Geographic.*"

Holly had to smile. "So did mine."

Despite the years gone by and the addition of boys, not much would have changed at Notre Dame. In Holly's day, even the lunch tables had status levels. She gave Janice an understanding nod. With a more flattering hair-do, a touch of natural makeup for those zits and some less intrusive glasses, she might be a late bloomer...if she got a personality transplant. "High school is an artificial world. I tried to forget it as fast as I could. And you're a senior now."

The girl leaned closer. "They're all losers. They just don't know it yet." Her tone was bitter, with an undercurrent of strange confidence. She saw someone in the crowd and brightened. "Do you have any more questions? I need to ask Mr. Gable something."

Holly set her free and reviewed her notes. She couldn't see Chipper.

Gable walked toward her a few minutes later. "Have you talked to the students you mentioned? I've been making some calls from the restaurant phone. The parents will be at the school in an hour and a half to pick up their teens." He brushed a hand through his hair and sighed. "God, the place will be buzzing. At least, that's what happened when we lost two boys to an auto accident last summer. Alcohol was a factor. And speed."

Holly turned at the diesel rumble of an elephantine motorhome in blinding chrome entering the campground. She was hardly aware of the fact that she spoke aloud. "Now's the worst part."

He cocked his head, a concerned smile on his lips. "I don't follow."

44

"Telling the family," she said, turning to a fresh page. "Do you have an address, offhand? Nate's the father, you said? Same last name as Angie? I have to ask these days."

He touched her arm, an honest plea in those grey eyes. "Listen, could I come along? Nate and I have been good friends since I moved to the island. We've both raised money for the Lions Club."

She thought for a minute. This should be her task and hers alone. No shortcuts to this heart-tugging ritual. But Gable knew the man. The father might need someone to stay with him. People often said that of women, but men were equally, if not more sensitive. A man was more likely than a woman to commit suicide after a love affair gone bad, partially because his choice of weapon was more fatal, a gun rather than pills. The romance of death supped from the blood and bone of the young and impressionable.

"I'd appreciate it." Gable would be the first contact person should more information be needed. There was nothing suave or smooth about him, just an earnestness that proved he cared about his charges. The stereotypical job of vice-principal put him in control of discipline, a dull but necessary job outside of the inner city. Presumably he had his eye on a principalship, either at Notre Dame or another Catholic high school. Even now, were there any woman principals in the parochial system?

He rubbed the bridge of his nose in a thoughtful gesture. This would be a brutal assignment for him, too, she imagined. "Maybe I should call Nate first. Normally we'd be watching the Major League playoffs together. Boys' night out. Pizza and beer." He shoved his hands into his pockets and stared at the ground.

"Thanks, but we prefer to tell the family ourselves." Not only was it a courtesy, but in the odd case where the parents might be involved in a crime, it was necessary to gauge their reactions.

Gable paused for a moment, then blew out a breath in frustration. "But I—"

"Protocol." She gave him a sincere but professional smile. Her vocabulary was beginning to assemble a category of helpful terms which made an officer sound efficient but still human.

"Okay, I guess that's best." He pressed his palms together. "Can we meet at the Grant Road turn at four? They live on Rhodenite. Nate works as a senior manager at Costco in Langford, but he has weekends off." He paused as if something else bothered him. "Sure I can't even call him? Give him a minute to prepare for the bad news."

Holly closed her notebook. "Think about it. That would be even worse. Letting the man stew for an eternity, wondering about the details. We're counting on you to help us do things the right way."

As they returned to their respective vehicles, she could hear him mustering the youths to pack up. Clearly, the entry of civilian personalities could compromise even the most straightforward situation. She remembered how Ben Rogers had played a distraught family like a sweet piano until he got the necessary information. An older boy had been molesting the neighbourhood children, often through his sessions as a babysitter. The fact that he worked cheaper than the girls had made him popular. Avid churchgoer and boy scout, he was the last person to suspect. The children adored him and his gifts of candy. Apparently he was quite gentle, convinced that his affections were welcome. Recalling that sad monster gave her the shivers.

"I'm going to call in," she said to Chipper. When the radio failed to work, she added, "I thought we were on West Coast Repeater west of Sooke."

Chipper fiddled with the controls and shook his head. "It's in and out like a yo-yo."

Cells also out of range as expected, they found a pay phone at a service station. Holly didn't like the feeling of being hung out to dry. What if something went seriously wrong? The techies had been working on the problem for years. At the end of the line, Port Renfrew was stricken when their phone lines went down in storms. Last week a car rushing a patient to hospital had crashed, leaving two victims to the failures of telecommunications along a rocky, forested coast.

Back in Fossil Bay, she and Chipper completed their paperwork at the detachment. Late reports were an officer's bane. This would be a good test of the man's determination... and his grammar. Careless errors which emerged in court cast doubt on the investigatory skills of an officer and could toss a case into the garbage can. Ann had left on their arrival, taking her aching back to an early bed.

A few hours later, she rendezvoused with Gable at the busy corner of Grant Rd. Noticing that he drove a venerable VW bus with large flowers painted on the side, she couldn't help but comment when they parked on Rhodenite Drive in a tidy suburban enclave. "I know," he said with a grin as he bumped the rusty door with a hockey hip block. "Got it from the collection of an aging hippie draft dodger. Runs an organic farm in Duncan. As old as the Vietnam War, but it still ticks like a Timex. While the weather's still good, I plan to do some exploring on the island. Strathcona Provincial Park, Cathedral Grove. Come winter, I might get over to Whistler for some skiing."

The Didricksons lived in a pink stucco storey-and-a-half home, judging from the rounded brown shingles, probably built in the early nineties. A towering monkey puzzle tree grew on the front lawn. As they walked along the bricked path, Holly gazed up at the heavy fruits ready to fall. Late-blooming azaleas and plump rhodos added riots of pink and purple to the tropical effect. Greater Victoria benefitted from the Japanese current, which moderated temperatures. Neither too hot nor too cold. The perfect porridge. A glossy black vintage Mercedes sat in the drive, ready for a Sunday parade. Islanders pampered their classic cars, freed from the salt and wear of winter driving. Forty-year-old Mustangs mingled with Gremlins, Bonnevilles, Pintos and the odd Studebaker Golden Hawk.

More nervous as they approached, Holly reviewed her courses in Interpersonal Communications, Crisis Management and Grieving. What had she learned about breaking bad news? Empathy. Eye contact. No box of tissues to replace the charming but unhygienic handkerchief. She hoped she wouldn't stutter.

"Ready?" Gable gave her an encouraging look. For a moment, she thought he was going to squeeze her hand.

She knocked firmly, and the door was opened by a large man with broad shoulders. He had a slight beer belly, but the fitness genes announced themselves, and so did the aromas of bacon and fried potatoes from a late breakfast. In comfortable jeans, he wore a polo shirt and carried a copy of the *Times Colonist* under his arm, a welcoming smile on his round face, thick brown hair pulled back in a ponytail. Seeing her uniform, he furrowed his brow, then looked at Gable, a question in his cool blue eyes.

"Paul? Anything wrong?"

Gable shifted his glance back and forth. "Nate, this is Corporal Martin."

Her pulse off to the races, Holly stepped forward, her hand extended. Their shake was a mere gesture of civility. *Out with it. The swift cut is the kindest.* "I have bad news. Your daughter, Angie, has been in an accident at Botanical Beach." Damn. She hadn't breached the battlements of the cruelest truth.

He stepped back as if struck, placing a workingman's large

hand on the door frame. His unshaven face paled, and his jaw hardened, a muscle at the corner pumping. "A car wreck? Damn those kids. I told her not to ride with anyone with a novice license." He paused, staring in accusation at Gable. "You said you were taking vans. Call this responsible chaperoning? What the hell—"

"It's not that, Nate," Gable said, putting a hand on his shoulder and blinking, moisture in his eyes.

Holly swallowed back a sob. "She drowned, sir. I'm very sorry for your loss."

As they stepped inside, she let Gable take him aside for a moment, opening her notebook in an automatic gesture. What did she really have to ask him anyway? A few muffled groans came from Nate, the paper dropping to the handsome fir flooring. Behind him, a polished mantelpiece was covered with shiny gold and silver trophies. On the wall, candid pictures of Angie poised at the starting blocks at her meets displayed the progress of a champion. Hadn't Gable mentioned a son? An ancient golden retriever rose from a cushy corduroy pillow in front of the fireplace, shook its arthritic body, and ambled toward Nate to nuzzle his hand.

He straightened and cleared his throat. For a moment, though he opened his mouth, no words came. Suddenly he became aware of the dog and let his fingers brush the silken ears. "Buster. He's nearly blind now. Got him when Angie was three. He was her guardian angel."

Holly made sure that the dog saw her first before she stroked it. Like most goldens, it was quiet and amenable. A perfect therapy dog. Not as serious as shepherds, nor as bright, but a winning, dippy smile that made it one of North America's favourites.

Nate pulled himself from Gable's steadying arm. "When can I—"

Holly adjusted her voice for the gentlest tone. He was handling the death of a child better than she expected. Yet what else could he do? Keening and wailing was a woman's province. Men had such burdens. No wonder they snapped. Her father had been dry-eyed throughout the crisis with her mother. For her a solid knight. But in private, she knew he mourned at every sunset, staring out to sea, alone and frozen in grief.

"Angie is at the Jubilee. There are formal procedures. An autopsy perhaps."

"Is that necessary? She drowned. It seems simple enough. Why put us through..." His voice trailed off, and he finally let his legs shuffle him to a seat in a leather armchair.

"They're ordered thirty per cent of the time. It's rare but possible that physical causes were responsible."

"What physical causes? She was a goddamn world-class athlete. She should have lived..." His voice trailed off, and his fists squeezed into themselves.

Holly took from him only what she needed for the time being, the evidence of a life. "We'll give you a call tomorrow. And Mr. Didrickson, I'm so very sorry."

As they walked to their vehicles, a boy about eight with a vocal VRRRROOOOM tore down the street on a mountain bike, bumped up a curb, and turned into the driveway. Gable gave a wave. "That's the son. Robin." He wiped at a tear in his eye. "I'm going to stay with Nate for awhile. That's okay, isn't it?"

"It's kind of you. I was going to suggest it if there isn't local family. This is no time for him to be by himself."

"He has a sister in Metchosin. Very nice lady. I'll get her over here."

Back at the detachment, Holly passed Chipper heading for his elderly Sunfire. He'd been taking the bus, but had recently got a loan from his parents to buy the thousand-dollar beater.

Under his arm, he carried a manila folder. "Taking my report home for another read," he said. "One class assignment I wrote: 'She said that she had been gone for fifteen minuets and that her ex-husband had stolen the cat for breading purposes.'" He spelled the offending words.

Despite the grim day, Holly produced a genuine laugh. "Spellcheck was invented to lull a writer into a false sense of security."

"You've got that right." He held up a battered Strunk and Whyte style manual. "Ann gave me this. Said she nearly wore out the pages. I never can keep *affect* and *effect* straight."

At least her staff got along with each other, she thought. Inside, she organized her notes and rerouted the answering machine to her house as officer on call. Then she set the security cameras and locked up. As quiet as Fossil Bay was, keeping the detachment open for more than one shift wasn't feasible.

"Hello, baby," she said to the 1985 Honda Prelude. When her Civic had coughed its last breath at 250,000 klicks, she'd traded it in at Sooke Motors, adding a new sound system for CDs. The Prelude was cherry in colour and condition, having been owned by an eighty-year-old retired jeweller who drove it only on weekends. The sound system was top of the line. She rolled back the sunroof and slipped in a disk of Sheryl Crow's duet with Kid Rock. Holly's mother had been no faithless spouse diving into a bottle, but lines from "The Picture" made her throat hurt. "I called you last night at the hotel/ Everyone knows but they won't tell." Did someone on this tight little island have information about Bonnie Martin? "I want you to come back home." *As if she could.* From the beginning, Holly had known in her heart that her mother was dead.

She headed east a few miles on winding West Coast Road toward Otter Point, where her father lived. It had been too easy to accept his generous offer to share the large home. With her fledgling career and modest salary, buying a property was impossible with average prices shooting past four hundred thousand dollars. Legal (or illegal) suites were available only through close connections, and apartments were scarce. Park trailers were an alternative, but she wouldn't be stationed here for more than a few years and didn't want the hassle of selling.

Reluctant though she'd been to return to a place with bad school memories, she wanted to be sure her father was as well and happy as possible. The quintessential professor, he nursed his absentmindedness like a fond character trait. It allowed him a certain aloofness, especially from women. She wondered if he was lonely, because he'd never admit it. Neither did he mention female companions. Perhaps, with her dismal dating history, she was closer to him in personality than she thought. The social whirl never had meant much to her, busy and content in her own company.

She passed Kirby Creek, Muir Creek, Tugwell Creek, pioneer names from settlement. A metal sign on each bridge flagged the salmon habitat and urged people to protect "our" resource. Many feared the fishery might collapse, due to overfishing, sea-lice transfer from fish farms, or hungry seals staking out claims near spawning areas.

At Gordon's Beach, a curious string of miniature homes perched on the narrow shoreline, elbowing each other like in a Disney film. Some were flimsy shacks, others brand new whimsical hobbit houses with gables, turrets, nooks and crannies valued at over half a million. With fifty feet frontage or less, they clung like limpets to the strip of land. Turning on Otter Point Road, passing a llama farm and saluting the dark brown shaggy male who gazed into another pasture at his harem, she took a left at Otter Point Place, a sunny hillside dead-ending in a turnaround. With the opposite side of the street still pasture returning to bush, it had an unsurpassed view of the ocean.

She stopped at the new mailbox pavilion. Nothing from Kevin in Nunavut. Why did she expect him to write? Even though they'd dated in Port McNeill, he'd made a deliberate attempt to keep their relationship casual. At first she'd been seduced by his gourmet Italian cooking and black belt in karate. Then, near the end, enter that new file clerk with the low-cut blouses and high-cut hemlines. He'd had such an odd look when she'd met them leaving the evidence lockers. After that, he'd been slow to return her calls, pleading the need to attend sessions of a court case.

As she opened the box, Telus, Shaw and B.C. Hydro bills spilled from the metal cubicle. Obviously, her father had neglected to collect the mail for at least a week.

Unlike the cottagey New England style of its demure neighbour, his was a white Greek villa, huge windows in the solarium, two decks, a hot tub, a rampant kiwi and a stand of banana trees. The lawn was dry and brown, even with the flushings from the septic bed. The monsoons couldn't arrive soon enough. As she passed the peach tree at the side of the house, she smiled at the flourishing holly bush her mother had planted and her father had nourished. Tempting red berries protected by prickly leaves, a wry allegory for any independent woman.

Norman Martin taught popular culture at the University of Victoria and steeped himself in a different period each semester. The concept anchored his life and removed him conveniently from the realities of the present. A savoury stew infused the hall as she entered, a mysterious ingredient teasing her nose. Her father loved to cook for his research, and she loved to eat. She blessed him for waiting for dinner. Reunited only a few weeks ago, already they had an understanding that if she wasn't back by seven, unable to call due to her remote location, he'd chow down.

"Get in here. Your old dad's nearly faint," he said, waving a wooden spoon from the kitchen. He wore a gingham apron over his chinos. Definitely not her mother's. Bonnie Martin had never made a meal in her life. Food was a fuel to reach her goals, the simpler and faster the better, often no more than fruit, bread and cheese eaten on the go in her Bronco and washed down with cold green tea.

"Let me climb out of this gear. The vest is smothering," she said, taking the winding staircase to the upper floor. Oblivious to its view, his nose in books, he had given her the master suite, taking the two back rooms for his bedroom and study. It gave her an odd feeling to have her parents' room, but its double occupancy had been short. Perhaps her father wanted a fresh start, too. For all she knew, he'd abandoned that room to far-off memories. But he hadn't sold the house, though he knocked around in its sprawl. Did he hope Bonnie would come home?

After a quick shower, she tossed on shorts and a T-shirt. At the pine table in a sunny, adjoining alcove overlooking the strait, she sat down to a Fifties meal. Shelves in the oak kitchen were lined with cookbooks, from Mrs. Beaton to Betty Crocker to *Joy of Cooking* to the Barefoot Contessa. He served a rich beef stew made with beer, boiled potatoes and a can of green peas. Starving, she dug into the meal, pausing only for appreciative nods and sips of the rough red wine he made at a local do-it-yourself vintner for three dollars a bottle. No need to make conversation. His commentary would be forthcoming.

Norman blotted his mouth with a pure white cloth serviette. "If they couldn't get to a market or raise their own, even in summer canned vegetables would be welcome.

54

Birdseye had just brought in the frozen variety." He scrutinized the soft, mushy pale-green balls. "A different animal, but I crave them from time to time. Takes me back to my boyhood in Sudbury. Had a friend in Little Britain there whose mother served them mashed with fish and chips."

Holly was transported to her childhood. "Mushy peas, I remember."

Norman, never Norm, Martin was closing in on sixty, but she knew he'd retire only when they wrenched the cold chalk from his dead hands. Whip-slim at six feet, recently his shoulders had assumed the beginnings of a stoop, and his sleek blond hair was shading to grey. She doubted that he got regular exercise, though Otter Point had many excellent walking areas, from residential streets to clear-cuts, and the shortcut to the beach. Except for his professorial mien, an off-putter for some, he was an attractive man. She could imagine him fending off advances from middle-aged female staff. Sometimes she wondered about the unmarried departmental secretary, Frances, who baked him blackberry pies and used to call in a worried voice when he was running late.

Like companionable stablemates, they quickly slipped back into old familiar routines. "How did everything go, little freckle-pelt?" he asked. That curious lichen had been her pet name, a step up from the ubiquitous frog-pelt which Bonnie had showed her in the *Plants of British Columbia* guidebook, a gift for her twelfth birthday.

On the stereo in the tiled solarium down the stairs, a CD of Kate Smith played "When the Moon Comes Over the Mountain", then "Be My Love", and "Danny Boy" as she gave him an update. His tastes in music were as eclectic as his many rotating historical periods. One semester he was enjoying Scott Joplin, the next the Beatles. "That woman could belt them out," he said, pumping his fist in an unusually assertive gesture. "Whenever I hear 'God Bless America', I could almost march off to war myself." An incongruous comment from a peace-living NDPer who drove a Smart Car, she thought as she managed another swallow of ghastly wine. If it had been in the bottle three weeks, she'd be surprised.

"Sorry, what did you say about the poor girl? That must have been a rough introduction on your first day. This is supposed to be a quiet place. I was relieved when you got the post. Never liked it when you were so far from civilization in that darn bush."

"Sometimes the bush is safer. Give me bears over brawls. We'll know more when the medical examiner takes a look," she said.

He seemed pensive, shook his head and pushed the last pea to the side. "Terrible place for young girls. The morgue. So wrong. Any woman..." He paused and gazed across the strait to Washington State. A bank of clouds was dissecting the landscape, suspending a cruise ship in the air. Each year five thousand vessels used the passage. The possibilities for accidents were becoming exponential. Another Exxon-Valdez waited around every cove.

She knew he was thinking of her mother. Ten years had passed since she had disappeared, past the legal time for a person to be declared dead, such an artificial line. She knew nothing about what life insurance the woman might have had. To ask would be not only crass but an affront to her father.

Her mother had First Nations blood, growing up on a Coastal Salish reserve near Cowichan. When Bonnie had failed to return from a trip to the Tahsis area to start a safe house for abused native women, a search had started. At first they thought she'd driven off the road in a snow storm, but days had gone by, then weeks. Even when spring had revealed the landscape, her Bronco had never been found. The months that followed had been grueling. It had even been whispered that her father had played a role, not surprising, given the statistics in domestic killings. Normally he was peaceable, but her mother's long absences in her social causes exasperated him, and the neighbours beside the eighty-foot lot had heard arguments, she suspected. Nor did Bonnie appreciate his career. "A waste of time," she would say, considering the plastic black-cat clock he had found at a garage sale and mounted in the kitchen. "Why chew old bones? Do something for the *living*, for god's sake."

"Those who don't remember the past are condemned to—" He'd retreated into professor mode. Fifteen-year-old Holly had been outside on the deck, but with the thin walls of the house, she heard every word.

"Give me a break, Norman. I know all about the past...and so do the women I help. We're trying to make a difference." Bonnie left to answer the phone, one of many calls which arrived at all hours.

Coming back inside that sad day and trying to feign ignorance, Holly had never forgotten his defeated look. With his tenure assured at last, he'd bought the Otter Point Place house for Bonnie, a sunny change from their dark A-frame in East Sooke, where the sun cast a fleeting glance down through the dense firs, and lights burned in the daytime. But it hadn't helped. She cared little where she hung her hat, straw in summer, a warm toque in winter. Holly supposed she got her contempt for fashion from her mother. Bonnie would have liked the freedom of the uniform. Imagine starting each day with a series of bothersome decisions about what to wear and what makeup might complement it.

After dinner, they took their desserts and tea to the TV room for his favourite channels, Turner Classics or American Movie Classics. In keeping with his Fifties theme, they were watching *River of No Return*. Robert Mitchum was solid and upright for a change, even if he had killed a man in self-defense. Marilyn was buxom and casual, a wasp waist cinched in her blue jeans. Her scenes with young Tommy Rettig, Jeff in the *Lassie* series, were honest and touching. "Weren't we watching this movie when I left for university?" she asked.

"You can never see this couple too many times," he said. "Mitchum wasn't just the dope-smoking bad boy in the tabloids. He was talented in many directions. Did you know he composed a symphony that was played at the Hollywood Bowl? Orson Welles directed it," her father said, a master of trivia.

A sea change from Mitchum's villainous roles. Even here in a quiet backwater, chances were strong that a sociopath lived within range, whether or not the person would ever act violently. "No return, no return, no return," the theme song warned as she thought about her mother. Was he thinking the same thing? She shook her head and finished the prune whip. Not as good as his floating island.

When the movie ended, she looked at her watch. "Damn."

Norman yawned and stretched. "What's wrong?"

"I should have written up my notes at the station. That's going to take me at least an hour and a half."

He wagged a finger at her. "You always were a bit of a procrastinator. Unlike your old man."

She stuck out her tongue and headed upstairs to her bedroom, where a new Dell computer awaited. Once seated, she opened the palm-sized notebook. The routine had been laid down at the academy. Dates of each notebook on the cover, ink only, no erasures, any changes initialed. Crucial for a court case.

Then the transcription into a formal report. No secretary for that, they were warned. Her handwriting wasn't the best; she tended to think faster than she wrote. In university, she'd used a shorthand which helped her to take notes in heavy-content courses like Abnormal Psychology and Sociology of the Family. If she hadn't memorized the Criminal Code, she could cite numbers on command. And not everyone realized that Canada didn't have the official Miranda warning like on American TV shows, but a caution based on the Charter of Rights. Each notebook contained a glossary at the end, which included radio codes for incidents and other standard information.

She was a long time getting to sleep. And the half moon was rising, not over the mountain like Kate's, but across the water, pulling Orion and its triple-star belt in its numinous wake. Her mother had said that when it formed a C for coming, it was actually waning. She got up, slid open the patio doors, and walked onto the deck to contemplate the strait. Cruise ships took polite turns with freighters to ply their way west toward the Pacific or east to Puget Sound, the lights on their wires and superstructures like a mobile amusement park. Getting back into bed, she burrowed into the down pillow. Tomorrow wouldn't be pleasant. She could take a pass on the autopsy, but how bad could it be? Telling the family was worse, and she'd leaped that hurdle today. She wondered how Nate Didrickson was faring. His daughter had seen her final moon.

Three

Boone called the detachment the next morning. "Daso's got the autopsy scheduled for nine thirty. Just got around to checking my answering machine. Late night at the legion." Holly washed down the thistle scratching her throat with bitter coffee. Chipper had arrived first, and apparently he liked his brew strong enough to trot a deer. "I'd like to be there. Do you think that—"

"Hell, we can still make most of it. Traffic's light now. Pick me up fifteen minutes ago."

He was standing in front of his doublewide behind the Kemp Lake store at the Olympic View Park when Holly drove up minutes later. The ocean-view spot catered to retirees, who owned well-kept modern units with elaborate porches or sheds, even a small plot of land. A white cat twirled around his feet like a fluffy fog. "Cassandra's deaf," he said, stroking its head. "Many white cats are. She doesn't wander far. Knows she'd make a nice snack for a cougar."

"Apparently there's a wounded one at large in the John Muir area. Nearly took out a chihuahua."

"Keep your voice down," he said with a mock-worried look. "The old gal lipreads."

At the first stoplight, they turned left and cozied in behind a strip mall. Nestled there was the latest Sooke coffeehouse, the Stick-in-the-Mud. Run by trained barista Dave Evans, a neighbour of Holly's, it sold the best java in town, not a bitter bean in a carload.

The regulars were lining up, while others were in leather armchairs reading the *Times Colonist* or the free *Monday* tabloid with its radical Seventies flavor. Laptop computer keys clicked. While Boone went to the washroom ("prostrate," he said with a chuckle). Holly ordered an Americano for herself, and a daily special, Kenya, for him, doctoring them at the depot. Then a raucous voice took her back to the past with the zing of a bungee cord.

"Holly! Holly-O. Damn! And check that uniform. You look maaaaaavelous." Valerie Novince kissed her manicured fingers and planted her hands on her broad hips. Her dark brown hair was now platinum blonde and teased. The dimples in her merry face cheered any room.

Holly gave her a warm hug, flattered that Valerie remembered the "O" for Oldham, a family name dating back to their ancestral home in Devonshire. "Hello, friend. This is a wonderful surprise. What have you been up to?"

Valerie explained that she had spent two years in the army, then returned for real estate training at Camosun College. A curvaceous eyebrow spoke pages. "I was a baaaad girl, but the army gave me discipline. Remember when I got expelled from ND for smoking?"

Holly laughed. "Twice, wasn't it? I was glad to see the back of that place, too. But how did the army survive your invasions?"

"Hey, I made master sergeant on my riflery alone. Every time I went to the range, I had that ugly old gang of skanks in my sights." She raised her arms in a shooting gesture, attracting some attention from a white-haired lady carrying a Pomeranian. "Pow, pow."

"Uh, Val, I think—"

Valerie gave a thumbs-up. "Slim as ever, you. And I've gained the last ten pounds since I stopped smoking. Hey, do you still rescue banana slugs? Damn, that was funny."

Despite the stares surrounding them, Holly couldn't help smiling. "To serve and protect has always been my motto."

"So it has, and you figured it out. We've got to get together." Valerie padded wicked coral nails on her shiny lips. "Say, do you need a house? Meet Sooke's top seller."

"You're out of luck. I'm living with my father on Otter Point Place."

"Woo, woo. High rent district." Valeria plucked a card from her elephantine purse. "If you ever want a place for yourself, short term, easy-sell, consider a mobile, uh, manufactured home. It's an investment. I have one for only $79,000 in Wells o' Weary. Right on the ocean. Lapping waves will sing you to sleep."

"And when the big wave comes?" Tsunami warning signs along the coastal road had made realtors furious and alarmed local businesses so much that they were removed within a few months. Now tourists could travel the road at their own blissful risk.

Valerie elbowed her way into the lineup. "You'll be the first one to know, so call my cell!"

Back in the car, they passed the Log, a grassy meeting place, which anchored the town. A fifty-foot Douglas fir post displayed two carved loggers, one balanced with an axe on a springboard perch aiming at a cut above the thick butt and the other climbing to the top using a strap and cleats.

The forty-five minutes into Victoria went quickly. Delayed only for a moment behind one of the signature red double-decker buses, they took Sooke Road, Route 14, through Milne's Landing, skirting Metchosin and entering Langford, then merging with the Island Highway in View Royal.

The Victoria Metropolitan area consisted of twelve municipalities with a total of 335,000 people. Long a retirement mecca, it also attracted tourists with its "More English than the English" atmosphere, or lately a controversial campaign promising better orgasms. Sadly, urban crime had made serious inroads in the small core of 74,000. The spectres of substance abuse and homelessness were more evident in the balmy climate than at the frigid corners of Portage and Main in Winnipeg. Low-cost housing had been a promise for decades, but only million-dollar condos were shooting their floors skyward.

Then they followed narrow Bay Street east all the way to the venerable Royal Jubilee Hospital, serving the city since 1890, when the old Queen reigned. Leaving the car in the lot, they entered the front lobby and took an elevator to the basement to the morgue and autopsy rooms. "I left a message with Daso's secretary. He'll be expecting us," Boone said.

Holly had to remind herself that this was real, not a staged event. Anyone with a sense of humanity was never fully prepared. They pushed through into the office and were given green gowns, paper hats and shoe protectors by a young technician. Through a glass portal, a white-coated man waved.

The room was large but low-ceilinged, a typical old basement. At least ten tables waited. Two held bodies, each covered with a large white sheet. Immaculate if claustrophobic, the room was cool. Fluorescent light banks lit the room, along with spots on angled arms at each site. She heard something frisky. Salsa music?

As if preparing for an exam, she scanned the instruments on a side table and tried to recall their names and purposes. Scissors, but beginning with E? Enterotome, used for opening the intestines, the blunt bulb at the end to prevent perforation of the gut. Scalpels, rib cutters, toothed forceps, skull chisel, and the famous vibrating Stryker saw, which had revolutionized autopsies. Those tools on a white cloth were clean, those on the next rolling table bore the inevitable effluvium of the body. A third shelf held surgeon's needles, Hagedorn by name, and heavy twine, coarser than ordinary suture threads, for the workmanlike closing. Realizing with embarrassment that she was moving her lips, she looked down and noticed that the floor was flecked with blood. She presumed that the organs had already been removed in some Russian-sounding method that escaped her. Once, a neighbour had gutted a deer that had crossed their path in untimely fashion. To her astonishment, once connections were cut, everything lifted out in a neat package.

Boone introduced Holly, who stuck out her hand in reflex until Vic held up a soiled latex glove and shook his head with a smile. Her breathing was shallow, but she noticed a strange peppermint smell. Vic cocked a thumb at an air-freshener device seen on television, puffing out occasional drafts. A white-sheeted form, blotted with a few stains, lay on the steel table. "Virgin?" he asked her.

Her face reddening, and tempted to bluff, Holly conceded. "Yes and no. I've seen the procedure on...interactive videos."

"Those little cartoons where you move the mouse and pick up the organs? Modern version of that game where you had to pull out body parts with an electric tweezer without touching the sides of the opening. Got that for my seventh birthday."

Boone cleared his throat. Holly felt a pressure in her chest, as if she were under the massive boulder called Sir on Muir Beach. She was not going to faint. Concentration was all. Focus.

"About time you got here. I was just going to put Angie back," he said. "All done."

"Anything conclusive?" She noted with approval his use of the name. Before much longer, nothing tangible would remain of the girl. She was already gone, the carapace merely a rebuke to her attendants. Like an efficient waiter, Vic's chubby assistant was already packing up the instruments for the autoclave in the corner. She remembered the historic word for the examiner's helper, *diener*, translated from the German as *servant*. Not an inapplicable term, but no longer PC.

He gave her a skeptical look. Vic was in his late forties, fuzzy brown hair in an Afro. He had a small, precise mouth and the ears of an elf. A cleft in his chin added a winsome touch. "Mr. Conclusive is a creature we seldom meet, a birthday present wrapped with a shiny ribbon. Life down here in the crypt isn't like that."

Left feeling like a television script writer in a cancelled series, Holly shuffled her feet. "Sorry, I..."

Leaving Angie's head covered, he pulled back the sheet to breast level. "No need to compromise her dignity. We'll use the relevant areas."

Holly pulled up her own gown to dig notebook and pen from a pocket. "Shoot. I mean go."

"It's all on tape if you want a copy," he said, pointing at the dangling microphone. "But as for highlights, she presents as a well-nourished and muscular female of seventeen. You can see the strong development in the upper arms and shoulders. In the neck, too."

Holly added, "She was a swimmer. That's what makes this acc—"

"All the organs are in top shape. Last meal some sort of chili. Also chocolate, marshmallows, crackers. What do you call that campfire stuff?"

The idea of eating repulsed her, but Holly answered, "S'mores. Nothing unusual there."

Boone sucked on his empty pipe, this time a Meerschaum model. As a smoking deterrent, she supposed it wasn't far removed from those plastic cigarettes. "Tox scan?"

"Some alcohol. About .03. Well under the breathalyser. Couple of beers, I'd say. We're still waiting on the drug reports. They'll go to Vancouver to the lab."

"So she couldn't have been drunk and fallen into the water."

He levelled dark little chameleon eyes at her, black, then brown as the light shifted. "You don't have to be drunk to fall. Broke my damn ribs in the tub one night. Pathetic."

She bit her lip, feeling shorter than a garden gnome. "I guess not. And the head injuries?"

"Ready? One rookie fainted and split open his scalp only last week. When you see the face, it gets more personal...at least in the beginning."

She blinked and nodded, locking eyes with Boone for a moment. His gaze sent her a blessing.

Gently, Vic pulled back the sheet from Angie's head. Holly wondered why it had been necessary to examine the brain in a drowning. Could they determine some type of seizure? Strokes were rare in young people, but they did happen without warning. On closer inspection, she noticed no signs of cutting. Angie's eyes were tactfully shut, and if anything, she looked peaceful though pale.

"So you don't do a full autopsy? Take out the...brain?" she asked. Boone had a wisp of a smile on his face. She felt like a source of entertainment, then chastised herself for self-focus.

"Funny, that's the first thing people think of. After the Y incision, it's so classic. Bet neither of you knows when the first autopsy in North America....amend that...the first autopsy over here by Europeans, took place."

They both shook their heads. "That's why I love you, Vic. I always learn something new," said Boone.

"Winter of 1604-5. St. Croix Island down in Maine near

the New Brunswick border. At a settlement of Champlain's, nearly half of the seventy-nine settlers died over a harsh winter. Panic set in."

Holly wondered, "How did anyone discover this?"

"Champlain's memoirs a few years later described how he ordered his surgeon to 'open' some of the men. Excavations by the National Park Service in 2003 found skulls cut just like they are today. Neat as can be. Turned out it was scurvy. No need to look at the brain for that." He gave them a grin. "Should have followed the native diet. Perfectly balanced. Now ours is killing aboriginals."

Holly wanted a better answer. "So why *not* examine the brain?"

"How many tax dollars do you want to spend for little payback? It's not that simple, either. First off, the brain fresh out of the skull is very hard to work with. It needs to firm up in formalin for week or two."

The image brought a sudden queasiness that tugged at her gorge. "That long? So then the family can't..." Her voice trailed off.

"That's a tough decision. Funeral, burial, cremation might be delayed. For a useless formality, do you think they want their loved one sent to heaven without a brain?"

The floppy scarecrow in the *Wizard of Oz* danced across her memory. "I see. It's a very emotional issue." The terminology was returning. The calvarium, the vaulted part of the skull that protects the brain. A lyrical word, from the Latin *calvaria,* skull. A Catholic education scores again. Her father would enjoy that piece of trivia. She realized that she was babbling behind her own curtain and gave herself a mental slap "upside the head."

"Anyway, in this case X-rays revealed no skull fracture. Drowning was clearly the cause of death."

The skin on the girl's face was untouched, but to the side, a section had been probed to examine the wound. "What did you find around the bruise on the temple?"

"Rock debris. Small marine pieces. Algae. The usual beach suspects. I put them under the microscope and later did a scan."

Cautious, Holly searched for another option. "Could she have been hit with a rock?"

"Are we talking meteors? Anything's possible, but is it probable?" Vic shook his head. "You can knock yourself senseless from a fall. Hell, I lost consciousness for five minutes banging my head on a snowpack when I bombed out running moguls."

"What else makes you think it was an accident?" Why was she pursuing this? Was it Ben Rogers who had told her that mindless but useful saying about "assuming" making an ass of you and me?

"Hard to say. Whether the stone hits the pitcher or the pitcher hits the stone—"

Holly gave a knowing sigh. *Man of La Mancha.* My father's favourite musical. 'It's going to be bad for the pitcher'."

Walking on uneven ground in coves in the dark could have sent Angie off balance, given those few beers. Holly tried to remember if there had been a moon that night. "The beach has some very rough spots. She could have taken a tumble. And at that time of night, the tide would still have been high."

"Seems to fit. She was still breathing when she went into the water. Her lungs are full of sea water."

"Of course." She folded her arms. *Let Occam's razor settle the case.*

Vic gave a soft snort. "Not really. There is such a thing as a dry drowning."

"Our coroner told me about that," she added with a nod to her companion.

Boone replied, "It's one in a million to fall a few feet and kill yourself. Better odds at winning the lottery. Still, people fall off ladders cleaning moss from their gutters. It's the where, not why and how. The water was waiting. Without that factor..."

"Fill me in a bit more on the scene. Nobody saw anything? I understand her school was camping near there. Why was she off alone?" Vic asked. With an unexpected sigh, he replaced the sheet as if to trouble her as little as possible. Then he clasped his hands as if in silent prayer.

Holly searched her memory and took a deep breath. She wanted to help this man as much as he wanted to help her. "A good question. The campsite was a long hike from the beach, but we think that she used a bike, and she was an athlete. Fifteen minutes, twenty. Maybe she just wanted to get away by herself. As for the others, it was dark except for the campfires and an occasional flashlight. No one started to look for her until the next morning."

"Why so sure that she was alone?" Vic asked quietly.

"We interviewed everyone involved. Are you suggesting... sexual activity?" Holly wondered about the logistics. "But if she'd been in the water—"

Vic clicked his teeth together twice. "The vagina's plenty tight when it wants to be. Sealed like a clam."

Was Boone smiling, or was it her imagination? Holly felt her face flush.

"We did the usual swabs. No sign of sperm, though she's not technically a virgin. Hymens are tricky, especially in active women. It's not usually a topic of dinner conversation, but a freakish blow to the vaginal area, gym equipment such as monkey bars, even bikes can have the same result."

Ouch. Holly recalled the condom wrapper by the site. It could have belonged to anyone, and it might have been there for days. Still, she was glad that she'd had Chipper comb the area before the winds rose.

Boone checked his watch. "Anything else, Vic? I've got some surveillance to run later this afternoon. Old fart pensioners like me have to earn a living."

Vic glanced over to where one of his assistants was pointing at the wall clock. "Guess we'd better wrap this up." He shifted the sheet and lifted each arm and leg. Rigor had released its grip. Holly winced again at the tissue shredding on the arm. "The abrasions are consistent with exposure to rocks...and to crustacean nibblers. Every animal's an opportunist. Can't blame them."

"So are some people. At least she didn't die hard," Holly said, remembering the tragic beating and drowning death of a teen in Victoria by a mob of students.

All the way back through the shadowy, winding hills, the silence was palpable. "Looks like we're going to call this one an accident, inasmuch as no one saw what happened, and the body hasn't told us different." Boone said. "Still got those tox scans, though."

The CBC was accumulating static the farther they drove towards Sooke. Holly grimaced and reached out a hand.

"Allow me." Boone tuned in a Bach cantata, an excellent choice for the mood. "NPR from Washington State has better reception. Just don't look for country and western unless the weather is clear."

"I grew up here, but I've been gone since I left for university." Holly shook her head as a transport passed them with a roar at the Humpback Road just before the four-lane ended. Before she could decide whether to delay them by pursuing him for speeding, she realized she was ten kilometres under the limit. Too much thinking and rote movement.

She took advantage of their final minutes together to

confess her doubts about handling the interviews. Boone was easy to talk to, on the gruff side but non-judgmental. "Maybe I didn't ask the right questions. It's my first time heading up an investigation. Being a foot soldier was easy. Do what you're told. I'm wondering if I'm too—"

He mock-punched her arm. "Don't be too hard on yourself. Why, I remember..." He launched off into a time machine of the Seventies and Eighties, culminating when he gave evidence that helped put Clifford Olson behind bars. In 1982 the confessed serial killer and child kidnapper had pleaded guilty to eleven counts of murder and was sentenced to eleven concurrent terms. He'd been up for parole several times but would never be free. The public outrage at his negotiating a payment of $100,000 for his wife in exchange for revealing the whereabouts of the bodies, deep in the British Columbia wilderness, had never cooled. There was a price for closure, Holly, thought, mindful of her mother. What would she pay to find her, dead or alive? Could Boone, with his connections and investigative skills, help? Should she suggest to her father that they hire him? What did the costs matter? Norman had pots of money tucked away in mutual funds.

She let Boone off at his trailer, then proceeded to the detachment. Chipper was talking to a pair of tourists in bright floral shirts and Tilley hats. The woman carried a camera and the man a fancy carved walking stick. A camper with Oregon plates was parked behind them, and a toy poodle barked out its brains in the rear window, flailing paws at the glass. Chipper was smiling as he pointed out places on their road map. The couple tried not to stare at his imposing figure, but it was a losing proposition. His outfit said everything the world needed to know about Canada's commitment to multi-culturalism.

Every "horseman" knew about the landmark decision in

71

1990 when Baltej Singh Dhillon had won his battle to wear the Sikh turban despite a petition from nearly 200,000 irate Canadians who defended their objections all the way to the Supreme Court. The five Ks were represented: the kes, kirpan, kara, kanghas and kachh. Turban and beard, steel bracelet, ceremonial dagger, hair comb and sash. All had profound meaning. Though some die-hard militarists still frowned on the adaptation of the uniform, others greeted it as a progressive nod in the British tradition of proud Gurkha regiments.

"See me in my office, Constable," she said as she walked by.

Inside, the door to the tiny lunch room stood open, and Ann sat at a table. The aroma of a spicy soup from her Thermos filled the air. On a paper plate was a slice of cornbread. She was reading a copy of *Maclean's* and wearing ear buds. Her son had given her an iPod loaded with country and western stars, the Dixie Chicks in particular, Chipper had mentioned. He and Ann were friendly, some sort of maternal effect, Holly imagined. As for Ann, perhaps she'd take that early retirement sooner than she'd imagined. The bitter daily pill of working through pain, directed by a younger woman who should have been her staff, might take an added toll. Holly didn't doubt that Ann had been a top officer, but the breaks had eluded her, and her time had passed.

The bulletin board featured posters of missing girls and women. Unlike the Vancouver prostitutes, whose disappearance had gone unquestioned for years, cases involving model citizens got higher priority. She glanced at a winsome school picture of a seventh-grade girl in Campbell River. Fifteen years ago she had gone to the convenience store for a video and never returned. Every province had its share. Except for the population strip along the U.S. border, the country was so vast that it was easy to make someone disappear. Was that what had happened to her mother? Would old bones in 2108 explain why she had left her home and family? Who would care enough by then to maintain the records? All the more reason for pursuing every thread. Yet where could she start? Should she take another look at the official reports? How much trouble would that be with a clear conflict of interest?

Chipper took a chair across from her desk. "What happened at the autopsy? Was it tough to watch?"

"You get used to it, I suppose, but I wouldn't want to." She explained the signal points of Vic's preliminary analysis. Slowly he took in the information, whistling softly. "Boone thinks the death will be ruled inconclusive? That's the term, right?"

"Unless something else turns up. The urine tox scans aren't in."

Chipper folded his hands, lacing long, supple fingers. "You're talking about pot, I guess, or coke. Hard to imagine them shooting dope on a Catholic school trip, twenty feet from a campfire."

She shifted, an uneasy feeling inching down her spine. First-time jitters in an administrative job? Would a man have the same misgivings? "I wonder if I should call someone in on this. Just to be sure. All they can do is say no, right?"

His dark eyes sparkled, and his voice assumed a confident tone. "I didn't like the ex-boyfriend. And I thought that Gable was creepy. But that's not enough, is it?"

She leaned forward, read the innocence and insouciance on his fresh face. "Creepy? Hardly a logical approach."

Chipper, blinking at the slight reprimand, took a sip of the tea in his mug, releasing a faint jasmine scent. "Want me to call West Shore? Don't get your hopes up. They've been bitching about being several officers short. A couple more joined the Victoria force in order to get permanent postings. Where's the loyalty?"

Holly took a deep breath and watched Chipper watch her.

It was protocol. If there were the slightest suspicions of foul play, it was her duty as the head of a small post to let superiors decide if more resources should be requisitioned for a blitz. The traditional first forty-eight, a cliché on its own. But how slight was slight? Wasn't it wiser to err on the side of caution? "I'll do it."

Sooke was the nearest detachment, but it had no inspectors among its fourteen constables, corporals and staff sergeant. If West Shore wanted to read her as a panicky rookie and said no, she'd bury this and return to traffic control and lost dogs. Or was nemesis looking for a bride?

Something pattered on the window, and she looked up. Rain at last, big fat healthy drops. After the long summer drought, September would see the precipitation double in each following month, then fall as precipitously in the new year. What was that verse?

If it's sunny in Victoria, it's cloudy in Vancouver.

If it's cloudy in Victoria, it's raining in Vancouver.

If it's raining in Victoria, it's pouring in Vancouver.

If it's pouring in Victoria, god help Vancouver.

Four

"Where the hell's Martin?" A short man with an Italian-tailored suit, off-white shirt and striped club tie banged into the detachment, clipboard under his arm and the door squeaking behind him. His pants looked as if they had been pressed en route from the car. Iron grey hair was barbered and slicked. A dark blue raincoat hung over his arm, Burberry by the classic brown-plaid lining. He took a slow assessment of the room, barely suppressing a contemptuous smile but allowing his nostrils to flare at the rustic decor. A practiced expression? Affixing a sheet to the bulletin board, Holly suppressed an instinct to salute, tug a forelock, even kowtow.

Her outstretched hand met a cursory shake, the fingers stiff and unwelcoming. "Welcome, Inspector...sir."

His cold battleship-grey eyes flicked up and down. "Whitehouse is the name. I've been sent out here by an officious boss on a fool's mission, and I intend to wrap it up as fast as I can. So let's be clear." He paused ominously. "What exactly do you have? What have you done? And don't omit the slightest detail. Some of it may have to be undone. More to the damned point, why the hell did you wait how many days before calling in?"

The building wasn't shaking, but she felt like an earthquake had struck. Fortunately, Chipper was off supervising down the road, where an accident with a delivery truck and a hikers' shuttle bus had closed one lane in the Sombrio Beach area. Having the top brass criticize either her actions or inactions undermined what little authority she was nurturing. "Two days, sir. But that's because—"

"Never mind the excuses. Get to the point, Corporal. And I'm not surprised that this is your first assignment."

He seemed oblivious to the fact that civilians were in earshot, two older women whose purses had been stolen from their convertible while they had stopped for a picnic lunch and detoured behind bushes for a pee. Holly passed a hand over her forehead, conscious of Ann's throat-clearing. The older woman sat awkwardly in her duct-taped chair and considered Whitehouse from the corner of her hooded eyes. Her lips were tight and her breathing deep, as if she were trying to relax stubborn back muscles.

"I think we'd better go to my...office and get comfortable. Would you care for coffee?"

He grunted a negative, and they proceeded. She shut the door as two bicycle volunteers came in to talk to Ann. They reported suspicious vehicles parked in out-of-the-way places, and those abandoned or without license plates. Since nearly half of the local cars and trucks sported dented fenders or non-disabling damage too costly to repair, standards were relative. If a muffler was dragging, a fender was loose, or a windshield was cracked, that was another matter.

Holly spent half an hour reviewing the few verifiable facts of the case, her mouth so dry that she stopped twice for water. Whitehouse took the copies she'd prepared but gave no mollifying signs of approval of her cautionary move, merely retrieved a pair of half-moon reading glasses, then ran fingers through his steely hair. The back of each hand was peppered with an angry rash. Eczema? A nervous man, then. That could explain his bluster. The small weakness pleased her.

"Goddamn waste of resources. Pulling me out of Major Crimes just as a sting operation was going down. Prisoner for the day. We need to talk to these students again, not on neutral or home ground. Here. As soon as possible." He folded his arms in an aggressive posture. "The atmosphere of a police station always loosens the tongue. Hit them fast, and hit them hard. That advantage is gone now, and don't think they won't know it." He glared at her as if she were a bothersome insect.

Did he expect her to play good cop-bad cop games? "I'm not sure Angie was out there alone. There's the condom wrapper. And I'm wondering about the sweetgrass we found?" Her voice seemed weak and insecure, especially the rising tone at the end of the sentence. Sometimes women made a question out of an assertion. She clutched the chair arm out of his sight and vowed to get back on track. "It's used for—"

"I know all about that." He raised a sharp, inquiring eyebrow, as good as a stab. "Very tricky. We don't want to get accused of racial profiling. When you interviewed the students, were there any Indians? Port Renfrew's known for that. They get into brawls with twenty people, and by the time we arrive, the streets are deserted, and we look like assholes."

"All the Notre Dame students are Caucasian except for two exchange students from Sierra Leone. Others could have been at the beach. We have First Nations tribes in the area." With his outmoded terminology, she could guess what he called Chipper's ethnic background.

"Go on. You have my undivided attention." His tone was less than sincere. "What did the park staff say?"

With some consternation, she related that Tim Jones had mentioned the possibility of boys camping illegally on Botanical Beach. Why hadn't she followed up on that? A raucous Steller's jay scolded as she looked out the window.

Whitehouse's voice jerked her back from her thoughts. "What's the matter? For god's sake, pay attention. Don't waste my time."

"Sorry." She felt herself blush crimson, the heat moving from her neck to the top of her head.

On his clipboard filled with yellow lined paper, Whitehouse made a note with a silver pen, underlining it decisively. "So talking to that Jones fellow, that's something your people can handle. What else do you do around here in Malibu but give parking tickets?"

Were it possible for a woman to feel unmanned, Holly knew the sensation. "Well, I—"

"Now what about these students? What's your contact number at the school? Who's in charge? I'll do those interviews myself. Let you see how it's handled. Turn on the speakerphone and make the calls."

Assigned to her place as a secretary, Holly picked up her notebook, one hand shaking slightly. She'd have to watch everything she said and did. Chipper was right about Jeff Pasquin. If anyone had a grudge against Angie, he did. But what about his alibi? She reached Paul Gable at the school after someone had gone looking for him.

"Cost cuts throughout the diocese mean that I have to teach a class in auto shop to fill in for a man out on sick leave this week. I used to be pretty good with cars, but I've forgotten more than I learned."

His complaining voice made her wonder if teaching, for all its perks, was such a breeze. She was still thinking about those boys on the beach.

"But listen to me droning on. What can I do for you?"

Whitehouse was leaning forward and motioning to her,

speeding up his hand like an old-fashioned movie camera. She told Gable that West Shore had sent someone to investigate the case.

"A detective?"

"We call them inspectors. British touch, I guess."

A hmmmmm came over the line. "I hate to see the students going through this again. They're just settling down. Still, you know your job. Guess the top brass wants you to be as thorough as possible." She could see Whitehouse narrowing his eyes. Why didn't he take the call? Though she sat still, inside she wriggled like a worm on a hot griddle. And this was making her look like a fool to Gable, not that she cared. Why did Chipper think Gable was "creepy"? Some male thing? He wasn't her type, but some women might find him attractive.

"I doubt that we'll need to talk to more than a few students." To save time, she decided to pick his brain while she had him on the phone. "We'll be sending a car for those we want to interview. Anyone under eighteen needs a parent or guardian."

"What, today? This may take time."

"We don't have the inspector with us for long. I'm hoping this can be arranged."

"You're taking them to the station?" Incredulousness made its way into his mellow voice. "Isn't that a little harsh? Last time you only—"

Whitehouse snatched up the phone. "This is Inspector Whitehouse. I need to lay a little groundwork here. I'm sure that as a senior administrator, you'll cooperate fully." He looked at the names on a sheet Holly had indicated and adjusted his glasses. "What can you tell us about..."

Gable needed to access the records, but in a small school, he soon had what he needed. Jeff Pasquin had been an A student until the last year. Then, except for phys ed, his grades had dropped to B's and the occasional C. Teachers blamed the extra hours of swimming training. And at home, his parents were in the late stages of a divorce, albeit amicable. Paul added, "Divorce is always a heartbreak, especially for a Catholic family. Used to be you could get an annulment if you had connections." He paused as if unsure whether to go on. "Ray Pasquin converted for his wife. Guess it didn't take. Marriage is no picnic. You have to work at it."

Whitehouse started to rub his hands, then stopped as he saw Holly watching him. "Yes, yes, now let's move on, please."

When they had finished the call, they heard Chipper returning, talking to Ann. Whitehouse said, "Send the constable for Pasquin. We'll take it from there." He folded the glasses and massaged the bridge of his nose. "He'll be our focus. We'll get some answers."

After her nod, he rose and stretched. His stomach gave a low rumble. "Where's a decent place to eat? Is there a tapas restaurant? Anything ethnic?"

"We don't have the population year-round for much variety. Try Mom's. Turn left in Sooke between the post office and the stoplight. You'll see the sign. Their specials are good, especially the sirloin sandwich *au jus*. Huge burgers, too. Great pie." She felt defensive, like a self-appointed ambassador for the tiny village. This was the only human trait he'd exhibited, and she couldn't accommodate him.

In the bathroom, she wiped moisture from her face and applied an extra layer of deodorant. That man could wring sweat from a dried codfish. And catch that classy suit. Except for undercover officers, inspectors wore the same uniform as she did, except for a white shirt and a tie in the summer.

Rummaging in her bag, Holly unwrapped a bologna sandwich on rye and checked out one fact that had bothered her. She found Tim Jones's number in Port Renfrew and caught him at home, bringing him up to speed. He mentioned that the night that Angie had disappeared, two boys named Billy Jenkins and Mike Baron had come into the park with their bikes. He'd cautioned them not to take the bikes to the beach and watched them chain their rides to a post. Never having seen them leave later, he suspected that they had camped in the park. "Not too much you can do about it," the ranger said. "Too big a place. But they could have been way down the beach. Lots of driftwood for campfires around the point."

"Do you know them well?" she asked.

He gave a hearty roar. "Hell, everyone knows everyone here. I can tell you whose marriage is shot, who's sleeping with who, who's broke from online gambling, and who will front at the liquor outlet to buy for minors." He paused. "They're decent boys, though. Polite, and big as they grow. Seniors at Edward Milne. Gotta give 'em credit for sticking with it and not dropping out."

Not much had changed on the south coast. "Farther west you get from Victoria, the tougher the kids," she added.

"Damn straight. Grow up in Rennie, you take a lot of shit," he said. "Wonder what kind of education they get, spend half the day on the bus. Can't do homework with that rough road."

He gave her Billy's address east of town. His father did carvings and had a small fish boat that took tourists out for salmon and "hali" in the summer. The rest of the year, they put food on their table by selling wood and shooting the odd deer. "Wouldn't put it past them to have a bait yard with apples. But we can spare a few Bambis. Better than ending up on the grill of a car." Leaping deer road signs crisscrossed the area, and everyone knew someone who had had a close encounter.

Not long after, Whitehouse returned with a sleepy expression and a trace of ketchup on his upper lip. He must have ordered the cartload of fries. She told him about the Port Renfrew boys. "You can handle that. I'm not driving out to hell and gone." He left her office and headed for the restroom. Water ran for several minutes.

"Bringing in Jeff Pasquin," Chipper said in an unusually formal voice. "And his grandmother, Mrs. Faris. The parents are in Vancouver on some legal matters." His face was without expression, except for a nuance of a rise in one sleek brow. He caught Holly's glance and gave a silent click to his heels.

"Come in, please," Holly said. She and Whitehouse had set up in the interview room.

His prim glasses nowhere in sight, Whitehouse sat at the scabbed wooden table while Holly took a chair to the side, once again prepared to act as secretary. She wasn't averse to learning interviewing techniques. Whitehouse's experience gave him the advantage. She also realized that she might discover what *not* to do, and she smiled to herself.

Mrs. Faris, a nervous woman under five feet and bent from osteoarthritis, took a chair with a padded seat in the corner. She wore an old-fashioned housedress and running shoes, one of the toes cut out for a monster bunion. Her pudding face had bright red lipstick and a heavy coat of powder. The atmosphere was charged with tension underlaid by her laboured breathing.

Jeff strutted in and let himself be seated in a cheap plastic stacking chair by Chipper, who then discreetly closed the door as he left. Even four people made a crowd. An old leak in the ceiling from winter monsoons had left a streak down one cinder-block wall. Quick-fix painting had covered the mark, but it reasserted itself like a persistent evil in a Grade D movie. A single yellowed bulb dangling from the ceiling cast an ugly glare on the table. Both Holly and Whitehouse had oak chairs with cushions, a pecking order impossible to ignore. Desultory air currents carried the telltale earthy smell of black mould from under the suspiciously discoloured linoleum. Holly made a note to herself to arrange for budgeting to address that serious problem, a minefield for those with allergies. The building had originally been bought at auction and moved to the site, a cheap deal but a recipe for structural disaster.

Holly noticed that Whitehouse cast a quick disapproval at the dusty light, but kept quiet as if to set the stage. The young man gazed around and gave a theatrical cough at the stuffiness. "So whassup?" He pronounced it like a joke in a slurry, smart-ass fashion. Mrs. Faris cleared her throat in the mildest of reprimands.

Whitehouse shifted his shoulders, sending a masculine message from the lead bull. "No time for showing off. I'll ask the questions. Corporal Martin may have a few of her own." Since Jeff was under eighteen, Whitehouse took some time in reading him a number of forms to make sure he understood his rights. Then he asked the boy for feedback on whether he grasped the terminology.

"What's this all about, anyways?" Jeff asked after he had "passed" the test. He tried to present an open and honest face, but it was a grotesque contortion with duplicity below the pretty surface of a boyish grin.

Whitehouse gave an imperceptible nod to Holly. "Angie's drowning may have been a tragic accident," she began with a casual frown. "But Inspector Whitehouse wanted to make sure of the facts. He's an experienced investigator from West Shore." *And who are we in this third-rate detachment, parking attendants with a more lucrative salary?*

Jeff came to with a start, flexing his broad shoulders. He wore dark pants and a white shirt, apparently the school uniform, but the musculature underneath left little to the imagination. His strong young neck had a flashy gold chain. "Why me, then? This is nuts."

"Some of your friends say that you weren't too happy with Angie lately."

"Hey, I never hit a woman in my life. Only cowards do that."

Whitehouse stuck out his chin, his voice like a cobra hiss. "Nobody said anything about violence. Seems to me you're rather defensive."

Despite her efforts to remain neutral, Holly approved of the inspector's score.

The boy shot back. "I take psych, and I get your point, but you're way off. We dated last year. This year we were history. Happens. 'Sides, I was in my tent with Lindsey Benish. Ask her. She's got the guts to tell you the truth."

And to lie for you, Holly thought. Small wonder that spouses were not allowed to testify against their mates in court. The whiff of a conspiracy piqued her interest. Holly scanned the list of those they had interviewed at the park. She tried to picture Lindsey and came up with a brash, unlikable girl. "Benish, you said?"

Whitehouse clicked his pen. On. Off. Three times like a mantra. "Say she backs you up, any other suggestions? Who else might have seen Angie after dinner?"

"Try Kim Bass. Angie had a crush on her." A sharp intake of breath came from the officers, but Mrs. Faris wore a bland expression, perhaps not following the implication. Aware of the repercussions from that depth charge, Jeff gave a contemptuous snort. "Lezbo. What a waste. They all oughta be fat, ugly cows." It seemed to Holly that he gave her an oblique look.

"Mind your language. Your bigotry is showing. And show some respect for your teachers. We're not here to discuss idle gossip." Whitehouse leaned forward and made a note, circled it. "Anything of substance to your charges, or are we talking only about your own self-doubts and shortcomings."

"Nothing short on me. I was with Lindsey all night. Get my drift? We made a deal with our tentmates and traded off." He lowered his voice in a conspiratorial fashion that made his grandmother's face puzzle. At least, he seemed to have some sense of shame in front of her.

Jeff's bravado was slipping. He began examining his short fingernails, sucking on one. Holly noticed that it was broken to the quick. "That must hurt," she said.

Abruptly he folded them on his lap. "Did it diving down to get a rock crab. Stupid thing died later." Then he smiled at her with straight white teeth, the incisors slightly pointed. "They're nice and red in the ocean. Get them home, and they fade right out."

"I wonder why," Holly whispered. Whitehouse was checking a thick day-timer with a tooled leather cover. His squint was evident.

She wondered if Jeff had any idea of the sinister nature of his reflections. Then Whitehouse stood and clapped the book shut. "Constable Knox will take you back now, Jeff. If there's anything else, we'll get in touch. And Mrs. Faris, thank you for coming."

The older woman rose with a small groan and nodded. "Jeffrey, I hope you told the truth."

"'Course I did, Grans. That's what you taught me." Jeff lifted himself from the chair with a smirk on his sculpted lips, good-looking in a superficial way. He made a show of offering his grandmother his arm as he asked over his shoulder, "Aren't you going to tell me not to leave town?"

"Just leave *here* for now," Whitehouse said, and called, "Constable Singh. Come, please."

A minute later, Chipper closed the door behind Jeff and gave Holly an inquiring look. She shrugged. Whitehouse smacked a fist into his palm. "Cocky teenaged bastard. Even if I was one once. And by the way, for future interview techniques, stuff those reaction comments like the one about the sea urchin or whatever it was. Never let them know what you're thinking. Give them room to hang themselves. Capish?"

Though the cliché added unintentional comedy, Holly felt her face warm. "Right. So now what?"

"I'm going to give this one more day. It's a rat's nest anyway. Someone drowns at the back of beyond. No forensics to speak of, and probably for good reason. It was a bloody simple-minded accident." Letting a bored sigh communicate his feelings, he turned to Holly. "Did you talk to this Lindsey girl?"

"No, that was Constable Singh."

"Well?" Whitehouse turned to the young constable.

Chipper's voice cracked. Clearly he was as nervous as she was. "Just for a few minutes. I didn't think... I mean, at the time—"

Whitehouse held up a hand like a traffic cop. "You didn't think. And we'll need two thousand officers a year for the next five to fill the ranks. If you two are any indication...my god."

Neither spoke, but their heavy swallows were nearly audible. Whitehouse moved on. "As my father used to say, I don't like the cut of this young man. He's an insect, no matter how big he is. Get that Lindsey girl in here."

Chipper leafed through his notebook. "She lives on Henlyn."

Whitehouse shot his cuffs and scowled at the numbers on his heavy metal watch. "This is getting impossible. Tomorrow I'm due in Victoria for a conference with the crown attorney about my testimony at a very important trial. We're about to bring down a drug ring. You'll see it in the papers."

"Perhaps I should talk to Ms Bass, sir." Holly jutted her

chin towards Chipper. "If nothing else comes up here that the Constable can't handle."

Whitehouse pondered this for awhile, then he threw up his hands. "I hate to open that can of worms, but we can't leave it now that it's been raised. A woman might respond better to you. Take a subtle approach. We don't want any harassment charges from the Lilac Brigade, even if it's pure bullshit from Pasquin."

Holly nodded. If the woman were gay, she was either utterly dedicated to the parochial system or taking the world's biggest chance. However, Angie's crush on her, unsubstantiated at this point, wouldn't be the first time a straight teacher had been targeted by a gay student.

"We could bring Lindsey Benish in on Friday, if you're free then," Holly said. She was learning to follow Whitehouse by leading him.

In the foyer, he adjusted his French cuffs, silver shell cufflinks winking at the bottom, and reached for his raincoat. "I'm totally tied up next week, too. The province just got financial support for a crime squad to coordinate efforts all along the south island. I'm helping with the initial organization. In a few years, we'll have seventeen people."

"That sounds big-time."

"Damn straight. We're talking nearly a million a year."

"Don't integrated units already operate?"

"Sure, in dive teams, safety, organized crime and child exploitation. But not in property crime. A full-time analyst is going to crunch the stats and match career criminals with their targets."

"I hear you. The same five predatory bastards make the rounds of the parks every summer and steal everything that isn't nailed down and some that is." It was important that her territory be safe in appearance and reality for tourists and locals. One bad experience could make a negative impression that circulated like the flu.

He passed her a card and walked away, calling over his shoulder, "You and Singh handle everything. Do it right this time. Call me if anything turns up, which it won't."

Major Crimes. No wonder he was ticked at the bush-league assignment. Was it the lack of dedication to this case, or a prioritizing of tasks that took Whitehouse off down the road? His card had a cell phone number, but it had been crossed out, as if they were second-class citizens. Holly gave him a one-fingered salute as the door shut. As she looked out the window, his unmarked car, a comfy Buick, pulled away, spitting small stones. Ann seemed to be smiling as she shut a file cabinet. Was she laughing at Holly or with her?

Chipper looked at her, his face troubled. "That was rough."

"You can say that again. I wonder what he's like when he's really mad." That got a grin from Chipper.

An hour later, deep in paperwork, Holly heard Ann answer the phone.

"I'll transfer your call to Corporal Martin."

Holly found Vic Daso on the line, and the news made her spill a tsunami of coffee from her "B.C.: The Most Beautiful Place on Earth" mug. "The last tox reports show signs of crystal meth."

"Why so late? I thought you did blood scans."

"Meth stays in the blood for only four to six hours, so we didn't twig, but it can remain in the urine even after forty-eight hours."

"I don't believe it." Suddenly chilled, Holly envisioned the fine young girl lying on that cold metal slab. "She didn't look like a user. This makes no sense." A wall poster campaigning against crystal meth flashed a graphic picture of the haunting signs of the addiction. Picking at the face, dangerous weight loss, and the signal feature of rotting teeth that were the stuff of nightmares. Angie had been a star athlete. Could scans lie? Was there room for misinterpretation?

"Are you sure? What about a clerical error?" She didn't like to insult the man or his methods.

"Positive. I double-checked it myself." He let the idea sink in before continuing. "Could be it was administered without her knowledge. The drug can be snorted, smoked, injected, eaten, even injected into the vagina."

"What a horrible thought." A mental pebble sent widening ripples across a pool. Was this proof that Angie hadn't been alone? Way too many suspects. And that included the two boys outside of the group. What were their names? She reached for her notes. "Chipper collected an empty condom packet in the vicinity. We haven't done anything with it yet. You said she was no virgin. Could there be a connection?"

"There wasn't any sign of rough sex, nor any semen. If anything happened, she was a willing partner."

"I'm no prude, but her background doesn't sound like—"

"Don't discount the effect of meth. It increases sexual drive, leading to high-risk behaviour. People do things they wouldn't normally dream about. And afterwards, memory is sometimes impaired."

"Did she get the meth at the beach or at the campsite? How could she have been in any condition to ride that bike to the beach?"

"It's possible. If she left right away."

"The drug could explain her disorientation. Maybe she *did* fall."

"Or maybe someone knows more than they're telling. Meth can be a solitary experience, but in the first stages, people like company when they're experimenting."

"Chipper, listen," she said after she hung up.

As she filled him in, his soft brown suede eyes narrowed, a transformation from boy to man. "Very bad stuff. I knew a guy who went to sh—I mean fell apart getting on it. Gave up everything. He lost his job, went three times to a rehab centre. It never stuck. Don't know where he is, and I don't want to know." His sudden passion seemed to indicate that the person might have been close, a relative or friend. She thought of asking, but saw his jaw quiver as he grew silent, looking out the window to where a steroidal seagull was dueling with a crow over a crust of bread.

"Whitehouse is going to have a heart attack. He thought he'd seen the back of us." She left a message on his voice mail at West Shore. Accident or something worse, the development called for more interviews and certainly a search of Angie's room. Breaking the news at the Didrickson house, the last thing on Holly's mind had been an intrusive search. Had her bereaved father already cleaned out the room or left it intact like a family shrine? At one household she'd visited, the mother had showed her the perfectly preserved room of their baby who had died in its cradle ten years before. Angie's room probably had a computer. What about a diary or other information about her relationships?

She closed her fist as the wind rose and a flurry of rain smashed the window like bullets. Somebody knew where that meth came from. Suddenly she felt as if they weren't in Kansas any more. With drugs knocking at the door, even Toto wasn't safe.

Five

She drove down West Coast Road through corridors where massive Douglas firs had fueled life for over a century. Now that the rains and cooler weather had arrived, the smell of wood fires filled the air, despite B.C. Hydro's fourth cheapest power in North America. Many retired neighbours, who had long careers in the forestry industry and enjoyed access to the scrap lots, appreciated the free heat. Suddenly a clear-cut broke the sylvan dream, a few token trees left standing amid the wreckage.

Long rows of power poles marched by the roadside, fragile nineteenth-century technology. After every storm in which lines were taken by falling trees, calls came for the wires to be buried. In new subdivisions, they were. Otherwise, the cost was prohibitive.

The microcosm of the timber industry on Vancouver Island continued. On one side, like a miniature graveyard with tiny white stakes for monuments, were acres of trial seedlings. On the another, a forest planted in 1948. Trees a foot and a half in diameter for six decades of growth. Her mother had been born that year.

On Otter Point Place at last, she crested the sloping driveway and parked her car behind her father's toy-sized Smart Car, bright red with a bumptious attitude. A muted bark caught her attention. The hillside overlooking the strait resembled a bandshell, reverberating with sounds from all directions. Next door lived Katie, a black lab. Up the hill on the next parallel street, Randy's Place, were several dogs and a new litter of puppies. She pushed open the back door and found a furry head in her groin. A border collie, young and agile and ready for play. White paint seemed to have been spilled down its ebony head in perfect symmetry. Strange to see a dog in the house after all this time. Bruna had been part of her childhood, followed by Nikon. He'd gone to Rainbow Bridge a month after her mother had vanished. After that, closing himself off to all comforting connections with the excuse that any dog was too much expense and trouble, her father had lived a solitary life.

"What's going on?" she called as she ruffled its silken fir and traced its ribs ever so slightly, a sign of fitness. "Where did this guy come from? Is it a stray? It looks too healthy to have been on its own for long."

Her father came through the TV room with a dishcloth in his hand. The smell of liver and onions made her stomach lurch. Doing the shopping for him, she had stocked Chef Boy-ar-dee ravioli in the cupboard, her default meal.

"He's a rescue. Got him today," he said. "And he's been neutered already. A bonus."

"Why have you been keeping this a secret?" she asked with a nervous laugh. It was his house, and he could do what he wished. His occasional sadness worried her, though he always seemed to pull himself together. Company might smooth things out. As for the comical but shallow breed, there was no accounting for tastes. On the island, border collies could do no wrong. They had free passes for any mischief.

His lean and serious face seemed to relax as he petted the animal. His eyebrows were growing fuzzy and unruly, another sign of an old man. "Suppose I have. Just wanted to think it over. I've seen him over by Wink's at the soccer field. There's a rescue place on Sooke River Road. Run by a lady called Shannon."

"Why a border collie?" She didn't like to discourage her father, but everyone knew that breed was high energy. This wasn't a farm. It wasn't even fully fenced, with the front open and one side a hedge of cedars.

"Thanks to the wise breeding of working dogs, their health is excellent and their disposition generally good. I know you loved our sheps, but their health problems cost a fortune. And this man doesn't eat more than two cups of kibble a day. A few quality treats like bison sticks are allowed. Very economical."

"But what about exercise? Aren't they pretty demanding?" Watching her watch him, the dog wheeled, grabbed a rope tugger and presented it to her.

"Depends on the individual. But Hogan/Logan can settle down quickly, and he's already house-trained, so that's another plus. I'd never take on a new pup. Bonnie always kept each shepherd in bed with us and trained them in two weeks flat. She'd get up at all hours of the night to take them out." He reached over and pulled out a bag with tennis balls and Chuck-it wand. "Shannon suggested running him off his feet with this device. Modern version of the atlatl." He mimed a toss, and she ducked as she laughed.

"Hogan/Logan? Did a poet wannabe name him? Or does he have a split personality?" She succumbed and gave the rope a tug up and down and from side to side. The dog fixed her gaze with the same insane focus that genes had given him for sheep. Was he one hundred per cent nature, or would nurture play a role?

Her father sighed. "He's had a sad history. His first owner wanted a rescue dog to help her train for marathons, but was refused because she worked long hours. She got a pup from a breeder."

"Marathons. It's a dog's dream. Plenty of exercise."

"Shannon said that pups shouldn't run those distances. And the rest of the time she left him alone in a yard in Esquimalt fourteen hours a day. He barked his brains out."

"Who wouldn't?" Though not warming to the animal, she felt sorry for his bad luck.

"So she gave him up. Points for one good decision. For the last six months, he's been in foster homes. They changed his name to Logan."

"Enough already." Holly snapped her fingers at Hogan/ Logan and pointed away. To his credit, the dog stopped pestering her, picked up a ball and turned to the other human. "Logan's even worse. Any ideas?"

Jackie and Bryan's diesel truck chugged up the drive next door. The dog dropped the ball and gave a roaring bark. Thirty pounds of attack dog. "Small guy, big voice. Doesn't he sound like a warrior, like...a Shogun?"

But when she tried to pet him, the dog growled and veered away. "What's that about?" she asked.

Her father waved his hand. "He's talking. Mumbling. Typical. Means nothing. I've been on-line at a rescue site." True enough, Shogun picked up the tug again and presented it to her.

"Who's going to walk him?" She passed her father a questioning look. He had far more free time than she did. Ivory tower perks.

"I am, of course." He gave her an impish smile. "Unless you want to take a turn. Now and then. Be some company for you. Take him to work."

"I don't think so. He's not a service animal, and he's too

94

small to be a protector. On a good day, I could tuck him under my arm."

Excusing herself, she went upstairs. On the bedroom wall were pictures of Bruna at sunset on the beach, her noble head posed in profile like Nefertiti's. Then Nikon, a puppy gazing up from the green leaves of a salal bush, his floppy ears a comical beret. In his handsome youthful vigor, leaping over a log with a determined look in his eyes. She'd always remember those shepherd eyes, deep and sober, penetrating and wise, retaining that connection even when old bones creaked and flaccid muscles flagged. Not foxy like this young man's but full of purpose, asking, "What serious matter will we attend to today, mistress?" Not what can I pull, tug or chase to please myself? It's all about ME. No wonder border collies didn't appear in the ranks of guide dogs and other selfless creatures. They were too frivolous to be soulmates. Though she admired the sleek coat, white shirt and ruff with matching paws, handsome is as handsome does. Shogun reminded her of Jeff Pasquin, a shallow pretty boy in youthful plumage. She didn't trust either one.

Six

At ten the next rainy morning, Lindsey Benish appeared at the station with her mother in tow. The girl wore hip-hugger jeans exposing a flat belly with a red jewel in the navel. Her skin was clear and luminous, but her eyes were heavy with mascara and glittery eyeshadow. The liner-defined lipstick was charcoal. She wore blue plastic clogs, an island touch. Ann had provided them with coffee and a soda, and they perched like two hawks, their noses a genetic road map. Mrs. B had seventy pounds on her daughter and wore a bright, floral-print dress. Holly was sure she'd seen her at the Village Market, loaded up like a pack mule with chips, popcorn, soda and a bale of frozen chimichangas.

"You're early. Thanks for coming," Holly said, offering a stand for their umbrellas, ushering them into her office and hustling another chair from the lunchroom. She felt like a stage manager operating under an absent but demanding director. Whitehouse was overdue, perhaps due to the rain. He'd burned her ears over the phone when he'd called her back to discuss the new meth development. Obviously he preferred the case dead and buried, flawed or not.

"Are *you* going to interview my daughter?" Mrs. B asked. Lindsey took a lurid graphic novel from her backpack and began flipping pages as she popped dark brown gum. The air filled with chocolate. Her eyes fat slits, Mrs. B gave her daughter an elbow.

Holly managed an official smile. Had the crystal meth issue not arisen, she might have handled the girl alone. Whitehouse had been furious about having to reschedule his appointments. "Inspector Whitehouse should be here any minute. He's coming from the *city.*" *That in itself sounded impressive.*

While she was checking a list of questions, she heard a car roar up and a door slam. A few mutters from the main office, and Whitehouse came into the room. He wore a drenched beige raincoat spattered with mud. Puddles seeped from his shoes, and his pants were soaked to his knees. When he took off his hat, droplets fell from his dishevelled hair to his nose and down his jutting chin. "Flooding at Gillespie. I had to push a stalled cab. How does anybody commute from this no-man's land?"

"We all just got here anyway," Holly said. Maybe Chipper had some spare pants in his locker. Then again...she rather enjoyed Whitehouse's predicament.

With a shake of his head, he left, presumably for the bathroom. Five minutes later, he took his seat at the head of the interview table. Clearly he was unused to looking the least bit unkempt.

Holly composed herself and practiced a neutral look. Whitehouse was her leader, like it or not, and she needed to fall in behind him. There were no I's in TEAM, a platitude flourishing for good reason. So far she felt merely TAME, but she needed to toe the same line everyone did. Even her father had jumped through many hoops getting tenure. Suck it back or set up your own private-eye business like Boone had.

Introductions made, Whitehouse sifted a few papers and levelled his icy grey eyes at Lindsey. She presumed he'd read the statements, including Chipper's short interview. He wasted no time. "Where were you the night that Angie went missing?"

Lindsey turned another comic page. Whitehouse repeated himself. "Lindsey. Are you hard of hearing, girl?"

Her swollen feet crossed in cruel sandals, Mrs. B shifted in her chair, waves of a cloying vanilla perfume wafting across the room. She nudged her daughter. "Put that down."

"Where was I?" She sipped from the soda and wrinkled her nose at the bubbles.

"The whole night. Don't play coy. You're wasting our time." Whitehouse raised his voice another notch. Holly could read the anger in his eyes as a gauge neared the red zone.

"I don't see why I have to talk to anyone *again*. Been there, done that."

"We're not designing T-shirts here. Something new has come up. You'll find out on a need-to-know basis."

Holly approved the joke but not the jargon. This vacuous girl seemed a perfect match for Jeff. Babe and the Ox.

His face purpling and his breathing speeding up, Whitehouse added an ominous touch to his timbre, nailing each word. "So get to the point. A girl is dead. We're no longer sure it was an accident."

Lindsey sat up straight, the cogs of her brain finally turning. "So like you think she was...murdered? Get out."

A black storm cloud crossed his features. Whitehouse remained rigid, but Mrs. B flapped a placating hand and assumed an apologetic tone. "She says that all the time. It's just silly slang. No offense. Sometimes she says 'shut up', if you can imagine. Same thing. Kids. Go figure."

Whitehouse gave the mother a withering stare. She folded her chubby arms defensively and watched her daughter. Was Whitehouse married? He wore no ring, and he did not seem able to handle women except to bully them.

Cornered, Lindsey explained that she had sat around the

campfire with the gang. Then she'd gone to bed around eleven. Jeff came to her tent...at this point she had the wisdom to look a bit flustered in front of her mother...and spent the night.

Her mother tried to cross a leg and failed, so she sat up, mustering her dignity. "Lindsey's old enough to know the facts of life. She's on the pill and always insists on con...oh I hate that word...I mean protection. What can a mother do these days? Mine always said, 'Forewarned is forearmed'."

"Did Jeff tell you about us?" Lindsey's beady eyes narrowed, and she stuck out her pointed chin.

"You're a bright girl. What do you think?"

"Well, he was there. I'm not saying he was himself, though." She tugged on an earlobe. A *tell*, Holly thought. But what was the message?

"Explain that," Whitehouse asked.

She gave an annoying, tittering kind of laugh. "He was wasted. He passed out before...anything happened."

Her mother placed one hand on her ample chest and took a deep breath. "Lindsey, you told me he was a nice young man. When he came to dinner, he even volunteered to wash—"

"Mother, please. They don't care about that." Lindsey swung her flat face back to Whitehouse. "Jeff didn't go anywhere. Had a super headache the next morning, too."

Her mother assumed a hurt tone. "Were you drinking, too, Lindsey? You promised after the last—"

Lindsey lifted one finger. Like its fellows, it was long and pointed, a gel job in fluorescent green. Holly had had her nails done once. The next day, three broke off when she had to change a tire in the bush. "One beer. I swear. It's no big deal. How many margaritas do you pack away before Dad gets home?"

The mother swallowed with difficulty and looked out the streaky window, twisting a large diamond wedding ring ensemble.

Within the short sleeves of her dress, bat-winged arms threatened to flap free.

The dynamics weren't working. Holly caught Whitehouse's attention, seeking an opportunity to ask a question. He gave a curt nod. "What did you think of Angie? We need all the information that we can get from her friends," she said.

"Huh. I wasn't her friend. Used to be before she got snobby. Big friggin' swim star and all."

Mrs. B frowned. "Lindsey, watch your language."

"Were the other girls jealous of her success?" Holly asked.

"No way. Unless they were jocks. Who cares about that stupid stuff? No girl wants to look like a weightlifter."

"Was she dating anyone?"

"Jeff. Last year. He got sick of her, too. Stuck-up bitch. Somebody should have..." She blinked at their expressions and looked at her hands. "I didn't mean nothing. He just stopped dating her."

"Whose idea was that?"

"His, for sure. He tells me everything. We're close."

"Was Angie *close* with anyone else?"

A mischievous smile creased her face as if she had found a secret jewel. She batted her furry lashes. "There were rumours."

"Rumours?" Whitehouse came to attention.

She lowered her voice and looked around. "Ms Bass. The English teacher."

"Go on."

Lindsey crossed her legs theatrically and gave her gum a workout. "The L word's no big deal now. Ms Bass is okay. Angie never really said anything. But she was always in there after class with her English themes. Brown noser."

"Your cooperation is appreciated. One last question." Whitehouse shifted in his seat, tensing his muscles like a cougar preparing to spring. "Where would Angie get crystal meth?"

The girl's hand moved to her face, then she brushed back her long brown hair in a classic avoidance technique. Whitehouse twitched. "We don't mess with that sh—" she said.

"Lindsey, really. Your father will hear about this." Mrs. B settled into a pout.

Whitehouse stood, cracking his knuckles. He seemed to look down on them like a colossus. "Come on, Lindsey. Blade. Black beauty. Crypto. Pink. Tick tick. Do I have to run down the alphabet?"

Holly stifled a grin as she remembered those bizarre names from a Victoria meth website. Whitehouse had been fishing in the same pond.

Lindsey's eyes glittered, but the idea seemed more humorous than threatening. She began giggling, putting her hand over her bee-stung mouth. "Excuse me? Is that New York language from TV? Shard's more common out here. Maybe jib." She dropped her eyes. "I mean the kids that hang out in Victoria down around Cormorant and Blanshard call it that. Older people call it meth, same as the other stuff."

Whitehouse tapped a pencil and broke the point, startling Mrs. B. Picking up a small cube sharpener, he began grinding, testing the point until he was satisfied. "How do *you* know so much about the terminology?"

Lindsey folded her arms. "TV, movies. Plus we learned about it in Contemporary Problems class."

"So as far as you're concerned, there's no meth out here in sweet, innocent Sooke." Whitehouse tried a smirk. It didn't look good on him.

Lindsey threw back her skinny shoulders, revealing two fading hickeys. *A present from Jeff?* "I...can't say for every kid in town. I don't hang with anyone from Edward Milne. The Port

Renfrew gang go there. Everyone knows they're a rough bunch. Some of them have been in *jail.*" She spoke with a wide-eyed amazement that bordered on admiration. Bad boys were always an attraction. Even good girls paid the price.

When the Benishes had left, Whitehouse snapped shut his file and made a sour face. "We have two problems to track down. If anyone saw Angie on that bike that night, and where she got the meth."

Something had twigged in Holly's memory. "What about the Port Renfrew boys camping in the park?"

He shot her a caustic look. "I thought you took care of that. What did they say?"

Her stomach flip-flopped. "Well, I haven't—"

"Jesus. Get on it, then. You're a government worker, not some local yokel on island time." He stood and wiped at his damp pants, the knife crease a memory. "I'm going to Angie's house to check her room. Her father said he'd meet me there in an hour. And follow up on this English teacher, too, now that we have another confirmation. If you'd done your job right in the first place, I wouldn't be doing it for you."

"But at the time, we only—"

He stood and brushed at his wrinkled pants, scowling. "Need I mention that you called *me* in?"

Holly seethed for at least ten minutes after Whitehouse left, then found Kim Bass's number. Her home phone had no answering machine, so Holly made a note to call the school and find out her free period. In their interview at the beach, Bass had looked entirely normal except for dark circles under her eyes. Insomnia, she claimed. She had admitted taking an over-the-counter sleeping pill. Holly traced a few contemplative patterns on her note pad and wondered whether the teacher had been dealing. The morning's troll of the online *Globe and Mail* had reported a principal in Detroit selling drugs, not to students at least, but distributing from the school itself. Unheard of in Canada, but for how long?

"I'm going to Rainbow Elementary with Sean Carter to start this year's DARE instruction. Andrea should be here in five minutes to take over the desk," Ann said. Larger posts had many civilian positions, but Andrea operated on an on-call basis. DARE stood for Drug Abuse Resistance Education, a ten-week program.

Ann's face was pale, another line etched into the broad forehead as she leaned against the doorway out of necessity, not languor. Holly asked, "Are you feeling all right? Are you okay with the duty?" She regretted her quick words, though prompted by concern. Officers didn't consult their staff as to whether they were equal to ordinary assignments. They assumed it. For insight, Holly had searched the Mayo Clinic website to learn about the symptoms of DDD. Standing for long periods was as painful for Ann as sitting. Walking was easiest, though fast movements weren't advised. No wonder she couldn't assume active duties.

"Of course. Why do you ask?" Ann's tone was defensive, and her spine stiffened, though Holly saw her wince.

Flashing a smile that she hoped looked reassuring, Holly added a casual gesture. "No reason. That's fine then. Tell me how it goes."

Fossil Bay was too small to justify the many programs of a larger division, such as Restorative Justice, Drug and Alcohol Counselling, or Family Counselling, but friskier retirees liked to combine their daily exercise with bike-patrol duty. Those who could drive to French Beach or China Beach worked the Park Watch, writing down license plates for reference in case thefts occurred. Young Sean Carter kept an eye out for "suspicious" activity, including abandoned cars and trash dumping. Garbage collection was privatized in the area and cost about twelve dollars a month per household.

Ann lined up a pack of bright, kid-style brochures fresh from headquarters. "I like going to the school. At that age they're still open to ideas."

Holly remembered Ann's boy and saw an opportunity to reach out. "I guess you learned that raising...your son."

In a rare gesture, Ann searched her eyes, as if to ascertain Holly's sincerity. Apparently she found positive signs, because she continued. "The greatest school on earth. But Nick was a handful for awhile."

Holly's pulse jumped a few kilometres. How far should she go towards establishing friendship? Keep her radar open and pull back at the least sign of discomfort, banana-slug style? "That's hard to believe. He's a teacher now, isn't he? You must be proud."

Ann nodded, apparently warming to the conversation. "He could have become a serious problem at one point. Got in with a bad crowd. I was posted to Wawa when he was fifteen. Home of the giant goose, and I speak in a social sense, too. Absolutely nothing to do if you had no money for a snowmobile, boat, or motorcycle. We couldn't even afford cable. Our rabbit ears pulled in one patchy U.S. station."

Holly perched on the side of the desk in a casual but interested pose. "So what happened?"

Ann did an impromptu stretch. "Booze. He was picked up drunk after a house party gone bad. Three thousand dollars in damages. Two young girls nearly died from drinking punch from contaminated windshield fluid jugs. When he sobered up, I told him I'd sign him over to Children's Aid if he pulled a stunt like that again. I arranged with a colleague to take him to the agency for an interview. Showed him some legal papers already filled out."

Holly's mouth opened at the imagination and the desperation. "Shock therapy. Would you really have..."

A thin smile crossed Ann's mouth, the first so far. "I was very tempted. You have to know when your resources aren't equal to your responsibilities. But he smartened up. First he got a part-time job at a motel, then a scholarship to Acadia University."

"So your bluff worked. I wouldn't have had the nerve. And where is he now?"

"He teaches high school up around Prince George. Third year already. English. Can you believe? He wants to be a novelist but knows he needs a day job."

"Sounds sensible." Holly had enjoyed their surprisingly productive conversation. Then as the wall clock ticked, she said, "Guess I'd better get moving. I thought we'd seen the last of Whitehouse, but now—"

Ann gave a dismissive snort. "I knew Phil Whitehouse when we were on the force together in Richmond. He's a bully, but he usually gets the job done, methods aside. Don't think he'd remember me, though."

Holly had seen a graduation picture of Ann in the files, fit and determined, a world away from those extra twenty pounds. "He's over fifty, old enough to be a Superintendent or even Chief Super. What's holding him back?"

Ann assumed an owlish look increased by the two small puffs of hair over each temple. "Hot temper. He socked another inspector shortly after making the grade. Seems the other guy blew a case he'd worked on. They've had their eyes on him ever since. He never backs down. Gets his teeth in like a bulldog on a bear. Problem is, if he's wrong, then there's no steering him off the road to hell."

Gravel crunched outside from a braking bike. Ten-year-old Sean came in and walked up to Ann, admiration clear in his shining butterscotch eyes. His round cheeks were pinked with exertion, and he could barely catch his breath. "The school sent me over. Are you ready? Can I carry anything?" He gave her a winning smile. Like many south coast youngsters, he wore long, baggy shorts well into the fall. Holly had seen him walking in a downpour with no umbrella, just a hoodie over his head. Immune to rain, with the high metabolism of youth. His sweatshirt bore the picture of a familiar detrivore: Nanner Slugs Rule!

Ann handed him a bundle of flyers and bookmarks. Clearly she had bent the principles by making Sean an honourary member of the Bicycle Patrol even though the official age was nineteen. He couldn't have a uniform, but she'd found him an old badge for his jacket. It read: RCMP GRC: Gendarmerie Royale Canadien POLICE, with the crown at the top adapted from St. Edward's for Her Majesty Queen Elizabeth II.

"I hear you've been doing a great job as our...auxiliary member in training." Holly shook Sean's small hand, then gave him a salute.

He saluted back in smart style. "I'm going to be a horseman when I grow up. Are you called a horsewoman?"

"Close enough. Though we drive our ponies now."

"Cool. I have my own horse. Daisy's fifteen."

Many households with acreage kept horses, the benefits of a rural zone. Holly felt his enthusiasm blow through the detachment like a healthy breeze. Working with the community made a strong alliance. "Then you might like to try out for the Musical Ride."

Ann's face relaxed. With the distraction of the boy, Holly was enjoying the interaction. Had the tension been broken?

With talents like Ann's, Holly could imagine the humiliation of a desk job. Was there another way she could contribute? The small team could start to build on its individual gifts.

"Pardon us for one more second, Sean. Official business." While he put a finger on each of the Wanted posters on the bulletin board as he read the information, Holly pulled Ann aside. "This crystal meth connection. See what you can learn from your students."

Ann reached for her jacket. Her large hand had strong, blunt nails. "Oh, come on. They're too young."

"So I hope, but they have brothers and sisters. And younger kids are always underfoot. They may have heard something."

"That's true." Ann opened the door for Sean. "And for the best picture of drug use out here, call Sooke. Ask for Corporal Hoicks."

Andrea Bonhomme passed her and settled into the front desk with a large thermos. She was tall and willowy, a retired loans officer. Her strawberry blonde hair was gathered in one gorgeous braid down her back. Like them, she wore traditional shirt and pants with a volunteer patch. Without people like Andrea to fill in the gaps, life would be much more difficult for the detachment.

As Holly learned when she called, Corporal Hoicks had worked with the Drug Unit in Victoria and had his finger on the pulse of the Capital Region. The man's voice was ragged with concern. "Christ, yes, it's a regular epidemic. And we haven't even seen the tip of the iceberg yet. Sorry for the lame joke. Meth is as bad as crack any day." He explained that most people thought that the drug was limited to scabrous nether regions of urban areas. But even suburban housewives could become addicted. The unparalleled rush, hours of euphoria, the cheapness at ten dollars a "point," or tenth of a gram, and the availability made a toxic and fatal combination.

"So it's here after all. My case isn't just an anomaly." She felt an undercurrent shoot through her core, like turning over a mossy rock and finding a den of poisonous newts.

His laughter was grim and ironic. "It's in Sooke, guaranteed. Didn't take long to snake its way over from the street scene in Victoria. Their Specialized Youth Detox Centre has seen meth victims increase nearly six times in the last few years. Over seventy per cent of admissions are for meth. Average age, sixteen."

"Average," she said with a sigh. "That means..." Her voice trailed off as another thought entered her mind. "Could they be *making* it here? We've had our share of pot farms, private and otherwise." B.C. bud, the legendary provincial product, made up a sizable percentage of the British Columbia economy. Taxing it might pay for health care.

"Brush up on your terminology. They 'cook' it. A whole new ball game for investigators. Get the guidelines report after that explosion in Vancouver? You gotta be careful as hell taking down a meth lab. Blew the house halfway to Whistler. Buddy of mine got second-degree burns busting down the door."

"I was just posted here from way up north, Corporal. Pardon me for being naïve."

He laughed in a friendly way. "We had a forum in Sooke last summer at the school. Showed that 'Death by Jib' video. Over fifty people came, parents mainly. Were their eyes ever opened. Should be a yearly experience, but if you overdo it, kids turn off."

"I can understand that. Any other initiatives I should know about? Or is the ferry sailing away without me?"

"Our Staff Sergeant, Roger Plamondon, was instrumental in getting the Sooke Council to pass a bylaw to help authorities detect not only grow-ops but meth labs. Municipalities on the lower mainland anticipated us by a few years on that."

"Good thing I asked. I assumed we'd be operating under the Controlled Drugs and Substances Act." A sheen of sweat gathered on her brow. How close could she have come to looking like a fool?

"Getting search warrants under that relic could take weeks. The perps could be gone overnight."

"Sounds like a great idea. Very proactive. I left here long before this drug scene. What's your take on the area and its possibilities for 'cooking', as you put it?"

"I live in Saseenos, and I do volunteer work for the salmon hatcheries. It's pretty wild country, despite the acreage in clear cuts. Five miles from town, all the better for an isolated lab. Abandoned farms, forests, ravines and twelve-foot brambles make a better deterrent than chainlink. All natural and very easy to camouflage from occasional helicopter flybys like the one that helped us find a cannabis patch on Farmer Road."

"True. And out this way? Past Otter Point to Shirley and Jordan River?"

"In the interior, away from the coast road and tourist stuff, you might as well be in the northern bush. That's the way they like it. Nothing can be seen from the road. Junkyard dogs. Keep a few chickens, goats or llamas to justify the fences. Maybe even call it an organic farm, the new rage. For a small place, high electrical use is a tip-off. But often they're cheating and getting juice for free. That's my next point. Fire's one of the worst hazards with grow-ops. Bare wires going to the breaker box."

His comprehensive e-mail attachment an hour later illustrated signs of a potential meth lab. She read it with interest, instantly suspicious. As opposed to the stereotypical, more staid citizens of Victoria, with their legendary Empress tea room and haggis on Robbie Burns' day, people from the

Western Communities were mavericks. Irate over creeping suburban bylaws regulating open burning, the average man would stand up in council and say, "It's my damn land, and I'll do what I want with it." Her father had quipped that "Anything Goes" was the local anthem. Laid back, super casual in dress, a large proportion were hippies in their early sixties. They ate "slow food", organic if possible, and knew their homeless by name. Many had artistic sidelines like woodworking, pottery, weaving and painting, which they advertised by the roadside along with jars of flowers for sale on the honour system. Holly didn't see any of these gentle folk as possible lab rats, but that didn't mean that someone evil couldn't move in. The population doubled in the summer from tourists and had added a permanent two thousand in the last three years.

She thought of the trash angle of meth production. Recycling was free, and most property owners took advantage of the Blue Box program instead of trucking cans and bottles to the depot for nickels and dimes. Were the Capital Regional District trucks keeping an eye out for large quantities of discarded packaging, stained coffee filters, blister packs from cold remedy packages, lantern fuel containers, evidence of manufacturing? But what meth lab operator would locate on a well-travelled road? As for the other signs, strong odours similar to cat urine, ether and ammonia could be masked by burning wood as fall came on and fire warnings dropped to "green". Windows blacked out with plastic or foil? If the place were unseen from the road, who would know?

Ann returned around three as school let out and the lone bus began ferrying home the children. "I hate to think any of those babies are doing drugs." She sat down heavily, rubbing at her back. "Still, I guess twelve is the new twenty. Why do they want to grow up so fast? You're only a kid once, then it's game over. Pop stars are the exception to the rule."

"I made copies of these for you and Chipper." Holly handed Ann the meth info sheets. "Didn't you say that Sean rides all over the area?"

"He has a paper route before school. Delivers by six, poor kid. But on weekends he loves to tour the back country on his mountain bike."

"I know it sounds like we're training young Gestapo members to spy on their parents, but tell him to watch for this kind of thing." She pointed out a few paragraphs she had flagged with red ink.

Ann frowned, leafing through the warnings. "Isolated. Rural. Sounds like most of our district."

Holly had another, more alarming thought. "Tell Sean to be very cool about it. Under no circumstances is he to approach these places. Strictly ride-by at normal speed. Do you think he can handle that, because if not—"

Ann pursed her lips. "I know Sean, and I trust him. If the younger generation were more like he is..."

"Say no more. Your opinion is good enough for me."

An hour later, Paul Gable called. "I thought you'd like to know that the school is having a memorial service for Angie. It's tomorrow at eleven. In the gym. Sorry about the short notice. I'm glad I caught you in the office."

"And the funeral?" People usually wanted closure. That was another frustration in her mother's disappearance. Her father had refused even a memorial service, another reason why Bonnie's family had severed contact with him.

He cleared his throat. "Nate thinks it's a waste of time and money, making businesses rich. He's opting for cremation. But the kids have really gone all out for this service. A celebration of her life. Videos of Angie swimming at tournaments. Our choir will perform, too. Some of the kids will speak. And a few staff, too."

"Thanks for thinking of me. Of course I'll be there."

She should have checked about the service herself, if only as a courtesy. Tomorrow would be a good time to catch Kim Bass and Coach Grove.

When she got home, she saw her father sitting at the kitchen table in the bay window staring out at the waves etching white on the waters. Butterflies frolicked around the late dahlias on the deck. The rich and savoury smell of her father's premier dish filled the room. Shogun was lying on a plush cushion by the counter, looking like a baby rajah. His paws held a large rawhide chewie. Down the stairs to the solarium, the sound of Patty Page singing "Old Cape Cod" drifted up like a balm.

From his posture, she could see that he was looking at a picture on the wall. Then she remembered. September 30th. The anniversary of her mother's disappearance. How could she have forgotten? Slowly she came forward, trying not to disturb him. The picture had been taken at Bonnie's graduation from UBC. This was as formal as Holly'd ever seen her, black gown, hair rolled under just touching her collar. What did they call that style? A shag? Hadn't her mother once joked that she had worn rollers to bed like a thorny crown? Soon after, Bonnie had adopted a no-nonsense short hair cut which required a quick brush kiss. "Ready to wear," she had called it.

Bonnie Rice had gone on to law school at Osgoode Hall and met her father while he was doing his doctoral work at the University of Toronto. They'd married and followed his job to Victoria, not far from her family in Cowichan. Holly ran through her memories like a bittersweet movie. Bonnie had never been the pie-baking, stay-at-home kind of mother.

They'd laughed over her effort to make rice pudding like her grandmother's. But she'd never parked Holly in a day care. Despite the awkwardness, she had taken Holly to work whenever possible. Content in a small law firm arranging simple wills and real-estate transactions, she made little money. Then when her own mother died from tuberculosis just after Holly was born, the special needs of native women and children began to claim Bonnie's attention. Remote areas had unique challenges due to the isolation. First a safe place, then healing, education and goals for the woman and her children. Finally a job to maintain independence. Bonnie had fought long and hard for funding, appeared before the legislature, spoken until hoarse on television and radio. "Pro bono" must have been tattooed on her heart.

Her gift was an ability to assess needs, then locate and funnel resources where they would do best, interfacing with literacy people, doctors without borders, prenatal care, shelters for the homeless and especially for battered women. She had worked for Victimlink, Cherie's House and the Sexual Assault Centre, stirring many well-guarded pots on the way. There wasn't a millionaire she hadn't approached to sponsor a room, or buy furniture or business machines. As her profile grew, so did the number of people who wanted women kept in their place. Countless times, she'd fielded threatening phone calls from abusive husbands.

Often she was gone for weeks, but she never forgot her daughter's birthday, April 1st, a family jest. A brown paper package would arrive in the mail, a beaded jacket, an eagle feather carefully wrapped, a polished agate. "I'm sorry not to be with you, darling," she'd say on the phone, when she could find one. "A word of birthday advice. Modern wisdom has it that a woman should never learn to type. It will enslave you. But I've found it handy. And your father's such a good cook that you should get his recipes before you go off to school. Those two talents should sustain you. If you need guidance or are in trouble, call on your spirit animal, the deer. And don't tell me how helpless they are. An antler in the heart can kill a man."

Holly could still recall how Bonnie had arranged for a huge divorce settlement for a woman whose arm had been broken and her vision compromised due to beatings in front of her young children. Her husband, owner of a large car dealership in Nanaimo, had avoided jail by agreeing to the terms.

"I should have shot him when I had the chance," Delores Ash had said behind dark glasses as she'd sat in their living room. Ten-year-old Holly had just brought her a cup of coffee and made sure it was safe in her shaking hand. She wasn't sure if the sad lady was joking, but her mother's face seemed serious. "I know you would have gotten me off, Bonnie. Probably with a gold medal."

And her mother added with a wry smile, "You have my number if you change your mind. But the bastard's better off alive, where he can continue to pay for his crimes. Being dead is far too good for him."

Holly shook off the memory. Sometimes she imagined her mother by her side, offering advice, but she knew it was her own conscience, however shaped by the lost woman. Her career had taken a one-hundred-and-eighty degree turn when she might have been out saving stands of Garry oak. Much though her mother loved nature, she put people first, and she would have applauded the change.

Her father's shoulders gave a slight heave, and she heard him whisper, "Holly's home. You'd like the woman she's become. But where, oh where..." He wore a gift from his wife, a thick and warm Cowichan sweater in muted browns and greys.

Holly backed up and closed the French doors behind her as

she passed through the TV room to the kitchen. Disturbing his thoughts without warning would be like interrupting a prayer. "Hey. What's for dinner?"

Norman seemed to slip something into a folded newspaper. When it came to emotions, he was a very private man. Some thought he was oblivious to matters of the heart. She knew otherwise. Even though her parents had drifted apart, something golden and good had brought them together to usher her into the world.

"If I've made it right, your nose should tell you." He grinned and tucked the paper under his arm.

She lifted her chin to the ceiling and moved it back and forth like a flavour-seeking sensor. "Mac and cheese. Am I ever glad I found you in the Fifties. Hardly low-cal, but simple and comforting."

She saw Shogun roll over for a belly rub and obliged. His slanted eyes fluttered shut as if drugged. All men led with their groins, in honest fashion but often against their own interests. Perhaps even her father when he was young. "Did you get out with the dog?" she asked.

"Soon as you left for work. Took him up Randy's Place to the old gravel pit. Short and sweet." He looked at her as he stirred a pot of Harvard beets. "But he wouldn't mind another go, so to speak. If you're not too tired."

She recognized the gentle blackmail. The old man was trying to get her to bond, not to forget her shepherds, but to move on, something he still couldn't do with her mother. She gave him an arch glance to indicate that she was wise. "Let me get out of this combat gear, and we're in business."

"No hurry. You've got half an hour."

A short time later she came down the stairs in capri pants and a CourtTV T-shirt, grabbed a leash, and whistled to the dog. They left the house and headed for the turnaround. A covey of quail, tiny, coroneted busybodies, were flushed from the blackberry bramble hedgerow. Holly made a note to collect some late berries for their dessert. Her Salmon Kings ball cap would serve for the collection.

The turnaround at Otter Point Place led to an old path downhill through bushes, across from a small public access for Gordon's Beach. This historic strip often attracted wind surfers and ocean admirers bearing the island signature cup of coffee. Her father's home and others dotting the uplands had once been part of the Tugwell, then the Gordon farm. The family's salmon trap had sat offshore at this point for many years. In December of 1912, the Gordon family awoke to a roaring sound. The barque *County Linlithgow* from London had mistaken the new Sheringham Point light for Race Rocks fifty kilometres east. Instead of turning into snug Victoria harbour, the captain found his four-masted vessel gone aground. Accorded the best of hospitality from the surprised Gordons, the sailors refloated their boat at the next tide. Now an award-winning meadery occupied part of the property, with tastings and tours during peak season. The hives were often relocated into the clear-cuts in summer when fireweed was in bloom.

But slenderly trusting the obedience of the young dog, Holly latched him on to cross busy West Coast Road, scramble over the high-tide flotsam and jetsam, then let him loose on the beach. The waves thrust fingers up the sloping cobble, then retreated in a curtain of noisy white effervescence. Shogun spied a woman edging the surf like a tightrope walker and instantly ran forward, deaf to Holly's cries. Everyone he met was a friend, a charming but annoying trait indicating a lack of control by the owner. "Sorry," she said to the lady who was carrying a colourful golf umbrella. "Everything that looks like a stick must be one."

"Border collies. Gotta love 'em. Smartest dogs in the world," the woman replied, ruffling the dog's fur, then setting off up the bank to a tiny driftwood cottage no bigger than Norman's woodshed.

Open to debate, Holly thought, a matter of wiring, not problem solving. GSDs were the Einsteins of the dog world. Border collies were clever card-counters at a poker table, peeking out from under their green plastic eyeshades.

Shogun waded in and began herding waves, snapping and barking. The comic sight gave her the first laugh of the day. Along the shore, great mounds of seaweed had drifted in, kelp tangled like huge mounds of fat green spaghetti with bulbs at one end. A small tug miles out pulled a vast mat of chained logs. The captain chose his times with care. Serious wind and wave action could break the bonds and cause a shipping nightmare, not to mention the loss of tens of thousands of dollars of potential board feet.

She sat on a sun-bleached log and collected smooth white stones, placing them artfully as beachcombers often did, watching for the true prize, a piece of time-polished glass. The rote motions helped her think. Police work wasn't all action. *What if* often helped, but *that's funny* was an even better phrase. Who had given Angie the drugs? Would anything turn up at her house? If they found a meth lab in the bush, would that bring any answers? She shuddered, knowing that arrests often spread like a poisonous tide, revealing the rot underneath the pleasant surface. But progress beat stasis.

Shogun trip-tropped toward her, something odd in his mouth. His jaws were working like a baby's with a soother. "What's that?" Suddenly she froze. It was a splintery rib bone, probably from someone's picnic. "Leave it!" She might be driving to the vet instead of forking down mac and cheese.

He caught her excitement and gamboled down the beach, glancing back in an insolent dare. She followed, tripping on the cobble, angrier by the moment, mostly at herself for a lack of vigilance. Finally, a wave caught his small body, and he dropped his morsel, eyes slitted and his prick ears floppy with water. She waded in, soaking her feet, and grabbed his collar. "You're under arrest for possession of a controlled substance." "Biting" him with her hand as his mother would have, she gave him a gentle shake to let him know who was in charge. "And you'd better not have swallowed anything. Ve haf vays."

Seven

Whitehouse called that morning. "I had to stay at the Didrickson house until after eleven. Jesus. I hate that Sooke Road. The berm is crumbling between a couple of rock cuts, and the oncoming jackasses are over the line. I deserve danger pay," he said.

Holly wished that she'd been invited to the search. "No surprises in her room, then?"

"Not one secret diary." He paused. "Ferreting around in underwear drawers like a pervert. I didn't sign on for this."

Holly suppressed a smile at the more human image. "If you're sure. I can go over it myself. Maybe a woman—"

"What do you mean, 'sure'? Listen here. I've done a hundred similar searches. There was no sign of drugs of any kind. Are you suggesting that I take the Canine Unit over there to sniff the place out?"

Did dogs include crystal meth in their repertoire? Was this his idea of a joke? "Of course not. What about her computer?" Safe to assume every teenager had one.

His tone was gruff. "That's the first place I looked. Her password for booting was automatic, so no problem. Doesn't look like she had anything to hide."

"Proves that she trusted her father. He seemed like a decent guy."

"My kids zipped their lips around me. But while they lived

in my house, I gave their rooms a thorough and unannounced search every month. Kept them honest, I'll tell you."

Holly couldn't imagine her parents in this invasion of privacy. What kind of relationship did he have with his children? And where was his wife? "What about her history?"

"Just swim stuff. Didn't even belong to Myspace or Facebook." He paused. "That's unusual in itself. She was no joiner, I guess. Her word-processing program was used for school assignments."

"So she was serious and didn't waste time. That fits with what we know. How about the Favourites command?"

A deep sigh came over the lines. She could sense him drumming his knobby fingers. "Winter Olympics. Swim information. University websites like Calgary and Waterloo. Nutrition. Crystal Meth B.C."

"What?" Hair on the back of her neck prickled.

"She was a contributor. Signed in to the forums, even under her own name. Her posts were extremely anti-meth. That's what the website's for. To help addicts and inform the public."

"What about the password?"

He sniffed in disdain. "Angie had a tiny notebook with all her dedicated passwords. Good thing no one tried to clean out her bank account."

Holly remembered a few classes from basic training. No computer geek herself, she knew enough to protect herself from phishing. "Erased files can be retrieved."

"Are you telling *me* that? I collected the hard drive to send in to Forensics. That'll take another week." He let a moment pass. "A waste of time. All we're doing is looking for a small-time pusher or someone who passed on this crap. This case has had all the resources it deserves."

She told him about the memorial service. "Fine, fine," he

said before hanging up. At least he hadn't asked her again about whether she'd contacted the staff. Clearly he was moving on.

The secretary at Notre Dame said that Kim's free period was at ten, same as Terry Grove's. That gelled with the memorial service at eleven. Taking her car, Holly reached the Sooke limits, turned up busy Grant Rd, then over to Church past one of the few surviving farms in the core. A small herd of beef cattle grazed the stony ground, oblivious to the rampant development around them. A familiar old black bull with a broken horn raised his head and lowed. That's when she realized that she was driving the same route that had taken her to high school for three years. An assembly line for the petty kingdom of girls.

Notre Dame Academy on Warren Street had capitalized on a strong Roman Catholic presence in the post-war period. It had been well supported by the timber and fishing barons who wanted their daughters safe nearby. When enrollment gradually dropped, not long after Holly had left, it went coed. Now the ballooning population of the Sooke area, with its cookie-cutter developments for younger people and their children, might inject new blood.

The Romanesque red brick building with white trim had two stories, a gymnasium at one end, and a fenced athletic field out back with a baseball diamond and soccer goal posts. In Holly's day, the Saints soccer team had excelled. She remembered watching some of their games at Fred Milne Field. Opponents came from all over the province. Today a homemade sign read: "Game of the Year. Comox. Meet at the Log. Bring your helmut."

She entered the building as a bell rang, signaling a period change. The students paid her no notice, probably imagining that she was here for the service. The uniform was short kilts on the girls and dress pants for the boys. Both wore white shirts and dark ties, though a cardigan was allowed. Only on weekends did Notre Dame students experiment with Goth or gangsta couture. She'd seen them gathered around food joints at the Evergreen Mall, talking on cell phones and passing around cigarettes.

Notre Dame hadn't been Holly's choice. Her family had been free-thinking agnostics, but her father had perceived that a better education might be hers, religious instruction aside. Sending her all the way to Victoria to historic St. Margaret's was too expensive. "It's time you had a fresh perspective," he would say. "The island is a small place, and you don't want a mind to match."

"What about the heaven, hell, and sin stuff?" she asked, sprawled on the sofa and leafing through the school brochure. "This says we have to go to mass every Friday. Even confession?"

He chuckled. "Fairy tales, my dear. But mind your manners and don't make fun of them. Catholics don't like that. You're there for the small classes. And the Latin. A good basis for any discipline. What's the name for skunk cab—"

Holly didn't need to open her threadbare *Plants of Coastal British Columbia*. "*Lysichiton americanum.*"

Her mother flipped a rolled-up *Mother Jones* magazine onto the table. "Say what you will about public school, "she told Norman, "it's moving forward instead of being rooted in the past. A live culture. Not like dead languages and the frivolous things you teach." Her voice rose, and she paced the room, gesturing passionately.

"Snobs are better than thugs, Bonnie." Sitting in his recliner in the solarium, her father rattled the *Sooke News Mirror*. "Look at this police-beat report. Drinking and vandalism at the old graveyard again. Tombstones broken and defaced. No pride in their pioneer heritage. If they had more homework, they wouldn't have the time to get into trouble. And at least Notre Dame keeps a sharp lookout on absenteeism." He shot a smile at Holly. "Not that we need to worry about that."

On the way to the main office, she passed a familiar mural depicting the timber industry, in this community everyone's "friend". The long panel in Grandma Moses style showed a stream full of shimmering, leaping fish. On one side, trees were being cut, logged and hauled as neatly as a pack of yellow pencils. On the other, an army of jolly planters was investing in silviculture futures. A picnic with happy children was arranged in the final corner. No clear-cutting, no run-off, no burning and no diesel fumes. Did anyone really believe it, or were they glad to keep their jobs in the faltering industry? The alarming fact was that the companies owned over eleven per cent of the island, and eighty per cent of the old growth had been logged in the last forty years. Other than inaccessible mountain passes and a few protected areas like Cathedral Grove, little of the original beauty was left.

"Office", the sign on the smoked-glass door read: "Visitors please register." Holly had gone there every day as a student. Finished her work in half the time, she had made an ideal messenger and often carried supplies around the school. The secretary, an older red-headed woman with buck teeth but a welcoming smile, told her that the principal, Dave Mack, was at a conference in Burnaby. Brightening as he saw her face, Paul Gable came from an adjoining office. "Corporal Martin. Good to see you again. I'm so glad you could make it." He gave her tailored suit and low pumps an approving glance. "You didn't wear your uniform. That's probably better. In this age, the days of Officer Friendly are over, sadly enough. Much too adversarial now."

"I'd be glad to give a talk on Career Day or whatever it's called."

He beamed then pulled out a pocket planner and made a note. "What a super idea. I'll give you a call in April. And I'll have our counsellor reel in the girls. We need more female officers."

"I'm afraid I'm here on business, too." She sighed. "We have an inspector in from West Shore and some new developments."

"I heard about the interviews and hoped that they were just a final formality." He straightened his striped tie and adjusted the folded handkerchief in the pocket of his sportcoat. Then he pulled out a pack of gum and pushed out a square, popping it in his mouth. Nico-Ban. "This isn't going to be good for the students. What a nightmare."

Holly nodded in sympathy and tried for a confident smile. "I need to talk to Ms Bass and the coach again."

Gable looked around as the secretary bundled papers together and went into the hall, leaving them alone. His voice lowered, and he leaned forward, checking that the door was shut. "Is it true that crystal meth was involved? Lindsey Benish spread the word, not that I trust that little...girl. Meth here, for god's sake. And brought on the class trip? I blame myself." He twisted his face in embarrassment. She imagined that he must have faced serious criticism with the drowning happening on his watch.

"How could you have prevented it? Strip-search the students?"

He shook his head in concern. "We try to keep current, but even our drug awareness programs can't offer total protection, not when a new chemical thrill lurks around every corner. Our nurse is only part-time, but she monitors the drug scene. Listen to this." He told her about "cheese", the latest high. A combination of black heroin and cold medication, one snort for a couple of dollars. Problem was, the unreliable nature of the purity of the heroin had killed several youths in Vancouver.

"Alcohol is still the main problem, though. Teenagers are picked up every weekend, usually remanded to their parents. How would you say Notre Dame stacks up?" Holly was making the logical connection between any kind of mood-altering substance.

He gave a furtive look around the office and into the hall. "I'm going to level with you, but I'd rather you didn't spread the word around, because who needs that publicity? Sure, we have a few bad apples. Bring beer to school, take off on their lunch hours. For a second offense, they're expelled. Three so far this year, no matter how their parents bitched. And we're working with the liquor stores this spring for a Dry Grad. The system's far from perfect, but we're as proactive as we can be."

It had been the same when Holly had been a student. With all the aging hippies in Sooke, getting marijuana was as easy as buying a pop. Beer was also in quick supply. She remembered tasting her first after a soccer game at sixteen. She'd kept herself clean after changing majors, knowing that a career in law enforcement had no room for substance abuse. They'd been warned that even a misdemeanor could prevent them from entering the RCMP.

"People blame the school, they blame the parents, but everyone's in charge of himself. We tell the students about these critical choices." A worm of a question crossed his large brow. "Do you know any more about how she got it? Do you suppose she came in contact with someone in Port Renfrew? It's a tough place. The students mentioned seeing a few local boys the first day at the beach."

"I have a couple of names to follow up on." She wondered if he knew about Billy and Mike and guessed that he was grasping at any opportunity to pass the blame away from his own students. "We have doubts that she took the drug on her own."

He gave a sharp intake of breath, then exhaled slowly. "My thoughts exactly. Certainly not Angie." A frown passed across his features like a dark cloud. "But who would do such a thing? I see now why you need to re-interview people. How can I help? Can I show you around?"

"I graduated from here...more than a few years ago." She pointed at the old regulator clock, out of place in a digital world. "Several times I sat out a detention in this office. Skipping religion class."

He assessed her with a smile. "From your age, no disrespect meant, you must have been here in the glory days. Five hundred students. They came in from Victoria, even Duncan. We offered more electives then, the drama club, band and choir. Fewer sports, of course. All girls. I can't imagine that. Half of the teachers were nuns, I hear."

She made a brandishing gesture. "Let me tell you, they wielded a mean pointer and weren't afraid to break it over your head. How about you? When did you arrive?"

"This is my second year. The wife was sick of winter and wanted to move to the island, and they had an opening, so I transferred from a diocese on the mainland. Pulled a few connections, and the timing was good. We hit here just before the housing market went bananas. Forty per cent assessment increase in one year." He mimicked a rocket. "But I didn't know about the enrollment crisis. We're scraping by with only two hundred and twenty-five. If we don't see a substantial jump in numbers...let's just saying I'm praying as hard as I can."

"The new housing developments might save the day. Who says sewers aren't a blessing in disguise?" Many plots in the core which had no percolation for septic systems could now be parcelled out and sold. Money in the bank for retirees.

"Let's hope so. I like it here. So does Elanie."

The clock ticked on, prodding her. "Is Coach Grove in his office?" She remembered the layout of the school. Holly had played intramural baseball. Right field. She always cringed when the ball came her way. It was a self-fulfilling prophecy. Imagine you'll drop it, and you will. Still, her hitting and base running had compensated for that embarrassing weakness. Was that choking mechanism waiting for another opportunity?

Gable's stomach rumbled, and he gave it a rueful pat. "Oops. Shouldn't have skipped breakfast. Terry should be there. With a small staff, we know where everyone is at any time. I'll give him a buzz to stay put.

"I guess you know your way to the gym, Officer," Gable said, giving a slight scowl to a student with a mohawk, who entered and thumped onto a bench. He looked as if he had been sent there as punishment. "Not you again, Len. Same old story?"

"It's a bunch of bull, Mr. Gable. I was only..."

His words stuttered out in the changing voice of a young man as she went off down the hall. A bell rang, and students poured from the classrooms in a noisy but vibrant flow. Some went to the water fountains, others jostled each other. They all carried spine-challenging backpacks. A couple of whoops echoed, and a male teacher with a trim moustache emerged from a door. "Settle down. This isn't the circus. I have a nice fat pack of detention slips," he said, patting his pocket in a mock threat.

She could smell the gym before she got there. Cold, sweaty, with the silent cheers of thousands over the years and testosterone embedded in the walls, the varnished wooden bleachers that pulled out from the wall, the caged clock for basketball. Opponents. Saints. Banners on the wall from tournaments when the school was larger. Dingy grey padded mats and weight equipment. A thick rope snaking from the ceiling. The locker rooms hid at the far end. In the back corner was the coach's lair. "Terry Grove", a paper nametag said on a door. Not *Mr.* This man wanted to be a friend as well as a mentor. She knocked smartly.

At the request to come in, she found Grove with a Dagwood sandwich, as her father would say. No doubt it beat the dismal cafeteria fare. Mayonnaise dripped down his chin.

"Paul gave me a call," he said, reaching for a pile of serviettes. "You have more questions about Angie. I've already heard the rumours. News travels. Small community, smaller school."

The layers of meat and cheese made her stomach churn with hunger. "I'll be fast. Don't want to keep you from your lunch." Once again she'd forgotten to make herself something to eat.

She took the institutional wooden chair that he offered. He put down his sandwich and pointed to the coffee machine on a side table. When she nodded, he filled a cup for her. "Decaf okay? Fair trade. Got it at Serious Coffee."

"Perfect." She sipped the brew, making a mental note to pick up some for her father. At her mother's request and his own thrift, he'd always boycotted Starbucks.

Holly opened the notebook, turned to a fresh page and dated and timed it. "I came back to the school to try to track down this meth connection."

He shook his head, eyes deep with sorrow. "Those tests must be mistaken. Angie was a dedicated athlete. A brush with pot or a beer maybe. But meth? She gave a terrific talk on it for her health class. She was dead set that kids stay away from it. Even handed out cards with the B.C. Meth website. And the pictures of addicts. Holy crow. Put me right off my lunch."

Whitehouse had found research for the speech on the computer. "That's what I hear. But suppose someone slipped the drug to her."

Terry's face purpled, and he pounded the table. His eyes were wide with contempt. *Was he acting?* "That would be criminal."

"Exactly...coach. If she drowned as a result, we might have an involuntary manslaughter charge. Maybe even voluntary."

He looked puzzled. "I don't know anything about the law other than TV shows, but isn't manslaughter like murder? Like when a drunk driver kills someone?"

She gave a bittersweet smile. "One up the ladder from criminal negligence. Here's a similar case. A man let his son handle a loaded pistol. Showing off. A few days later, the boy took the gun from the closet and shot and killed his sister."

"I see. It's like the drug was a loaded gun."

A knock sounded at the door, and a slim young woman with close-cut chestnut hair came in. "Hi, Terry, I..." She caught a look from Grove, then noticed Holly. The girl gave her an unabashed assessment from top to bottom, as if measuring the competition. "Coach. Sorry. Guess I'm...interrupting."

He brushed crumbs from his Saints sweatshirt. "That's fine, Katie. I'll be free in..." He looked at Holly, and she held up five fingers. "A couple more minutes."

"Great. See you then. I brought the forms all filled out with my parents' signatures." She waved a bunch of papers. The door closed.

Grove cleared his throat with some difficulty. "Kaitlin Pollock. Katie. I've got her set up for a scholarship. She's our best swimmer next...next to Angie." He leaned forward and raised a thick eyebrow. "She's good, but Angie was one in a million."

Holly made a note. Had jealousy been a factor? "Was Katie on the camp-out? I don't recall seeing her."

He shook his head. "She had the flu that weekend. Left school on Thursday."

Holly asked Grove to keep an ear open. Then she gave him her card, recently arrived from headquarters. It seemed odd to read Corporal by her name, but it felt good, as if she were working toward a goal, not letting life pass her by. Her father was proud of her. Again she thought of Ann's bitter disappointment. Reg had mentioned a mother in a nearby nursing home.

Kim Bass was sipping coffee in the faculty lounge when Holly tracked her down. Lounge wasn't an accurate description. The stuffy room was small and crowded with stark furniture more suitable for a prison, hard wooden chairs and scarred melamine tables. The walls were an ugly pea green unrelieved by anything but a school calendar and a dusty bulletin board. Mindless elevator music burbled from two loudspeakers on the wall. Obviously people were not encouraged to linger here. A crusted coffee maker had a half-full carafe, and a tea kettle sat next to a tray of sugar and cream packets.

Dressed in dark brown slacks and a soft deerskin jacket with a beaded pocket, Kim was chatting with an older woman in her early forties. The merriment in their voices and relaxed posture indicated that they were close friends. Kim saw Holly and turned. Uncertainty flashed across her face, no guarantee of either guilt or blamelessness. Often the best liars had total control; they could also fake the nervousness of innocence, a double blind.

Introductions were made. Chris Wallace, the Spanish teacher, packed up her Tim Hortons travel mug. "Nice to meet you. Gotta run now. Grade elevens are getting ready to put on a play they wrote. Jennifer Lopez theme. Poor girl meets rich man. Typical fairy-tale world. What did we do wrong?" She winked at Kim, whose face pinked as she touched a beaded necklace featuring a double-headed eagle. Once, twice. Was she

130

trying to reassure herself with this totemic image?

Holly explained her reason for the visit. "Now that these complications have appeared," she said, "I need to know more about Angie as a student of yours."

Kim drained her mug with a wince, then gave a half-smile. Holly hadn't noticed before that she had a small gap between her sparkling front teeth, an attractive feature in the days of assembly-line beauty. "If this is coffee...you know the saying."

Holly let a beat or two pass. She liked this woman, but she remembered her initial days on the force. Several times she'd been one-hundred-eighty degrees wrong in her first estimates. Witnesses gave false information, sometimes not their own fault. With an endless variety of focus and five complex senses, people saw things different ways, could even be led in the wrong directions. Drained by hours of steady interrogation, confused by the options, innocent people confessed to murder, especially young people and the mentally challenged. "It's a rather delicate situation." She told Kim about the accusations. "Two students...and I consider their testimony as biased as the typical teen's—"

"Probably less biased than an adult's." Kim passed a broad hand over her brow. It was stifling in the room, the sun streaming through the glass. She got up and levered open a window, and a cool breeze rushed past them. The instructor sat back down and levelled her olive black eyes at Holly. "It's possible that Angie had a crush on me. Nothing was ever said or written. It's something you sense. And even so, she might not know her own mind at this age. I was in love with my Grade Eight history teacher, Mr. Bradshaw."

Possible crush, Holly wrote, leaving her face impassive. It was critical to keep opinions out of reports. Stick to the facts and let the justice system sort them out. If this woman had nothing to do with the death, "outing" her served no purpose. "Did she try to talk to you after class? Or outside the school?" She hesitated. Two questions at once. Bad form.

Kim's voice was even and serious. "Sometimes when school let out, she'd come by the classroom for a few minutes. She walked home, so she didn't need to catch the bus."

"Was she discussing her schoolwork?" Holly winced again. Leading the witness. Her techniques needed refining, but at least she knew that.

Kim gave a sigh. "Angie was an overachiever. She brought in her essays for my opinions on improvement, not to argue about the marks. In the normal scheme of grading, the huge numbers, sometimes two hundred essays each week, I don't have time to make thorough comments."

Holly nodded. Her father made the same complaints. "I don't envy you. Maybe gym teachers made the right choice."

A soft smile greeted that humour. "Often she wanted to move deeper into a point. And she brought some poetry."

"Poetry? Part of her assignments?"

"I teach Canlit, but I don't mind looking at creative writing from my students or any others in the school. We're starting a little magazine this year. *Spawnings.*"

Holly sat up. "Pardon me? Did you say—"

Kim was laughing out loud, apparently at Holly's expression. With her broad smile and a touch of crinkle at her eyes' edges, she was even more attractive. "I know. It's provocative. Sounds like Allen Ginsberg and those one-word Beatnik titles. But who around this fishing community could dispute it? I thought it was very clever. Angie was on the screening committee."

The scenarios might be multiplying. "Does that mean she had a say about what was included? Could that have made her any enemies?"

"About poetry? Who would think? It's the antithesis of violence."

"Or should be. What about rock lyrics and rap music?"

Kim gave this some thought. "I suppose. Do you want me to send you a list of the students whose work she read, those who didn't make the cut?"

"Might be an idea." She passed Kim her card. "What were her poems about?"

"The normal teen angst. 'Misery, companion mine, to my depths you do entwine'."

Holly winced. "Ouch. I see she had no career there. But no one else has suggested that she was unhappy." For once, Holly wondered if they were on the wrong track, if Angie had taken the drug herself. Even that theory didn't explain where she had gotten it.

Kim gave her a wordly look that revealed her greater experience with teens. "She wasn't unhappy. She was just exploring the concept. Young people think that writing about the small things in our lives, a flower, a delicate lichen, even a pet, is a trivial pursuit. They'll learn. I sent Angie to that William Carlos Williams poem about finding a plum in the...fridge...icebox. So simple, so pure." She closed her eyes. "Know what? There was a lovely fresh plum on my desk the next day."

"Back to my original purpose, I have to ask...I mean...off the record..." She swallowed back her hesitation. Kim Bass was a likable person, trustworthy and credible, or so it seemed.

"I get you. This is a Catholic school, Charter of Rights be damned. It's not exactly Don't ask. Don't tell. But close enough."

"I understand."

"I live with another woman who writes romance novels. We've been together for three years. I was glad to take this job to repay my student loans. I don't know if you've noticed, but

133

the boomers have been retiring in droves. I'll be out of here in June. I have an offer back home in Canmore. With her occupation, Judi can relocate anywhere. Oddly enough, I miss the snow and cold. It's so much cleaner." She looked out the window, where it had clouded over. Sooke weather changed on the hour. Fat raindrops teared runnels down the window. "How I hate the rain. I think I have SAD. Thank god they put in those special lights in the library. Fifteen minutes a day, and you cheer right up. I'm overdue for my fix."

"Your personal information will be confidential." Holly heard a bell ring. Her watch read eleven. "Time for the memorial service, I guess. One more question. Did Angie confide in you about other students?"

"Absolutely not. She was no gossip. All the same, Angie was mature for her age, but she wasn't one to make a teacher a pal. We're supposed to be leaders, not friends. I looked over that essay on meth for her. It was passionate. No way in hell she took those drugs herself." She checked her watch. "Guess I better make sure I have some tissues. If that's all, I'll leave you now and hit the bathroom before the service."

Minutes later, Holly found herself in the last row of the bleachers. At least half the seats were empty, a far cry from the old days. Perhaps the school would close after all, just desserts for the discomfort it had inflicted upon her. Standing in for the principal, Gable began the service as the crowd quieted. A large screen showed videos of Angie's triumphs in her swim meets. She poised on the starting blocks, intent, focused, a picture of youthful perfection. Then the video faded to black. Across to the podium came the president of the senior class, a boy with Harry Potter glasses, poking them back on his nose every two minutes. For his age, the comments were surprisingly mature. He ended by reading Housman's "To an

Athlete Dying Young". Had Kim given him the idea?

Then came the head counsellor, followed by Coach Grove, awkward in a role other than pep talks. She noticed that his gaze kept gravitating toward the statuesque Katie. But the girl next to her, Janice, was it? was fixated on Paul Gable. Such temptations lay in wait in the educational minefield. Now female teachers were being accused of seducing young male students. Women were proving to be as reprehensible as men when it came to sexual foibles.

The choir finished the hour-long service by singing "I'll Fly Away". By then nearly everyone except the most stoic was wiping their eyes, and a chorus of sniffs filled the air as tissues emerged among the females. Angie might not have had any close friends, but her peers recognized the tragedy as a harbinger of their own passing. A lone kilted piper played "Amazing Grace", walking out at dirge pace until the sound faded in the halls and the gym was totally quiet, except for the drip of water from the metal roof. Then the bustle of finding umbrellas began as people got up.

As Holly stood to the side, she noticed Nate Didrickson filing out, Buster the golden retriever plodding at his heels, bleary eyes searching the crowd for its lost mistress to part the clouds in its vision. Nate was with a woman with similar facial features, perhaps his sister, and had the boy Robin by one hand. The lad's dark suit echoed his father's, down to the white carnation boutonniere. Then the last handshake and hug had been accepted, and everyone had left for the cafeteria to take refreshments and sign the guest book.

Nate saw Holly and whispered to the woman, who then said to the youngster, "Come on, dear. We'll get some cake. Dad will be right along." They walked off as the senior dog slumped down with a relieved sigh and appeared to nod off.

Buster had been freshly groomed and given a bright blue collar ribbon, no slight chore under the demands of such grief.

"My condolences again. It was a lovely service," she said.

"Corporal Martin. Thank you for coming." He took both her hands in his in a warm embrace. "I didn't expect..." His voice trailed off.

"I understand that Detective Whitehouse visited your home."

He coughed into his hand. "Sorry. This time of year, the debris burning starts my allergies going. What were you... Oh, yeah. Whitehouse. What a know-it-all. You should have seen the mess he left in my little girl's room. Clothes and books all over the place. It took me..." Then he broke off and turned away, one hand shifting to his swollen, puffy eyes. "Funny, but I still think she's coming back."

She touched his shoulder gently, hoping that the light contact would be accepted. Common perception was that female officers had brought a new sensitivity to policing. Often they were of greater use in domestic violence cases because of the way they could defuse a situation without using brute force.

"He got me steamed, searching for drugs in my angel's room. There is no way she took that toxic junk or drank more than a beer, probably a light one at that."

There had been some alcohol in Angie's system, but he might have been right. For some, the excitement of the illicit beer itself was as much a charge as the small buzz of a single drink. She hadn't intended to bother Nate again after Whitehouse had done his job, but while she had him here... "I've been speaking with her teachers to get to know her better. Did she confide in you? I mean as much as a teenager does."

"She had some concerns about Robin. He's been her responsibility ever since her mother...passed. She went over his homework with him every night." Nate gave a nod to a very old bow-backed man and his wife with a walker who had been slowly making their way across the gym. The woman gave a sob as she hugged him. The man said, "We'll miss our girl, Nate. You come by to talk any time."

"Thanks for your support." Nate returned his attention to Holly.

"Sweet people. They live next door. Angie was like a granddaughter to them. Anyway, she said there were drugs at school sometimes. It disgusted her. I wanted her to tell the authorities, but you know how kids are about that. We used to call them squealers." His quiet tones took on an edge. "Now it's 'dropping the dime'. Gangster talk. Makes me sick."

"Did she mention any names?"

He gave a contemptuous snort. "If she had, I would have passed them on to the authorities. She knew that. That's the problem today. Everyone's covering up. The whole community has to work together to make this a safe place, and I'm not just talking about Neighbourhood Watch." He ran fingers through his hair, freshly trimmed for the occasion. "Just see out the year, I told her. Concentrate on your classes, your swimming. Get to university, and you'll forget there ever was a time called high school. Life will sort itself out."

Holly felt a kinship with this girl and her dislike of childish cliques. In a time warp, they might have been friends. Finding out why and how she died assumed the nature of a personal challenge, more than a job. Was that wise? She had no choice, and she hoped she never would.

She left the school wondering whether she should have dismissed Kim so quickly. Was she naïve to discard the gossip? Did this partner of hers even exist? Yet why plant the seeds of doubt in a father's imagination? She was beginning to understand how damaging passing on information in a case could be. Discretion was a narrow line between total candour and silence. And the coach. Loyal husband or playing his own little games with Katie? Should she do a background check, or was that overkill? She felt certain that the meth had come from someone at the school, a student or, god forbid, the staff. Then there was the wild card. The boys from Rennie.

Chipper met her at the Otter Point Bakery. They opted for the pizza buffet and started chowing down as the friendly owner brought more selections hot from the ovens. "No chicken pie for you today, Officer?" she asked Chipper, who grinned as he took another slice. The quaint room had Chinese antiques in wicker cases, along with silk scarves and carvings. They advertised a high tea as well as fresh meat and vegetable pies. Tourists crammed the place in summer.

Chipper nodded as Holly told him about the school. "Whitehouse checked in," he said. "He's off to Vancouver for a couple of days. Since there are no new leads in our case, I guess he's shelved it. Told me he thought that Angie took the meth on her own."

"Like hell she did. This is so frustrating."

"Too right. What does he care about us? No surprise, though. First lesson I learned in my first year. Ninety-five per cent of police work is dreary and routine. Glory boy wants none of that."

"And the other five, you get your head shot off and an official funeral better than you could afford." She munched on a Greek pizza slice, then selected a pepperoni piece.

"Don't forgetting shooting someone yourself." He wiped his mouth on a serviette. "Did you ever have to do that?"

Her memories had to be pried from their dark corners. "I drew my gun once...after a dangerous car chase. The guy was cornered, and I was afraid he was going to run me over or drive into a crowd. The warning shot stopped him."

Chipper stared at her. "Wow. You made the right choice and lucked out."

"It's not always that easy." She checked her watch. "We'd better get a move on."

"More interviews?"

"Just one. The boys from Port Renfrew. Maybe I can combine it with a speed check in the French Beach area. Sun's back out. Good travelling weather."

"French Beach. Good idea. The locals have been complaining to Ann." He looked at her uncertainly. "But the boys. By yourself? Do you want—"

She shot him a cool, sideways glance, and he backed off. "I've made a preliminary call." She explained that Billy's mother had sounded worried, until Holly had insisted that they were talking to everyone who'd been around the park that night in hopes of finding someone who'd seen Angie riding the bike.

They took the bill to the counter in the adjoining bakery where she picked up an apple pie and a loaf of seven-grain bread. "Routine. Do people still believe that? It's such a cliché on television and in movies," Chipper said.

"Even if it turns out that they were on the beach, we can't haul them in like felons unless we have a good reason. And don't forget that relations between the races have been prickly lately." In Sooke, a native man had been seen sleeping on a cardboard mat. Since he was in a bushy area with makeshift shelters where the homeless crashed behind the dumpsters at the Evergreen Mall, he was ignored. By the time he was discovered to be in a diabetic coma instead of drunk, he came close to dying. A tragedy borne of neglect. Good Samaritans were vanishing in a fog of perceived danger or possible lawsuits.

"That sounds like a double standard. We already brought in the two students from the high school."

She cleared her throat. "Because they were directly involved that night...or part of an alibi."

Back at the office, Chipper began reading the latest bulletins. Ann was under a pile of paperwork, requisitions for stationery and equipment. "It's so quiet here that I heard a hummingbird outside," she said. "Guess they didn't all head for California."

Just as Holly was leaving with the radar equipment and ticket pad, Ann answered the phone. A few tsks erupted while the other party talked in a voice nearly loud enough for all to hear. "We'll send someone right out," she said and hung up. "More theft from a construction site in Shirley. Six new strata homes with ocean views. Big money. But it's remote, so no one's minding the store at night. Broke into a metal storage shed. This time it's a generator, nail gun, a small table saw and a houseful of exotic hardwood flooring." Shirley was a small community formerly known as Sheringham Point after the picture-perfect lighthouse on the bluffs. When it had got its own post office, the name was too long for a stamp.

Holly whistled. "And they'd need a truck to haul that equipment." She turned to Chipper. "Take the Suburban and canvass the nearest neighbours. Ask the guys at the volunteer fire station. A few of them sit out front around lunch time. See if you can get any latents in the place where they broke into the shed." Thanks to his bush postings in Saskatchewan, Chipper had SOCO training.

He rubbed his neck. "A construction site? Fifty people have had their hands on things, not to mention deliveries."

She shook her head. "I know, but we could get lucky running them through CPIC. They should haul out an on-site trailer and hire a guard. A junkyard dog's no use if the place isn't fenced." The Canadian Police Information Centre catalogued the names of anyone currently accused, cases pending, probation and criminal records.

She headed back down West Coast Road, the window open, enjoying the warm breeze and the bright sun. In the summer droughts, when they held their breath that forest fires wouldn't start in the bone-dry duff, even logging was halted in the sere woods. Then the fall and winter brought exponential rains. Finally the precipitation slowed as March brought daffodils. Or so it had gone. Global warming was causing new weather patterns, and they weren't pretty. Her father had told her of a rare storm last April. One hundred millimetres of rain in a day. Some blamed the clouds of pollution from coal-power generation in burgeoning China.

Still uncomfortable from stuffing at the trough and feeling dangerously like a snooze, Holly settled in about five kilometres east of Fossil Bay. She cozied the car behind a rickety fence once belonging to a farm hacked out of the wilderness and now reclaimed by brambles and salal. Big city units had the new Stalker LIDAR laser guns, better suited to dense traffic areas. She used the old Basic Handheld K Band Radar, heavy but reliable. Some alert drivers saw her in time and braked quickly, slipping under the radar. Others must have been gawking at the stunning oceanfront or listening to music. Along with several gentle warnings, two of the three tickets went to tourists, one in a rented Mustang and the other in a Buick. The most satisfying citation tagged a yee-haw roofer flying low-level at 110 kmh in a battered Ford pickup. Like a primitive telegraph, the message would be received from other drivers, who observed the ticketing, that speeding in this area was unwise today.

Finishing the paperwork in a moment of pristine quiet, she recalled an article about the life of an average American officer in an urban department. "Twenty-five recently-dead bodies, fourteen decaying corpses, ten sexually assaulted children, and serious personal injury at least once on the job." Having refilled the government coffers and made the road safer, she closed down the unit and headed west for forty-five minutes. She was two kilometres short when she was flagged down near a shiny Toyota Sienna van. A balding man dressed in baggy shorts and a Yankees sweatshirt braced himself against the vehicle, while a woman of a similar age sat crying in the passenger seat. By the side of the road, a small deer lay still in a pool of blood. "Didn't mean to hit it. The poor thing came out of nowhere."

This year's fawn, all legs and hardly as large as a dog. As she bent over to look, the only living thing was her figure reflected in its glazed eyes. A brief candle snuffed out. At least no one was hurt. Roosevelt elk exacted a higher price. She glanced at the dented hood. "Happens all the time. I can help with your insurance claim." She gave him her card, grateful that the animal was out of its misery. Standard procedure in critical cases was to use the shotgun.

"We're from New York City. Zoo's the place we see deer. What should we do with it? Are you going to send for the SCPA or whatever you call..."

"Since we're out of the town limits, it'll remain where it is, as long as it's off the road. Even dead seals on beaches are left for the tides." She noticed that he looked disgusted. "Tell you what. Help me haul it deeper into the woods. Cougar or bear will probably come shopping."

His voice skyrocketed as he looked around. "Bear? Cougar?"

The disposal didn't take long. Holly pulled some towelettes from the console, and they cleaned up.

Billy Jenkins lived at the end of a long rutted road a few miles east of Port Renfrew. A homemade plywood sign at the turn advertised "Woodworking. Native carvings. Fishing Charters" with an arrow. Holly took care not to let the ruts damage her undercarriage but winced at the occasional thump. In a bigleaf maple tree festooned with lacy strands of witch's hair, a barred owl greeted her, usually a night bird but at home in the luminous curly hynum moss which coated the tree like a bayou beauty. A brown hare hopped to safety.

At last she came to a small clearing. Large firs had been trimmed or topped to prevent damage in a windstorm. In the yard, a circus of carvings caught her eye with their skill and majesty. Several rampant bears pawed the air. Despite the fact that totem poles had a more northerly origin, artful sculptures of all heights surveyed the quiet kingdom. Smiling in admiration, she discovered an eagle, a raven and a turtle on the posts. Two carved chests would make ideal storage for sheets and blankets. An artist coaxing buyers down this road probably did a good business in the summer.

The cabin with add-ons was painted a bright blue, a complement to the green moss which coated its cedar-shake roof. A huge woodpile was tarped beside it. On the shady side, sword fern nestled against the clapboard. A sizable garden wired against deer, in a common Stalag 17 effect, bore salad vegetables and potato plants. In a grassy patch, two mountain bikes lay on their sides. The recently-built deck had potted begonias in red, white and salmon. Showy burgundy dahlias, which lasted into the fall, added a cheery look.

"I'm Janet Jenkins. Come in," Billy's mother said, opening the screen door. She wore loose jeans and a red flannel logging shirt. "The boys will be back at three. They're helping my husband Tom with the firewood." Mike was staying with

143

them because his mother was in Victoria getting radiation for breast cancer. His father had gone north to earn money at a fly-in, fly-out mine in Yukon, she explained.

The house opened into a living room, kitchen at the side. A small television sat on a crowded bookshelf. The number of other doors indicated two more bedrooms and a bathroom.

"They aren't in any trouble, are they? You said this was routine," Janet said as she took a blue enamel pot of coffee from the stove. She added a can of condensed milk and a sugar bowl, urging them forward on the circular pine table.

Holly had a slight stomach ache from the pizza overload, but she couldn't refuse the hospitality. Her duty belt needed a bottle of Maalox. "Apparently they were on the beach at Botanical the night when a girl drowned. I need to know what they saw, if anything."

The woman's pleasant tan face shrank as she smoothed a crease on the freshly-ironed tablecloth. Rich black hair was pulled into a bun with an attractive shell holder, and her glowing, unwrinkled skin belied her forty-plus years. "My brother drowned. It's a bad way to go. His fishing boat filled up with a rogue wave, and he never made it to shore." She made a small fist, her hand worn from work, then reached for a tin of hand cream on the table. "Damn marine reports were wrong."

Holly nodded, managing a smile to ease the woman along. "That's so true. Weather changes by the hour around the lower island."

"And we're cut off out here. No cell coverage. Damn phone lines go down once a winter. Can't even call an ambulance." Janet finished anointing her hands and picked up her coffee. "Still, I prefer it to Victoria. It's freer, you know? Not as many rules, and we help each other."

A few minutes later, Holly heard voices outside. Through

144

the calico-curtained window she watched two young men walking toward the house, followed by a mixed breed, German shepherd and collie at a glance. The dog lacked one front leg but handled its mobility without complaint. One boy had an axe over his shoulder, the other carried steel splitting wedges and a maul.

Janet said, "There they are now. Do you want me—"

"Please stay here. I'll talk to them outside. Thanks for your hospitality."

She excused herself and met the boys on the deck, explaining her visit. The dog was friendly if muddy. She gave its head a rub but steered it away from her pants. "I'd like to talk to you separately, if that's all right. Maybe you could come back in a few minutes, Mike." She saw them give each other odd looks. Mike pulled out a pack of bargain-priced Canadian brand cigarettes, lit up, and strolled off, his short legs slightly bowed like a sailor's. Chances were that after all this time, they'd rehearsed their stories. She should have been out here earlier, from the minute they'd learned the results of the tox scan.

The taller at well over six feet, Billy wore green workpants and a hoodie. His clothes were covered in fir debris and the occasional oil stain. One temple bore a scar, the kind fashionable for nineteenth-century dueling Europeans. His nose was blunt but strong, and his hands could rip phone books in half.

She smiled to put him at his ease, but his eyes cut to her notebook. "The ranger says that he believes you and Mike camped in Botanical the night Angie Didrickson died."

"Angie?" he repeated. "Mom said something, but I—"

"Angie drowned that night." *Surely news would have travelled fast. What was wrong here?*

"Oh yeah, I heard about that. I was sorry." A nuance of

emotion passed over his face, raising a dimple in one cheek. Juvenile or ingenuous or both? Oddly enough, his voice cracked from time to time, mild as a girl's.

"Did you know her?" He attended Edward Milne, but they could have met at twenty teen haunts. The video stores, Willie Blues Snack Shop, the A and W, Sooke Pizza and Wink's, which nailed the student lunch trade. Aside from school, the Port Renfrew teens got to Sooke from time to time, hitched a ride, stayed with friends or relatives. Rock concerts in Victoria would pull them farther east. K-Os was playing at the Save-On-Foods Memorial Centre.

"Not really."

What did that mean? "You did or you didn't?" His hesitance made her suspicious, but the ambiguous teenspeak often meant "yes, but I'm afraid to admit it."

He looked off to where Mike was tossing sticks for the dog. "I might have seen her in Sooke...but we never talked."

"She was beautiful. I imagine you'd remember her."

"Yeah." He blinked but didn't meet her gaze. To some that spelled guilt, but the gesture was inborn in his people. It was disrespectful to lock eyes, especially a youth to an elder. *Did he seem nervous?* "What did you do that night in the park?"

Her begging-the-question technique worked. Instead of denying being there, he seemed to search his memory. "Made a fire. Cooked hot dogs. Went for a swim. We built a fort of driftwood." Common practice for beachcombers. More shelter from the wind than rain. But she didn't remember any food debris. Maybe here were two teenaged environmentalists.

"Can you give me a timeline? Start with dinner."

"Uh, six, seven. I dunno. Before dark. We just hung out and talked."

If she recalled correctly, dark came about eight o'clock.

"About what?" The devil was in the details, Roy had taught her. Once a suspect makes one mistake, he makes others. The cascade effect.

"Stuff. I mean girls, movies, school. Nothing important. The sunset was awesome. And we saw a couple of cruise ships. My cousin works on one. It'd be sweet to go to Alaska."

"Then what happened? See anyone else?"

"Uh-uh." He spread out his hands. One leaking blood blister dominated a finger, the price of working with wood. "Went to bed, I guess. Ten maybe. On the beach. We had sleeping bags."

"By the big butt stump of driftwood? Was that your camp?"

Suddenly a wary look crossed his face, as if he knew he might have said the wrong thing, placed himself in the wrong spot. Innocence and experience collided. "Maybe down a kilometre from that. The shelter wasn't anything special, more dug out in the sand. The main logs were already there."

Why was he trying to minimize the fort now? Distance himself from where the girl had died? The sun flickered behind a cloud, but she felt the heat coming. "All right, Billy," she said, and relief flooded his square face.

Mike took his turn next. The habit of reclusiveness wasn't as strong for him. His eyes weren't as intelligent as Billy's, more crafty like a fox, though those animals were oddly absent on the island. Mike confirmed much of what Billy had said. Perhaps they had practiced their stories. A total consistency often spelled collusion. "So you went to bed around—"

"Moonrise. Eleven-fifteen."

Strange that he named an exact time. Moonrise could be checked. "And you saw no one?"

"Guess we wouldn't." He toed his workboot over a knot in a board. "You're not allowed to camp on the beach. But we were here in the time long ago. It's really all ours." That he stopped without making derogatory remarks about whites spoke for his self-control, but perhaps he didn't want to antagonize the police.

"I don't disagree." She looked at her watch as if she were growing short of time and wanted to wrap up the interview. "That was a pretty cool shelter you made on the big fir root. Gotta hand it to you."

He seemed flattered, rubbing a hand through his thick hair. "I'm pretty good at it. Get the pieces to fit just right. Don't need no nails at all. Nice and tight. The wind gets up at night."

She excused him. So there was a discrepancy in their description of where they had camped and the time they went to bed. But both denied seeing anyone on the beach.

Before leaving, she dropped one more penny onto the table as Billy rejoined them. "I need your fingerprints."

They both tensed and looked at each other for a brief moment. Beads of moisture freckled Mike's forehead. Billy cleared his throat. "We didn't touch anything....not that there was anything to touch. Are you gonna check the driftwood?" He gave a childish laugh, then coughed into his hand.

For once, a lie came in handy. On a beach, with winds and tide, not many pieces of forensics would remain, and not for long. "Of course not. But a car was broken into in the parking lot that week. A couple of prints showed up. This will eliminate you."

Was that a visible relaxation in their muscular shoulders? "Sure, why not?" Billy said.

Normally the print kit wasn't carried in cars, but with distances making time a premium, Holly had changed the protocol. She took them to the Impala, opened the trunk and set up the equipment on a picnic table, offering them a wet towelette at the end of the process. Her real intention was to check against the prints on the condom package. Teenaged boys sure as hell didn't use them in a same-sex encounter. But as ubiquitous as condoms were, often given out free, one might have lingered in their wallets or backpacks. And if so, that might break their story. Had one of them, or both, had sex with Angie?

Holly pulled in to the detachment as Ann was closing up. "How did it go?" the woman asked.

"They seem like good boys, but something is going on," she said, explaining her procedures.

Ann gave a sign of approval at the fingerprint idea. "Why not? It's not impossible that they were involved with those thefts. Clearly, it's a local."

Ann's old Taurus chugged out in a cloud of blue smoke. With a sigh, Holly went inside to type her report. Then she set out the package of prints for the courier the next day.

By nine, her father had already gone to bed, but he'd left her a plate of meatloaf, garlic mashies and carrot coins in the fridge. She heated the tasty meal in the microwave, then sat in his recliner in the solarium. The wind had been up all day, the tides at a horrific 9.5, and from the beaches surf pounded the rocks like incoming mortars. As she finished the last juicy bite and stretched back in the fullness of comfort, she saw in a seat fold the newspaper he had been reading, a tell-tale piece of white sticking out. Inside was an envelope type-addressed to him with no stamp or postmark. Her hand hovered over it as she weighed the ethics. A plain piece of cheap copier paper lay inside. With hesitation, she read it. "I hope you're still losing sleep. You won't get away with it, you know. The mill of God grinds slow but exceedingly fine." Her heart chilled like a cold marble slab. No wonder he hadn't been himself. And the wording. "The mill of God." Hardly garden-variety prose. Who was harassing him, and for how long? Was he being blackmailed? She got up, her knees wobbly and her strategy uncertain. Secrets buried in more than one heart never kept their own counsel.

She climbed the circular stairs slowly, thinking at each step. Then she looked at his door, closed against the unwelcome night heat rising from the woodstove in the foyer. A slit of light appeared under it. "Knock knock," she said.

An umhmmm followed, so she opened the door of the smaller corner bedroom. Only a highboy dresser and bed table served for furniture, and piles of books and magazines leaned in pillars. Wearing striped pajamas and a silk paisley dressing gown, Norman was propped up by pillows in a monkish single bed. A patchwork quilt covered one end, his mother's work. Shogun lay on a soft foam pallet on the floor, his head sprawling, and his legs splayed, exposing his pink belly in a position of complete trust. A rope tug toy lay beside him. He was snoring. Another reason not to sleep with dogs.

The sight amused her, but she hadn't come for this. She sat at the end of the bed, focusing on her father's eyes, sad as an old bloodhound's. When the woodstove started burning in the fall, he developed allergies, a vicissitude of age, he claimed. "I have to confess something, Dad," she said.

"Oh my," he said. "Your old man's not a priest, though sometimes I live like one." He put down his book. *Peyton Place*. "Bestseller in 1956. We kids used to find the paperback copies in the drug store and read the forbidden pages."

Wasn't he a wizard at sidetracking, or was he covering embarrassment for the personal approach? "You're joking. Show me one."

A slight smirk on his lips, he leafed on, then passed her the book. Something about getting it up good and hard, Rodney.

"That's it? Pretty tame for these days."

He was chuckling when she touched his shoulder, a rare gesture, brought his sea-blue eyes to hers, fawn like her mother's but with emerald flecks. They saw the world so differently, he in his historical tower, she on the drawbridge tossing criminals into the moat. "This is serious. I found that note. Didn't mean to... No, of course I did. I was wondering why you were a bit thoughtful lately."

He said nothing, but reached for a glass of water by the bed. Then he took off his black horn-rimmed Mr. Peepers glasses. "Don't worry about...those letters. They mean nothing."

"Now *letters?* How long has this been going on? And no Judy Garland imitations, please." She tortured herself about the unspoken fact that her father had been a suspect, had no alibi other than being in his office late that night marking papers. An old maintenance worker had claimed to have glimpsed a figure in his office, but the man had serious cataracts, a less than ideal witness. With no sign of her mother or the Bronco and no other forensic trails, the police had been forced to declare the case cold.

"A poison little note comes every year around the anniversary of your mother's disappearance." In clear sorrow, he rubbed the bridge of his hawk-like nose where the glasses had left a mark like a bruise. "Anniversary. What an ironic word."

"Who's doing this? Where are the rest? You know, we could have dusted them for prints. Was the stationery always just copier paper?" She gave a laugh. "My god, we could have taken DNA from under the flap."

"Same paper and the same message, with minor variations. And the envelope's never sealed."

"Cleverer than I thought. How do these messages get to you?"

"They're left around the department, the offices, sometime in the week before the date. Often a cleaning person finds one and brings it to me. Last year I didn't get anything. Maybe it was thrown away by mistake. There's no proof. Hundreds of people pass through. We don't have a...what do they call those spy things?" He passed a hand through his thinning hair.

"Eyes in the sky. Closed circuit television." In the driveway, a caterwauling emerged. Felines from the surrounding houses made the front lawn a combat area. "Give me a name. You must have your suspicions."

He blew out a heavy breath. "Larry Gall. I'm sure he's behind this nonsense. That's why I never keep anything. Why let the idiot get to me?"

Shogun growled and raised a lid over one sleepy eye. She was becoming used to his grumblings. "So who the hell is Larry Gall?"

"He teaches social work at Camosun College, or so I presume he still does. He and your mother were quite...close, so some say. Activist causes brought them together. I wouldn't be surprised if he goaded the police into..." He sucked at his tongue as if a bad taste lingered. "You know. Their investigation."

She had another thought, but considered the phrasing carefully. "If they were...close, do you think that *he* had anything to do with her disappearance?" She refused to say *death* to her father. The lie kept hope alive.

"I can't believe so, but you know me. I like to think the best of people, not imagine that they could harm others. She always spoke well of him. I respected your mother's opinions on...most subjects. We were different, but we shared the important values."

Bonnie had a temper, but she rarely meant the harsh words she said and calmed down later. Norman was slow to anger.

But to protect what he held dear, nothing was beyond him. On one of their rare hikes, they'd met a cougar. Placing little Holly behind him, he'd raged and waved his arms, jumped up and down until the beast retreated. Then he sat on a stump and cried, shaking with relief. He'd saved their lives. She owed him one.

"Why didn't you tell me then about Gall? Why let all these years go by?"

He shook his head slowly from side to side. "You were working so hard at your studies. You wanted to come home and help search, but I talked you out of it. It was just gossip. I've never even met him." The hesitant look on his face made her sure that he was still trying to convince himself. "The man is harmless. He's just a wounded beast, striking out at the only person left."

"Even if he hasn't made any threats, this is harassment. I'm going to talk to him."

Norman folded his hands on his chest. "Don't do that, my girl. Waste of time. He'll never admit it...or perhaps he will. That would be like the man. Those kind think that they can save the world. Tell me, is it getting any better?"

Eight

Holly called the main number at Camosun and was routed to Gall's department. The secretary told her that he had office hours every day at eleven. She took Sooke Road to the Island Highway, turned off at Hillside, and drove ahead to the Lansdowne Campus.

Once at the college, she parked and walked to the main building of the small enclave of four thousand students. Gall must feel like a large frog in this pond, she thought. Postmodern and utilitarian. Nothing like the stately halls of UVic a few miles away, where her father taught. Was Gall jealous of Norman's prestige on the venerable university campus? To insiders, the hierarchy in post-secondary education was more than a matter of tenure or salary differences. University professors could be passport guarantors, while only an administrator in a college could sign the photo. "And they want to be called professors," her father once said in a huff, rattling the paper as he read about a recent strike at the colleges. "Few have doctorates. Some have no degrees at all. Professors of welding indeed." Her mother would have torn a strip off him for such elitism. For all Holly knew, she had.

Gall's office was tucked away in a cranny at the end of a hall painted a psychedelic sunflower yellow and purple. A scribbled paper sign on the door read "Larry Gall. Social Work." Posted nearby was his timetable with office hours highlighted in marker. Political cartoons taped on the wall featured George W. Bush, though a few involved the Prime Minister, to whose body were added horns, a tail and a long fork.

The door was closed, but she could hear vague music inside. Perky. Upbeat. Caribbean. Relaxing, sunny climes where fruit fell from the trees. She knocked.

"Come," said a low voice.

On a quick assessment, she was surprised to see that Larry Gall was much younger than her mother, in his mid-forties even now. In opposition to her conservative, fussy father, his thick black hair was tied in a ponytail, and he wore chinos and a denim work shirt with a pelt of curly hair at the V. The bookshelves were crowded, and hanging baskets of spider plants and ivy competed for the sun through the institutional window. On the desk were requisite piles of marking and a CD case reading *Songs of the Coffee Lands.*

"Great music," she said by way of opening the conversation.

"Putamayo. Always cheers me up. Especially in the winter. Live here, you've got to make peace with the rain. Nirvana it's not." His lean face was brown and weather-beaten, as if he spent much time outside. A carved hiking stick with a silver knob leaned in the corner next to a battered pair of boots.

Holly gave the usual answer which helped islanders bond. "Don't have to shovel it."

He looked at her uniform, one corner of his thin mouth rising. "Speaking of shovelling, if you'll pardon my French, you have me at a disadvantage. My name's on the door. I don't know yours, but you don't look like a student."

She extended her hand, and he gave it a perfunctory shake, earning 5/5 for comfortable pressure and duration. "Holly Martin. Bonnie Martin's daughter."

"Holly." He made no effort to disguise the fact that he was searching her face. For her mother? A muscle twitched at the edge of his square jaw, a slight haze of beard showing. He pulled out a rumpled pack of French cigarettes and fingered one out, offering it to her. Holly shook her head. "Then this isn't a social call."

"Not exactly. But it could have been. I know you were...good friends with my mother." Coy language sat ill with her, but she needed to find her bearings.

He groaned, tossing a glance of his head toward the wall behind Holly. She turned to see a large pastel portrait of her mother, expensively framed under anti-glare glass. Against her will, she gave a small gasp.

"I thought you might walk through that door some day. In fact, I hoped you would." Then his face grew colder, as if a band of steel had tightened along his spine. With a book of matches, he lit the cigarette and pulled up a small ashtray shaped like a pitcher's mitt.

Uninvited, she sat in an oak chair where many a student had waited. She expected no courtesy from this man, someone who had lurked in their lives all these years, yet she chose her words carefully. "Is that why you keep sending my father those notes? To bring me here?"

"I don't keep tabs on you. That would be neurotic, but I see that you're all grown up. Last I heard you were in university." He drew in a long breath of smoke and exhaled with apparent contemplation. The air filled with the strange tang of exotic tobaccos foreign to North America. "The coward. He'd never come himself."

She bristled at the insult, tempted to abuse her power. "Who's the real coward if you don't even sign these notes? You haven't threatened him in so many words, but this harassment stops now. And this has nothing to do with my position."

"The horsewoman rides to her doddering father's rescue. Precious." His lips appeared poised to spit. Yet he stood and went to the portrait, stroking her mother's bright cheek, which shone with youth. She looked the same age as Holly, but she must have been older, because the hair had grey streaks. When had she posed? Or had the portrait been done from a photo? The glimpse into her mother's other life frightened her.

"I loved her, you know."

"You *think* you did." She was still smarting about his comments about her dad. To many who didn't look deeper, Norman was the quintessential professor, no mystique, no romance, just a dusty cypher.

He turned with a vengeance. "You know nothing of this. She and I were to be married."

Standing abruptly, Holly mouthed the words like a death sentence. "Married. I don't believe that."

A desk drawer opened, and Gall lifted a pack of letters tied with a blue ribbon. "Here's proof. She didn't want to hurt your father, but by the time you left for university, our relationship had become serious. She was waiting for the right time to tell him. And she would have, except that..." He took a deep breath, then exhaled as if it were too painful to continue. "Anyway, I thought you were studying Botany, becoming a useless collector of information like the Professor."

"I changed my mind, and you can imagine why and when." She shot a finger at him. "So just before she disappeared, she was supposed to have told him?"

He cast down his oyster eyes, heavy with pouches, but creased at the corners from staring life in the face. The price of hard work, dissolution or genetics? "Does make you wonder, doesn't it?" Then he gave a dismissive gesture, and a long ash dropped to the tiled floor. "She and your father had nothing in common. I don't understand why the marriage lasted so long."

"I can't speak for either of them. But he would never have harmed her."

"And you know that I didn't. I was cleared from the start...unless you think I had a body double to speak in Calgary that week."

"Move on with your life. I have." Or had she? The past was returning to bite her on the neck like a loving vampire.

"Have you? I think about her every day, and if you're the daughter she deserved, so do you." He stubbed out the cigarette, punishing it until the paper separated from the tobacco. But though he said nothing, his eyes glistened.

"You said 'deserved'. Why the past tense?"

He barked out a laugh and coughed a cloud of smoke. "Oh, come on. You've been watching too many of those old movies with your father. Don't start living in other decades like he does. Christ have mercy. What a useless dreamer."

She ignored the gibe and took out a fresh notebook brought for this purpose. Hers alone, off the clock. "Tell me about that last week. Where did you see her? What did she say?"

He remained silent for nearly a minute. Then he firmed his lips. From under his shirt, he pulled an ornament that glittered as a shard of light punched from behind a cloud. "Recognize this?"

Holly tensed, steeled herself from reaching forward. She didn't want to appear weak, so she forced her trembling grip to the chair arms. The rawhide cord held a round silver image of a raven with the sun in its beak.

A corner of his mouth rose at her reaction. "I see you remember it. Your mother probably told you the story. It's one of my favourites, perhaps because of her."

Raven the Trickster was one of the most popular figures in native mythology across North America. Suddenly Holly was back in her childhood bedroom in that dark East Sooke property. The papery leaves of the eucalyptus whispered prelude to the croaky warble in the night. Her mother was explaining that when the world was in total darkness, Raven was tired of bumping about. He learned that an old man who lived in the woods with his daughter had a secret treasure, all the light in the universe packed into a tiny box. Spying on them as the girl was dipping her basket into the water, Raven turned himself into a hemlock needle. When she swallowed the needle, it grew into a human baby. She gave birth, and crafty Raven set to work coaxing his "grandfather" to let him hold the light. Losing patience, the old man threw the sphere to the child. Retransformed into a bird, Raven caught the light in his beak, flew out of the smokehole and escaped to bring sunshine to the world.

Suddenly she felt a squeezing in her chest. Was he admitting guilt by showing it to her? No one would be that stupid, or was it a clever ruse? "When did she give this to you?" It hadn't always been in her mother's life, though often it was unseen, nestled between her breasts to "keep it warm." Had Holly noticed it first around the time she left for university? A milestone? The end of her dependence on the concept of family? Did that ever end?

"I brought it back from a trip to the Queen Charlottes and gave it to her. It's Haida, a talisman. Very old. A hundred years, the seller said. It was tarnished when I found it, but I polished it. Cleaned up nicely." He gave an ironic shrug. "Little good it did her."

"And she gave it back? Why?" His alibi was solid. What did this mean?

"No. I found it."

"How do you know it's the same one?" she asked. He hadn't answered her question about "when," but she'd figured it out.

He pointed to a small scratch on the sun. "As I told you, it was an old piece. We thought that the flaw added character, a story within a story."

He was right. Her mother had postulated that Raven had bumped into an overhanging branch as he left the house. Suddenly her eyes felt wet, betraying her, and she blinked. She leaned forward, and he sat back, splaying his large hands on the desk. Clearly he had no intention of removing it. "Then how did you get...when did—"

One of his stubby fingers waggled at her. "Not so fast. Here's what happened." He lit a fresh cigarette and opened the window. "Thank god there are no smoke alarms in here...yet. Damn nicotine Nazis."

Holly felt pressure build behind her temples. Gall owned some precious part of her mother. She wanted to throttle him, to wrench the necklace from his chest. Bridge the gap to her mother with something intimate and palpable.

"She saw the rawhide getting thin. You can buy replacement strips at craft stores."

A flame long guttering sprang to life. "So then what?"

He sat back in an odd reflective mood as if puzzling out the situation step by step. "That's the funny part. I do some family counselling for the CASA in Sooke. They gave me clothes to take to the St. Vincent de Paul depot. That's when I saw it. Must have been a couple of years after she...left."

"Someone was wearing it?"

"No. It had been attached to a fresh piece of leather and was in their jewellery display. Costume junk for kids and teenagers."

It might have been there for a while. She knew the cramped little building that provided cheap clothes, bedding, furniture, the occasional toy or bike for those with meager resources. "Did you ask where it came from?"

"One of the part-time clerks at the depot washes cars at Westcoast Collision. Got sucked up in the vacuum, he said. He heard a funny sound but didn't think anything of it until days later when he changed the bag. The occasional spare change turns up. There was the amulet. The leather thong was broken. Didn't like Indian stuff, he said, so he donated it. Someone else fixed it."

Holly sat back in amazement. Back only a few weeks, and now this. If she'd been here from the first... Something hurt in her throat as her voice rose. "But the car, the truck, whose was it?"

With care and reverence, he tucked Raven back into his shirt. "I tried to find out. They do a hundred vehicles a week, more in tourist season. The kid's honest but not that bright. He thinks it might have been a luxury car, like a Buick, leather seats. Maybe an SUV." He tapped his temple in a "nobody home" gesture.

"That's not much help." She shot him a look. "Did you go to the police?"

"Bastards told me their resources were too stretched to expend any energy on a cold case. Years had passed. How did they even know this belonged to her? Others could have owned one. I lost my temper, tossed some papers around, and they threw me out. End of story."

She gazed out the window to where students trudged back and forth in the quad, burrowing under umbrellas in the pounding rain. Her thoughts running too fast to express in any coherence, she let silence fill the musty room. Gall's eyes followed her. From contempt or interest? Could she trust this man?

"Something occur to you?" His tone was cautious. As he lit another cigarette, his sleeve moved up his arm, revealing a medical bracelet, which indicated some vulnerability, from mere allergies to serious heart problems.

"Was she wearing it the night she disappeared? That's the important point."

He shrugged, reached for a cold cup of coffee. He hadn't offered her any, but judging from the rime on the cracked cup, that was fortunate. "The last time I saw her, yes. A few days before Calgary."

Rising slowly, she eyed the pile of letters. "I have to go. Any chance you'll let me look at those?"

"What the hell for? There's nothing relevant to her disappearance. You'll have to believe me."

"Why should I? I just found out that you exist."

He grinned. "Funny, but you sound like your mother." He glanced at the copier. "It might be painful for you. But if you're sure you can handle it, why not? You're a big girl."

He made duplicates of the letters, put them in a brown envelope, and handed it to her. Then he picked up another CD. *Women of the World,* acoustic music by some of the world's leading female artists. "Take this. I bought it for her last week. I'm always buying her things, almost forgetting that she's...gone."

Holly took the gift with thanks. She hadn't expected to like him, but the gesture was kind. He was exposing his wounds to her. "What do you think happened to my...to Bonnie?"

He took his time replying, as if the process opened deep wounds long scabbed over. "She was headed past Gold River, then up some backroads over to Tahsis on the west coast. Something about setting up an information centre, making contacts, that sort of thing. Helluva wild country, but she'd dare anything with that bloody Bronco. Last she called me was from a motel in Campbell River. The rains were bad that weekend. Even snow at the higher altitudes. It's possible that she might have run off the road and never been found."

"As simple as that?" The words were dust in her mouth. Somewhere, if she looked long enough... She couldn't finish her own thought.

"Despite the notorious clear-cuts and the publicity about Clayoquot Sound, most of this island is still wild and lonely territory. But think about this: If you're going to help good women get away from bad men, those men aren't going to love you. They're substance abusers, and they're violent. The worst have served time. Their women and children are their only possessions."

"Anyone come to mind?" How much did he know about Bonnie's work?

"So many ugly cases over the years. She didn't discuss names with me. Breach of ethics. And in a small community, I might even know the person." His eyes were slightly narrowed, as if sizing her up. "So now that you've met the ogre in his den, what are your plans?"

"I'm posted to Fossil Bay now, and I have access to records. There's a chance we might find out what happened to her." She was conscious of using the word "we", and suddenly felt traitorous towards her father. But surely they all had the same goal. "I'll stay in touch if anything turns up."

He tossed her one last question. Impertinent or frank. "Are you going to show the letters to the old man?"

The Old Man. She supposed he meant in it in the vernacular. Her father would never be old, would he? Mustering her dignity, with an even voice, she answered, "And break his heart? No one could be that cruel."

At the Kangaroo Road curve that night, she was nearly sideswiped by a logging truck over the line. Her blood pressure spiked, but the Prelude held the road like a cat in gumboots. She thought of her father and that damn tiny car. With the burgeoning population in the Western Communities, the traffic to Victoria was a crapshoot with loaded dice. He avoided rush hour traffic and travelled only three days a week, but she shuddered to think of how that toy might collapse like a billfold.

She mentioned it to him after dinner. "Gas has gone up to 1.295 a litre with hell between us and peak oil, and you think I should get a larger car? My dear girl." He finished the last crumb of chocolate layer cake and tossed down his serviette. "Follow me. I want you to see something amazing. I did not purchase that vehicle on a whim or because I'm merely...frugal. Give your paterfamilias credit."

They went upstairs to his computer, where he spent a few minutes clicking on Google, then Videos. Bouncing in his seat like a kid, he turned to her with a grin. "Here we are. Road tests of the Smart Car. It's made by Mercedes, you know. Precision German mechanics. They lost the war but not the engineering race." Then he turned up the sound.

She watched in horror as the unpiloted car barrelled down the road cartoon-style, hellbent on its mission, then smashed into a concrete barrier and bounced to a stop. When the dust settled, the cage was intact, the integrity complete. She let out a giant breath. "Whooee. I am so impressed."

Her father stood back, arms folded in an "I told you so" pose. "Now where am I going to get into an accident like that? Eighty miles per hour. I'm hardly driving over fifty kilometres most of the time. Your mother was the speed demon, remember?"

Later that night, reading in bed, she welcomed Shogun up with her for moral support. Then she started examining the letters. At first they were innocuous enough. Something about missing him, which could have a collegial interpretation. But the last two seemed to support Gall's scenario. Her mother's idiosyncratic angular handwriting made time disappear. "I'll need to think about your proposal," it read. "But my heart tells me that we have such little time on earth. Holly is on her way, building her own life as it should be." Then in the final letter, dated the week before she disappeared, she said, "I've made up my mind. Leaving will sting Norman, but his career will sustain him. And he's a good-looking man. It's possible he'll find someone else, given time. Next week I'll contact Richard Mayhue. If he can't handle the divorce, he'll know someone who can. This time in a few months, my love, we'll be together forever. Or as much together as my life can manage." Something rose in Holly's throat as lyrics from an inane disco song wormed into her ears. "Together forever, forever, we two."

Holly moved her legs under the quilt, and Shogun growled and jumped off the bed, looking at her accusingly. Had an event in his past spooked him about certain movements? Had he been kicked off a bed as a pup? She heard a toilet flush and shoved the letters under a pillow. Sometime she might tell her father. Perhaps he already knew. But that gave him a motive for...she didn't want to follow that thread. It would destroy her life.

The door, already ajar, opened as she heard a discreet "knock, knock." She looked up, afraid that the letters under the pillow were burning a hole in the mattress. "So there you are, Shogie. In a lady's boudoir, no less." Norman gazed at Holly in assumed innocence. "Are you two good friends now?"

She cast a suspicious glance at the dog, now lying on the carpet and grooming one foot in a meticulous fashion, the little prince. "Whenever I move my legs, he does this Charlie Manson act."

Her father chuckled, rubbing his chin. "Just a border collie. Ignore him."

She laughed. "Like you've been reading to me from the

forums on the net? My dog eats holes in the drywall. Oh, it's just a border collie. Barks my ears deaf if I stop to talk to someone. Oh, it's just a border collie. Rolls in dead salmon. Oh, it's... You get the point. These dogs get forgiven for everything."

Her father snapped his fingers, and Shogun got up to leave. "Be a realist, Holly. He's not a GSD. To serve and protect is not his watchword."

She fluffed her pillow, then sat back. "I wonder what his watchword is?"

"He'll let us know. Don't they always?"

She slept fitfully that night. Two geese, identified by their companionable chatter, had put her house on their flight path. Not at all migratory, the local flock flew daily rounds to visit farms and pastureland. Why bother with that north and south nonsense when they could stay in paradise? Where in this unnatural Eden did they nest safe from cougars, in swamps where the skunk cabbage grew? Their honking, at times canine and at others almost human, kept awakening her from the deep REM levels that would refresh her. Pounding the pillow, she remembered a news story about a grandmother killing her family after hearing "commands" from the geese. Now there was a unique excuse. Had it worked?

Nine

Ann came into Holly's office a few days later, bearing a fax. "This just in."

"Thanks." A smile passed between the women.

Mike was in the clear on the condom package prints, but Billy's prints from the left thumb and forefinger matched in twelve different ways, substantial proof. Disappointing news. The young man had seemed honest. Now he was in serious trouble. After studying the whorled diagrams and the arrows of comparison, she called Whitehouse. "It's still ambiguous. Maybe there's another girl involved. Maybe the package was there from an earlier rendezvous."

"Give me a break." He snorted. "But how did you get those fingerprints again?"

"Purely voluntary. There had been a car broken into at the park."

"That's one thing you did right. My compliments. Get those boys in this afternoon. I'll be right over. Our problems with this annoying case are nearly over. When they're faced with hard evidence, they crumble like burnt toast." He hung up with a perfunctory grunt.

Holly craned her head into the main office. Chipper was at one of the computers. She'd assigned him to looking into the sporadic radio connections on the southern island. In a crisis, communication lines were crucial, especially with only one coastal artery. A killer tsunami, well-documented in native oral history, could leave them as helpless as the Salish woman tossed into a tree. She fell from the branches and became a hunchback, but lived to tell a tale so amazing that it had survived without paper for three hundred years.

A mug of fragrant jasmine tea by his side, he was making notes, biting his lower lip in such concentration that he looked like a schoolboy. "Chipper," she called. "We need you over at Edward Milne for a pickup. Tell them to send a counsellor if the parents can't come. Whitehouse wants this done ASAP. And don't let the boys sit together. Put one in the front."

Holly gave serious thought to the way she had entrapped Billy, the specious reason for taking prints. But both boys had volunteered. If they had been innocent of that crime, why would they have refused? Did they play a role in Angie's death? Within legal limitations, bringing out the truth was the goal. An officer without compassion was a danger, but too much empathy was an emotional straitjacket. She thought of Mrs. Jenkins and felt strangely disloyal.

The boys arrived at noon. Whitehouse took Billy first and Holly sat nearby, along with a mousy female counsellor who seemed more attentive to the condition of her cuticles than the unfolding scene. She wore designer jeans, plastic barrettes in her unnaturally russet hair, and a peasant blouse, giving her the appearance of a student who had stayed too long at the fair.

The shabby interview room was silent as Holly began the recording at Whitehouse's nod. He didn't open the window but let the heat build. Holly's tie choked her as she fought the urge to adjust it. Sweating characters in search of an author. Opening with ponderous formalities, the Inspector stared down his long nose and used pauses like whips, watching Billy's pupils enlarge as an open condom package was taken from a labelled brown paper bag and placed on the desk.

His eyes sought Holly's, making her uncomfortable. "But I thought...you said—"

"We're ready to start," Whitehouse said. He turned to the counsellor, giving her a severe appraisal. "Ms Drew, is it? You understand that everything you hear in this office stays in this office."

The woman cleared her throat and shifted in her chair. "My profession involves confidentiality."

"Now, son," Whitehouse said in a curiously avuncular tone. "You've said you were alone on the beach with Mike. This is not consistent with your prints on this piece of evidence." He moved the package with a pair of tweezers, dangling it like an evil charm. "What were you both doing that night? This is your first and most important chance to tell me *your* side. We *know* what happened." Holly looked at the Rorschach watermarks on the stippled ceiling. He was using such a hackneyed bluff, from Thirties black-and-white films to *The First 48*. Sometimes it worked. Career criminals "lawyered up". Billy didn't stand a chance.

Holly watched the numbers on the recorder roll. A muscle on Billy's jaw twitched, but he said nothing. His oversized hands seemed frozen on the chair handles, until one finger began to tremble. Whitehouse narrowed his eyes like a veteran eagle toying with a rabbit. "Textbook case, Corporal. Wouldn't you agree?" he said. "The failure to make eye contact is very suspicious."

Billy inhaled deeply, flaring his nostrils. A pulse beat a frantic escape at the side of his neck. "I want to tell you the...the truth."

"It's about time, isn't it? You should have done that from the beginning." Whitehouse's fist pounded the desk, then he folded his hands as if nothing had happened. Tensions rose and fell with the tides. From somewhere far away, a time-challenged rooster crowed.

Like a beaten dog, Billy shook his head and ran fingers through his heavy black hair. "I know, but it didn't sound good."

"We'll be the judge of that. Go on. You're making an honest start."

"Not after the girl drownded...drowned. Who's going to believe me now? Even if Mike was there."

"Right, and he's your buddy. What's he going to say, other than to make you look as righteous as possible? I thought you said you were telling the truth. Smarten up."

Righteous. Holly winced at the Ebonics, or was it Mafiaspeak?

"He wouldn't lie for me. Not if I'd hurt someone." His voice forced against breaking, the boy sounded wounded. Under heavy black lashes, he looked down at his patched jeans more as an embarrassment, not a minor fashion statement. A huffing sound from Whitehouse caught everyone's attention. Ms Drew's eyes ricocheted back and forth as she sat rigid in her chair. A convenient prop, she knew little about why they had come together.

With a barely discernable motion from Whitehouse, Holly leaned forward, her voice soft and urgent. "So tell us, Billy, in your own words. What happened that night?"

Billy gave a long sigh, as if something deep inside ached. He tried to speak, but swallowed instead, then moistened his dry lips. "Could I have a glass of water, maybe?"

Whitehouse drummed his fingers. Holly went to the cooler, hitting the blue button and praying it wouldn't stick and flood the floor. "Thanks, Miss, I mean Officer," Billy said. He finished in a few gulps, then held the glass in his large hands like a chalice. She wondered if it would break into a hundred pieces like in the movies, but he cradled it gently.

"It happened the same as I said before."

Whitehouse leaned forward with a menacing snarl. "We're not here to listen to that crap again. We know what happened. We only want you to explain it. I told you to—"

Holly spoke quietly, trying to establish an atmosphere of trust. "I think Billy has more to tell us, right?"

"Yes, ma'am." He managed a sweet puppy-dog smile that girls would find appealing. Unlike many of his peers, his skin was clear and smooth, bronze with high cheek bones. "We had a fire on the beach. Mike was burning some sweetgrass, 'cause his mom's been pretty sick. Like a ritual."

"Sweetgrass. Not pot, then. Was alcohol involved?" Whitehouse's slash of an eyebrow rose like an unfurling snail.

He shook his head. "No, ma'am, sir." For seconds he sat silent. Outside, a heavy transport roared by. They cringed at the shrieking application of jake brakes, illegal in denser areas. Standing at rest in the corner, Chipper shot her a look as if asking whether to deal with it. She shook her head.

"Go on, boy," Whitehouse said. "And remember, we're not interested in small-time charges like trespassing on the damn beach or even smoking some dope. We want to know how this girl died."

Billy put the empty glass on the table and straightened his shoulders, a man under construction. "She came up to us. About moonrise."

Holly remembered the bike, abandoned on the path. "Walking?"

"Uh-huh." He squeezed his eyes together. "And I...lied to you about something. I did know her. We'd seen each other at a couple of soccer games. Said hi. But we never hung out."

"Don't worry about that now. We'll cover the fine points

later," Whitehouse said. His voice was speeding up, as if he smelled blood.

A quizzical look came over the boy's handsome face. "There was something funny about her. She was walking all right, but she wasn't herself. Maybe she'd been taking something, I don't know."

"Taking something? Like drugs?" Whitehouse asked, shooting a glance at Holly.

"I know she was an athlete. I can't see how she would have done that, but things happened pretty fast." He swiped a hand over his eyes with an ironic laugh. "Mike's no dummy. He went off by himself for awhile."

"By himself?" Billy gave a quick nod and dropped his gaze. "I see. And then?" Whitehouse asked.

"Yeah, we had sex. She was really hot for it. I hardly had time to...well, you know." He blinked in embarrassment. "No disrespect meant. I was like...what? She smiled at me last time I saw her at the July 1st fireworks. Gave me some gum. But she was with a big guy, another athlete like her. I didn't think we'd ever—"

"How long were you intimate?"

He translated the niceties and cleared his throat. "Not long. Maybe ten minutes. Then she said she was going for a swim to...clear her head. I found Mike and we went to bed. We were due back to cut brush for my uncle, and he starts work at sun-up."

Some enchanted evening, Holly thought. Premature ejaculation was common in young men. "And you didn't follow her? Make sure she was safe?"

"She wasn't staggering. She was talking slow, but she made sense. Anyways, wasn't she a big time swimmer? The water was calm that night, no waves or anything. When she went off in the dark..." With a groan, he spread his hands in a gesture of uselessness. Perhaps he felt that his performance had disappointed her.

"And what about the meth? Did you give it to her?"

"What meth?" His tone rose three notes, and his face paled to a milky coffee. "I don't do that stuff. Ask anyone."

Whitehouse stood. "Meth, Billy boy. We have definitive tests. We know she took it. You're the last person to see her."

Billy's face paled, and he was making an effort not to cry. It was as if he had been wading and now found himself over his head. "I don't care how many times you ask. There...was...no...meth. I wouldn't touch that shit."

Whitehouse turned his back. "Stay around Port Renfrew. We're not finished with you yet." He gave a curt gesture towards the door.

"But don't you believe...I mean I wouldn't hurt..." He got up slowly, brows confused, addressing his comments to Holly. "I'll take a poly...whatever you call it, a lie detector test. So will Mike. Isn't that good e—"

"Put him in the car, Chipper, and stay with him," Whitehouse said. The boys passed each other without speaking.

Mike came in next. At first he stuck to the initial story, but his head hung low, and he squeezed his hands together. Any bravado he might have had vanished as Whitehouse slapped a folder on the desk, making the boy jump. "Billy told us everything about your night with Angie. Help yourself out by confirming it. It's never too late to come clean."

Suspicions crossed his face as if in betrayal. Mike's self-control stiffened. "I don't know what you're talking about. Honest."

Whitehouse's voice sharpened into a steely edge that sparked words. "He confessed that they had sex. The condom pack had his prints, for Christ's sake. Don't waste our time."

Mike cleared his throat. A red flush came over his broad

face. Unlike Billy, he had a blooming case of acne. "I don't know. I left them alone."

"All right. That's better. And how was Angie acting?"

"Okay. Friendly. But I didn't know her." He squirmed in his chair. "Just to see around. At the A&W maybe. Who could forget a girl like that? She was a babe."

"And when you got back?"

"She was walking along the beach like she was going for a swim. She waved, even. We turned in then. Billy didn't say anything. He's a quiet guy. Not much for words."

Whitehouse added, "We know you gave her meth. She had it in her system."

This time Mike jumped from the chair. "No way, man. We don't use that shit. Billy never told you that. Never." He dropped his eyes. "Sorry, sir."

Whitehouse kept at him for another fifteen minutes, hammering the same questions every which way. Mike remained adamant that drugs had not been involved. Like Billy's denials, his words rang true to Holly. And naming an exact time for turning in, as if he'd been waiting and checking his watch until Billy returned. It fit. What other scenarios did that leave?

"That's enough, then. Have Ann transcribe the tapes, and get a statement for them to sign later. Take them back to school."

After the detachment door closed, Whitehouse turned to her. "Good bluff, and it worked, but only so far. They're the sole witnesses to what happened on the beach. They'll both claim she walked off of her own free will. And who knows, maybe she did."

Holly frowned and looked at her notes from an earlier telephone interview with a counsellor at Edward Milne. "I still don't get the motivation for any harm. Those boys don't have a record of violence. Billy is an honour student. It was opportunistic to take advantage of her, but—"

"Who wouldn't?" He made a rude noise. "Are we living on the same planet? Was 'Say no to sex' mother's best advice?"

Holly tried to keep her face neutral. She didn't want anyone guessing at her nun-like existence. Three boyfriends in ten years. "At least he used a condom. Score one for sex ed, or health ed, whatever they call it. Both boys agreed that Angie was acting strangely. From what I've read, she should have felt the effects of meth a lot sooner. Why was she able to ride that bike all the way to the beach?"

"Everyone's different. And maybe she brought it with her."

"From the profiles, first-time users wouldn't take the risk of experimenting alone."

"Anything else to suggest?" Whitehouse began packing up his papers, filing them neatly in an alligator attache case.

Holly folded her hands. Surely they hadn't considered every possibility. "Of all the ways meth is taken, what would be the slowest to reach the nervous system?"

He pursed his broad lips, a slight cut at the edge from hasty shaving. "Ingestion, I guess. Passing through the digestive system takes longer than shooting up or snorting."

Holly snapped her fingers. "So she could have taken it at the camp. Or had it given to her."

"To get the best rush, she should have been smoking it. Does this all matter?"

"Billy strikes me as an honest guy. He offered to take a polygraph test."

He snapped shut the case. "So do it. Get Victoria to send out the unit. If the boys fail, and I'm thinking they will...everyone believes they can fake it...we'll have more ammunition."

Holly left to give Ann the directives. When she returned, Whitehouse was answering his cell phone. "Yes, yes," he said impatiently, scratching the back of one hand until it bled. "Do what I told you, dammit." Then he hung up.

"Bad news?"

"A new case out of Royal Roads University. Some professor killed his wife. Tried to make it look like an accident. Pathetic, really."

Royal Roads, formerly a prestigious military training school, occupied a palatial estate in Langford. She swallowed, felt her blood charge through her veins at the word *professor.* "What kind of an accident?"

"Fall down the stairs. Trouble is, the blood spatters and prints don't agree with what he said happened. We'll nail the bastard to the blackboard, and it'll be a pleasure. Academics think they're so smart, but their heads are up their asses."

She kept quiet, digesting the information. Arrogance was Whitehouse's middle name. How comical that people despised in others the traits they nurtured. "I'm going to follow up that meth connection...all the way to Victoria if I have to."

"Try the parking garage off Government Street. At least that was last week."

Holly watched him leave...again, wishing that the wind would blow from the west to keep him far away from Fossil Bay.

Ann came into the office carrying what looked like a school blue book for exams. "I may have some information," she said, her face alive and almost eager. "About that meth. Sean's done a hell of a job. I'm proud of that kid."

Riding around on weekends, Sean had noticed something suspicious at the end of Munson Road. More a muddy rut, Munson abutted an old farm with rocky pastures unfit for crops, hardly prime real estate. Eli Munson, a childless widower, had once run a marginal sheep operation there after the Second World War, but with his death, the land had passed into the public domain for tax arrears. Over the last thirty years, the small farmhouse and leaning barn had fallen into disrepair. Its signal feature for a meth lab was total privacy. Thick cedars woven together with huge firs kept it well hidden from the road. Even the lane curved so that the house couldn't be seen. Ruts in the drive and the marks of truck tires showed that some recent traffic had passed. Teenagers looking for a private place to party? Ann paused with a proud grin. "Sharp, eh? Noticing those tracks. Not quads either. Too far apart."

"He's getting an A so far. Go on." She watched Ann read from Sean's notes. "Secret Report" was printed at the top of each page.

Sean had noticed a strange smell when he rode by. An unusual inland breeze was wafting odours from the property. Cat pee. "And my grandma has seventeen, so I know what that's like," he had added. When he crept closer, pulling himself on his elbows an inch at a time, keeping the bushes in front of him, he saw that the lower windows had been blacked out with tinfoil.

"Where's Chipper?" On full alert, Holly planned to visit the scene, even though the boy's imagination might be on overdrive. Still, his details were compelling.

"He went to Jordan River on a domestic complaint about ten minutes ago. It was pretty serious. Kelly Esterhazy might have a broken arm. Earl's drunk. She's drunk. Usually gives as good as she gets, just doesn't have the size."

"I'll wait for him. If it is a meth lab, it isn't going anywhere in only one day." This time she'd make no assumptions, but go by the book. With back-up. Given the three-person operation, that was like juggling plates on sticks. She tried to raise Chipper on the radio, but he was away from the vehicle, tending to the Esterhazys. It chilled her that they were so isolated and defenseless at this end of the island.

Ann got a strange gleam in her eye and went to the window. "Andrea's probably home. She could..." Then she turned too fast and winced. "No, forget it."

Holly gave Ann points for wanting to contribute in a more active way, but she let the woman set her own limitations instead of saying something patronizing. Meanwhile, she got on the computer and ran the Capital Regional District program, which allowed her to focus on the suspect area. Manipulating the controls, she zeroed in. The end of Munson Road looked like one giant Sherwood Forest. Trees in all directions, except for a few isolated meadows. The land had retreated to nature quickly enough, though much of the periphery was scrubby alder. At the maximum focus, she could make out a small house and several outbuildings. No vehicles were apparent, but that meant nothing. It wasn't a live feed. The satellite pictures came from a year or two ago. Maybe the house had been occupied then, maybe not. Squatters were rife in Victoria, but this far into the bush made an unhandy address...unless for good reason.

The only way in was the lane, one advantage for the law. Unless there were all-terrain vehicles, no one was escaping out the back. A deep V of a creek sliced the property in half. After jotting a few notes, she made a call to check municipal records for the owners.

An hour later, Chipper returned. "I've got Earl in the cruiser. Cross your fingers that he doesn't barf," he said. "He'll be off to the West Shore holding facilities. Sooke's full up."

Holly thought for a moment. Here was a safe chance to let Ann shine. "Call in our volunteer to man the phones, Ann. You take him in."

A small smile grew on Ann's face along with the nuance of a dimple on one pale cheek. It seemed to ease the strain lines and light up her personality. Holly had seen a yoga pamphlet on her desk with a couple of classes circled.

"Will do." Ann grabbed the phone and dialed, speaking quickly.

"Chipper, check your belt, then make sure the shotgun's loaded and the Suburban's full of gas. We have a house call to make, and the terrain might be rough."

His face lit up like a kid's as he looked at her computer screen. "Where are we going?"

By the time they were ready, Andrea was power walking down the lane as Ann was pulling out. With Chipper at the wheel of the muscular vehicle, Holly brushed aside chip packs, candy wrappers, and root beer cans from Reg's time. "Sorry, Boss," Chipper said, scooping muffin crumbs from the seat. "Haven't used the old bus since I got here. Tomorrow I'll take her into the car wash and clean her up."

In the late afternoon torpor, Holly's vest was punishingly hot. She filled Chipper in on Sean's information and the way they would handle the approach of the property.

En route through the rural backroads, they blocked an escaped peacock whose owner was pursuing it with a net, then took the final turn to Munson. "The island," Chipper said. "Gotta love it. Llamas, alpacas, therapy horses and exotic birds."

They had climbed a serious of long grades to amazing views of the strait to one side and the San Juan Ridge on the other. Despite the sun, mist rose like smoke from the dark hills. Holly agonized trying to understand why some of the island's premium coastal land had been tagged for logging or gravel pits. But twenty-five years ago, anything even a mile from town was "rural". The population huddled along the lifelines of the ferries to the mainland.

After parking out of sight before the last turn, she removed the shotgun from the clip. On a second thought, she put it back, then took it again and handed it to Chipper, who watched her with some confusion. Going in like gangbusters might be a mistake, but being unprepared for one time in his life had killed Roy. How many people were on the property? Perhaps if they saw more than one vehicle, they'd call for backup from Sooke. If the damn radio cooperated.

Chipper looked down the lane. "Can't see a thing. Just like you said."

She grabbed a pair of binoculars. "Let's approach from the side. There's a break in the hedging fifty feet down." Emerging through the tormenting Himalayan blackberries, both their uniforms torn, they crept toward the house, passing the outbuildings first. The open barn door revealed piles of rotting hay and rusty implements hung on nails. Chipper pointed to a small storage shed with a new padlock that gleamed in the sun peeking through the clouds. Otherwise the place looked deserted. They needed to get closer.

He followed her to a thick arbutus bush full of plump, pink berries with hard, raspy shells, where they hunkered down to inspect the house. Constructed over a century ago, when the area had fledgling farms, the building was thirty by thirty feet with a crumbling chimney. The mossy shake roof sagged over a dilapidated porch with boards missing like yanked teeth. The unpainted cedar siding had weathered to grey. Underneath was a stone foundation, merely a crawl space which might have served as a root cellar. Instead of storing beets, carrots and potatoes, now it might house supplies. A brisk wind blew in as the weather pattern shifted. A rocker missing one arm started to move back and forth in eerie silence as if entertaining a ghost. Someone had sat there, watching the sun go down.

"Smell anything?" Holly asked.

Chipper obligingly tweaked his nose, small for his face, giving him a boyish appearance. "I was a scout. Wind's blowing from behind us."

She pointed to the windows plastered with foil, as if some night shift worker lived there. "That's very suspicious. Sean was onto something." Records at the town hall had revealed that the owner lived in Vancouver and rented out the property. But he was in Europe on business, and his personal secretary at the appliance store could reveal no more information about the tenant other than that he had been there only a few months. "It's been vacant since the owner died," she had said. "Mr. Mitchell bought it for back taxes on spec. As a hobby farm, it's just a drain. He's been renting it out this year to people not particular about luxury, he says. When the re-zoning comes through, those lots will be worth a fortune." Holly recognized the strata concept, allowing four properties on every ten hectares. The CRD had been able to sustain a moratorium on that kind of growth, but with development pressure, how long would it last?

Mere suspicions and foiled windows aside, they had no search warrant and no probable cause. The reactions of the "tenant" would tell her how far to proceed. She couldn't see the debris Sean had mentioned, but perhaps it had been cleaned up. After a mute signal to Chipper, she knocked on the door. No response. Knocked again. Women's tones would be less alarming. "Hey, are you guys there?" she called casually. Certainly better than announcing themselves. Chipper gave her an approving nod.

Then they heard an annoyed answer. "You fuckwit. I said not to come before..." And the door opened. "What the..."

A skinny white man who hadn't seen a razor in days stood before them. His jeans were torn, his T-shirt filthy with stains.

He stepped back and made as if to shut the door, but Holly found a use for her tough boot. "Not so fast."

He opened the door slowly. "What is it, officer?"

She introduced herself and Chipper. The man's name was Neil Forrester. He had come to the island with a buddy who promised him a job on a fishing charter. The season was over for that gig, she thought. "And you're renting this house?" she asked.

"My buddy's sort of subletting to me. Not much of a place, but the price is right." He waved his hand and snickered. "Ever try to rent on the island? It's a brutal market."

"There have been reports that an illegal substance is being made on the premises."

He slapped the wall with the butt of his hand. "What? Wine? That's not illegal last time I heard."

Holly bit her lip. "May we have permission to search the building?" She added, "Please."

His lizard lids narrowed his reddened eyes to slits. "Oh, I don't think so. We have rights in this country." He gave the blue turban a once-over and made a contemptuous sound in his throat. "Too many, maybe."

Chipper tensed, shifting his glance to Holly. They'd lost the timing in this play, moved too fast with too little and no backup to keep an eye on the place. This crew could move on in a half a day, given a truck. Meth cooking was a drive-by-night operation.

"Excuuuuse me then." Neil prepared to shut the door, the smile broadening on his weasel face.

Then a booming voice called, "We're gonna need more red phosphorus..."

Before Neil could speak, Chipper moved in, pushed him against the door jamb, and put a warning hand over his mouth. "Beg your pardon, sir. I tripped," he whispered.

The voice went on. "Check out that source in Langford, Jason someone. And count on making the rounds at the drug stores, one pack per. That Methwatch program is bullshit."

Holly pulled out her handcuffs. "Hello, probable cause. Either that or a really bad cookie recipe."

Neil's brow began to sweat, and his eyes shifted in their sockets as they glanced down the hall. Then he freed his head and yelled, "Take off! Cops!" Chipper gripped his spindly arms, and Neil sank down on the stairs.

Holly secured him to a sturdy bannister while Chipper added leg cuffs. Then she ran toward a back room, where thumps were sounding, slipping on the scarred boards of the hardwood floor. A strong ammonia smell nearly stopped her breath as she entered. She had time only to register the lab equipment and to step carefully. Empty packaging dotted the floor, along with beer cans and chip bags. She was in a minefield of danger. With lethal chemicals, even a spark from a light switch could ignite the gas. Many meth labs were self-destructing, blowing up their cookers or maiming them for life. Following the sounds, she slipped through another door, her gun drawn, body to the side like an old-fashioned gunfighter presenting the narrowest target. "Stop now. Police. You're surrounded." A wish and a prayer.

Down a dark hall, a window opened with a shriek, and a grunt outside told her that someone had escaped. She followed, dropping to the ground and scanning the area. No one in sight, but the shed was open. A roar erupted and a small motorcycle emerged at full throttle. It raced past her a hundred feet away, slewing in the gravel. She had time only to record the B.C. license plate. MNR 657. It was gone in seconds, throwing dust clouds in its wake.

She cursed herself for not searching the buildings ahead of

time, merely assuming that since no cars or trucks were around, that there were no means of escape. But they had the lab, and they had Neil.

"Aren't you gonna read me my rights?" he asked with a sneer as he leaned against the wall. She could smell the stale sweat that soaked his shirt. His nose kept dripping, running down his chin. "I want a cigarette," he demanded with a wheeze.

"You watch too much television. I'm not Dog, the Bounty Hunter. He makes way more money," she said, then turned to Chipper. "Call it in, get a team from Sooke, and run his name through CPIC for wants. Run the plate, too. It could be stolen."

They secured Neil, with a complimentary wad of tissues, while Holly pulled on surgical gloves and went back to check the house. If a gas flame was burning, they could lose the place. Though the hydro was working, the house was barely habitable, and the water came from a shallow well dug before her father had been born. Wallpaper peeled in strips, revealing lath and plaster, and the pissy smell of black mould permeated the rooms and made her sneeze. The ceilings were hammered tin, a decorative touch from an age of craftsmanship and pride.

Once this had been a cozy farmhouse with a pump at the kitchen sink and an outhouse instead of indoor plumbing. Bedrooms upstairs, a nominal term, contained only soiled mattresses and blankets. The kitchen had a Coleman stove and an ancient refrigerator with a round apparatus on top, circa 1935. The thought of opening it made her gag.

On the wall, a framed needlepoint sampler, the glass cracked and yellowed, read: "To know how sweet your home may be, just go away but keep the key." Hard-working farm families had lived and died here, their only medicine a dose of honey and vinegar, their weapons a scythe, pitchfork and axe, their loyal partners a team of burly plow horses. In fifty years, perhaps forty, luxury homes would dot the hillside in this Victoria West.

She went back into the lab, a former parlour off the foyer, built to face the afternoon sun. Plywood and sawhorse tables held boiling substances in assorted carafes with tubing in all directions. On the floor were empty boxes of cold medication, salt, lithium batteries and Coleman fuel. Unbleached coffee filters sat piled next to a round metal cooking screen and wire cutters. Pitchers, wooden spoons and a carton of Ziploc bags completed the preparations. She saw no finished product. Perhaps they worked batch by batch. It wasn't a large operation, so chances were that gangs weren't involved. That might give her a bargaining coin. Whatever Neil might say in this unguarded moment could affect later strategies. As for an immediate confession, he was no boy like Billy or Mike, but he had been caught in the act.

Holly finished taking notes and joined Chipper in the car. Neil coughed in the back. Black mould could make someone quite sick.

"I called it in," Chipper said. "A specialty team from West Shore will be out here in an hour. After they make their report, this whole place is going to have to be assessed for the toxicity of the chemicals, the guy said."

"Glad our part's over," she said, then turned to Neil. "We have a date at the detachment. I have more questions for you."

Neil blew out a contemptuous breath. "Go fuck yourself."

"We expect you to cooperate. Meth isn't friendly like pot, which has some acceptance in the community. Public feelings are running high against this cheap poison. You're looking at some serious time here."

Chipper stayed at the site to secure the property and wait for the investigating team while Holly drove Neil back to Fossil Bay. Once in her office, she had determined the tack to take in the preliminary interview. If he started thinking too much, they might not get any more information. As they came in the door, Ann gave them an unusual look and passed Holly a file.

Holly gave the papers a quick scan. "Good work, Ann."

She sat Neil down in her office, leaving the handcuffs on as a reminder. "I see by your sheet that you come from Edmonton, but you did a year in William Head for dealing cocaine in Vancouver. First offense. You got off lucky in one of our Club Feds." William Head was located in pastoral Metchosin on the glorious strait. It had a stellar view of Hurricane Ridge. Times she'd driven by, the inmates were in the yard chopping wood as if they were on a rustic vacation.

Neil fiddled with the cuffs, contorting his face. "Can't you lighten up with these? They're making my wrists sore. And how about some coffee? I'm not a friggin' terrorist."

Unlike the empathy she had for Billy and Mike, here Holly saw a source of evil. Crime had its hierarchies, and Neil was a cowardly bottom feeder. What approach should she take? Lowering her voice, she chose her words carefully. "Consider yourself lucky that we took the leg cuffs off. I want the name of the other man at the house. I have his bike's license, so it's a matter of time. Make it easy on yourself and cooperate."

"Brad Pitt. Elmer Fudd. Take your pick." Then he added as his thin mouth curled into an ugly question mark, "I'm not afraid of you, babe. Whadda you gonna do, beat me up?" He shuffled in the seat and produced a pungent fart, watching her reaction.

A bottle of ruthless pine air freshener came to hand, and she sprayed it with abandon, nearly hitting his face. Sparring was fun with an ace up her sleeve. She tapped her pen on the desk, noticing that despite his shabby clothes, he wore a spanking new pair of two-hundred-dollar runners. "Maybe coffee would help, because you're not thinking too clearly here, Neil. We're not the problem. You need to be afraid of people who don't have our ethics and represent only themselves, not the public welfare."

He coughed pointedly. "Public welfare my ass. Horsemen don't need the Mafia to do the dirty work. The force is bent enough."

Holly ignored the flash of flame across her chest. Recent personnel scandals had proved a national embarrassment for Canada's Mounties, the latest a constable at a lonely outpost cruising sex lines while on duty and offering his patrol car as a bedroom. *Hot cop* had brought very bad publicity. "Something much more West Coast style." She got up and pulled off an information paper from the bulletin board, sticking it in his face.

A purple pimple rose from the side of his nose, volcanic in potential. "I don't read so well," he said. "Lady at school called me functional ill...ill..." His voice trailed off.

She re-tacked the paper. "If you're new to the island, maybe you don't know that most of the dope business is run by gangs. It's a billion-dollar business, and it's as protected as a newborn. The Hells Angels take a dim view of some amateur skimming their profits."

He paled, swallowing back a bobbing Adam's apple. Clearly he was running a penny-ante business. A few months, and he would have moved on, keeping his head low like a lizard. "What's that got to do with me? See any Harleys at the farm?"

She leaned forward. "Here's what. It's no problem to spread the word via our undercover officers that you're open for business and keeping all the cash. Don't think they'll ignore you because you're small. This is a question of disrespecting their operation. And *respect* is a very important word." Now she was whisked back to her father's Seventies period, just before she left for university. He'd organized a *Godfather* party for his graduate students.

He paled, and his knee started a spastic reaction, riding up and down. He crossed his legs to hide it. "I need a drink."

She brought him water from the cooler, placed it into his hands as he brought them to his mouth. "And they're not the worst. Just home-grown. Let's try another name. The Big Circle Boys."

"Who? You're making this up." Water spilled down his T-shirt. She reached for the paper cup and tossed it into the basket.

"Dai Huen Jai. Chinese gangs. They don't fool around." She sliced her finger across her throat in amateur theatrics.

"Enough already. What does it matter? Game was over when Dickhead opened his big mouth." He furrowed his brow, blood-flecked eyes moving back and forth in spasms. Had he been sampling his own wares? "But if I tell you all I know, you gotta protect me."

"As much as we can. Don't expect to get into the witness protection program on this petty information." With some leisure, she opened a fresh page, drumming her fingers in thought. "We might be able to send you out of the area to do your time. That's all I can promise. Prince George is lovely in the fall."

He took a deep breath and rattled off curses. "Dave Barnard. He's my partner. He'll probably run to his mother's in Nanaimo. Fucking baby. Dumb as a bag of nails, too. Damn near blew us up twice."

She tapped the pen on a yellow pad. "I want the name or description of anyone you've sold to in around here. Let's start with the high schools. Unless you went after younger kids, too."

"Jesus. I don't ask for passports." His tongue ran around his thin lips. "If they resell it, what can I do?"

"Poor you. The downside of distribution." She spat out the words, punctuating for emphasis. "As if you *care*. So give over, Neil." He furnished her with several names, scratching one seedy ear for inspiration. One struck a bell. "Did you say Jeff Pasquin?" She looked up abruptly.

"Met him down at the old cemetery one night. Dude never gave me his name, but I saw it with his picture in the *News Mirror*. Some swim-meet shit."

"How many times did you sell to him? And when?"

His upper lip rose, revealing an oral hygiene as dubious as the yellow-birch stumps of teeth. Even his tongue was furry. "A couple. Think I keep records? This is a friendly business."

Next he'd be referring to his poison as "product". "He's an athlete, and as far as I know he's still in training. Are you feeding me a load of manure?" She thought of the physical ravages of the addiction. Jeff was a poster boy.

A croaky laugh came from his chapped lips, a slit in his pasty face. "Oh hell. That's a myth. Some people can use it and lose it, then go back to pot, booze, whatever turns their...crank." He winked for a response but got none.

"That's not what I hear. Users look wasted in very little time." She pointed to a wall poster with an image of a young woman fit for a horror movie.

He used his thumbs and forefingers to frame the picture, then guffawed, nearly hitting her with a spray of spittle. "I tried it a few years ago. Rough high. I'm more of a mellow guy. Never used it again. Go figure."

Holly completed the paperwork to move Neil to West Shore, then loaded him into the car. He would be installed in a cheery cell with stainless steel sink and toilet and no sharp edges. Some luck would give him glass-block windows next to the busy thoroughfare of Veteran's Memorial Parkway. By this time tomorrow if he didn't make bail, he'd be at VIRCC, Vancouver Island Regional Correctional Centre. Her stomach growling, when she'd finished, she stopped for a pulled pork sandwich at nearby Smokin' Bones, adding a side of vinegary collard greens.

By five, she was back at the office. Chipper had caught a ride back from the Munson property. He brought cups of herbal tea, and they sat on the small sofa in the lunchroom. Neither cared to be wired by caffeine at that time of day. They had taken their boots off. Chipper was rubbing a sore toe, the hazards of the stiff footwear.

He told her about the crew that had arrived to secure the site and begin the cleaning process. "What a mess," he said, gesturing in excitement.

"The place was a sty, but I didn't take an inventory. What did you find?"

He consulted his notes. "Acetone, red phosphorous, lye, muriatic acid, anhydrous ammonia." He paused, shaking his head. "That's tough to get, but some people steal it from farmers."

"Chemistry background?"

"Not really. Lots of amateurs get into it. There are sites all over the web with instructions on how to make meth."

"What's the time frame for the cleanup?" she asked, wondering how to close the site to gawkers. "If Sean could ride over there, so could any kid."

"It might take a week to go over the property for toxic waste. At least in the boonies, they couldn't flush anything down the sewers. It's different in the cities. Eighteen to thirty grand per incident in Vancouver. A lab in Surrey exploded, and twenty people had to be evacuated. Methane gas from a lab blew up in a Kitsilano sewer line."

She blew out a breath at the nickel-and-dime budget at Fossil Bay. "Who pays? How could municipalities afford that?"

"They bill Ottawa, but here's the crunch. They get refunded only if there's a police report and charges are laid." The conversation petered out. Chipper picked up a *Blue Line* magazine.

Suppose Neil had made it out a window? What if Chipper hadn't been there to help? She turned back to her notes and double-checked for errors. Damn. Had she really written that he had "waved" his rights?

"You two look comfortable," Ann said, coming in with an envelope. The results of the polygraph test had arrived.

Ten

Beaming for a change like a proud father with teeth that looked like ceramics, Whitehouse sat with Holly in her office the next day. "We got several outstanding warrants for Neil and Dave. Break-and-enters in Edmonton. Auto theft. Failure to appear. Ran on their bail, which was too bloody low. Soft judges. The boys will do serious time. The Crown Prosecutor is rubbing her hands together."

"The Nanaimo force picked up Dave. But this connection to Pasquin has me thinking." She laced her fingers together.

"So she got the meth from him after all. Sneaky bastard."

"Not with her knowledge. I think he gave it to her in some food." She consulted her notebook from the day of the drowning. "That s'more."

"More what?" His face assumed a quizzical look, clearly not the picnic type of man.

"It's a campfire dessert. Graham crackers, marshmallow, chocolate bar. Everyone was eating them, and so was she, according to Vic Daso."

"So the food caused a delayed reaction."

"Depends on the health of the individual, but reaction time could be from thirty to forty minutes. Plenty of time to get out to the beach if she left immediately. She was young and strong, probably confused by the drug."

He nodded, rubbing his chin with his hand. "Where she

got up close and personal with our dark-skinned laddie in no time flat. Ripe for the picking."

She bridled at his course language, but it wasn't her role to teach the man tact or sensitivity. "The boys thought that she was acting strange. Makes sense now. We just got the results of the polygraph. Their stories didn't make the needle flinch. Maybe you were a bit rough on them, especially Billy."

He ignored her reproof. "Breaks of the game. Move on. Let's deal with this Pasquin scum." He reached for the typescript of the interviews, ran his long finger down the pages in speed-reading and stabbed at the last paragraph. "Can we break his alibi? Little Lindsey lies with him, and she'd lie for him."

"He had no way of getting to the beach. But even if he wasn't with her when she drowned, he's responsible for Angie's death. He must have suspected what happened. Didn't even go after her or report her missing, the son of a bitch."

The phone at the main desk rang. They could hear Ann answering, then some measured responses. "Corporal, you'd better come in here."

Holly approached the desk. The corners of Ann's mouth fell, and a crease appeared between her eyes as she muffled the phone. "It's Mrs. Jenkins. Billy's tried to commit suicide."

Between gasps and sobs, the mother was speaking so fast that Holly could hardly understand. "Damn all of you. Mike came over and found him in the boathouse. Cut him down as fast as he could. They're sending a helicopter from Victoria to take him to the General. Thank god my neighbour keeps oxygen for her emphysema. I don't even know if it's helping."

"Calm down. You're doing all you can." A muffled wap-wapping announced the rescue bird heading west. "It's passing here now. Better look for a place they can land. Is he conscious?"

"He's breathing, but there's no response. Why did you

193

make life hell for my boy? He didn't do anything wrong. It's not a crime to have consensual sex. Kids are kids."

"I'm so sorry. We...talked to many students. Mike and Billy were the last to see Angie." She felt sweat trickle down her back. But she hadn't given Billy the third degree. That had been Whitehouse's job. "I tried to be as easy on him as I could."

"You said it was routine. He told you he'd take that test, that polygraph. And he passed, didn't he? Did you want his life, too? Is that how you—"

They hadn't called the family yet with the results, but his mother knew he had been telling the truth. "I never thought he had anything to do with Angie's drowning." A minor lie. To be objective, she needed to suspect everyone.

"This is a very small village. Gossip is cheap entertainment. Some people are making jokes about how he was showing off with a white girl. Do you people have to make it so hard for us? We're not second-class citizens."

Holly bit back the fact that Coast Salish blood ran in her veins. A feeble way to establish rapport at this critical point. "Please tell me more. Has he done anything like this before? Did he give you any indication that he was depressed?"

The response was instant and strong. "Of course not. He's a great kid. Sure he doesn't talk much. Neither does his dad. They show their love for their family by hard work."

"I'll stop by the hospital as soon as I can. And I need to talk to Mike. Is he with you?" The circumstances of the discovery were critical. Asking more questions now when the woman was wondering if her son would live or die wouldn't help.

"Save your concern. I've got to go watch for the helicopter." She hung up with a slam.

Holly sat with a large rock lodged in her throat. She told Whitehouse what had happened. "Suicide rates are brutal for young aboriginal men, but more in the far north. I blame myself."

He made a scoffing sound and went to fix himself a coffee. "For what? Acting too fast? That's the way we're supposed to work. You don't sit on information for weeks and chew it like fucking cow cud." Then he tested the brew and added more sugar. "Pasquin admits that he gave her the meth, and I'm out of this kindergarten. Lord god, why me?"

Holly felt her stomach rise. That happy moment couldn't come soon enough. And with the polygraph clearing him, why had Billy grown so desperate? Was even a misdirected shame that powerful?

Jeff was brought in with a sneer on his face a few hours later, his grandmother in tow again. He wore his school clothes, but he'd taken off his tie and unbuttoned his shirt six inches down his smooth, shaven chest. He looked as if he had regular dates with a tanning bed, and Holly could imagine the golden pectorals. "This is getting boring," he said with an arrogant whine as they seated themselves. "I'm due at a swim meet in Richmond. Don't want to miss the ferry."

"You're due for a cellmate, Jeff," Whitehouse said, the cold arc of his voice slicing through steel. "We know you gave Angie that meth, probably without her knowing it. Several people have told us you supply the school, including the man who cooked it."

"Cooked it? What is this meth?" Mrs. Faris asked. She rose to come to his chair. Whitehouse waved her back to her seat, where she trembled with palsy. Her powdered cheeks were the colour of light purple hydrangeas. The thin hair had been recently permed and a pink scalp showed.

"Supply the school? That's a good one. Do I look like a friggin' drug dealer? Whoever told you that is a damn liar." A worm of a pulse began to beat in Jeff's temple, and he brushed at it like a traitorous friend.

Whitehouse moved closer, and put his hand on Jeff's arm. "You could face some serious time. Everything would go down the tubes for you." He paused and folded his arms. "But..." He let the word draw out.

"You're gonna take Neil's word? He's nothing but a..." Suddenly he stopped, his strong hands gripping the chair arms until the fingers grew bloodless.

"I never mentioned any names." Whitehouse's voice dropped so low that Holly had to strain to hear. It was more effective than a shout.

Jeff's brow broke out in a shiny sweat, and his pupils began to dilate. Holly hadn't noticed what tiny, round ears he had. "But what? You said 'but'."

"Admit you gave Angie the meth. You didn't know she'd wander off. Lindsey's already vouched for your whereabouts. Take a week or two of rehab. Everyone loves a reformed sinner. Get on with your life. This is your one chance."

As a car with no muffler roared by, all eyes went to the grimy window. In one corner, a tattered web held the desiccated remains of a fat fly. Holly heard the front door open, then the cruiser started, and Chipper took off down the road. Still Jeff said nothing. The wall clock in the main office beat ragtime with her heart. Whitehouse tipped back in his chair, inspecting his ragged and angry nails with cool bemusement.

Jeff finally shook his head and stuck out his lower jaw until the underbite made him resemble a bulldog. "I don't know. I think I need a lawyer."

"You're getting way too complicated. Do you want to be tied up for months, or do you want this over fast and neat?" Whitehouse gave an elaborate sigh and lifted a sheet of paper from the bulletin board. It was a flowchart.

Jeff looked at it as if it were printed in Sanskrit. "What's that stuff?"

Suddenly Mrs. Faris began slowly sliding to the floor, her weary little eyes rolling back in her head. Jeff shrugged and folded his arms, cocking one eyebrow. "She's only fainted. Whenever she gets upset. Says it's her heart. But the doctor said it's just nerves. Women."

Whitehouse sent for water as they helped Mrs. Faris back to a seat. When it arrived, she sipped slowly, and her eyes cleared. "I'm all right. Sorry to cause a fuss."

Reassured she could stay with the group, Whitehouse went on. "You're still covered by the Youth Criminal Justice Act, Jeff. That's your ace." He traced the flow, from the investigation to the report to the Crown Counsel. "If charges were deemed provable, two choices were possible. Extra-judicial sanctions, involving a contract which the youth could meet (end of matter) or not meet. "So if you didn't complete the contract, you'd go to court, same as if you fought the charges in the first place. There will be a bail hearing if you're in custody..."

"In custody? What if I don't make bail? We're not rich." For the first time, Jeff dropped his guard. In his exalted mind fed by Hollywood glamour, he probably thought that a million dollars was at stake. In Canada, bail was nominal. No sleazy cement-block bond businesses anchored backstreet corners. People put up the family home for surety.

"Calm down. You're a good risk, so it's a mere formality. Then at the bail hearing, you plead guilty or not guilty. One way there's a trial, the other a pre-sentence report and then sentencing."

Jeff groaned. "I'm all turned around."

"It's an easy out for you. Tell us the truth, and you could

end up with community service. Teach kids to swim. Along with regular school attendance and curfews, that could be part of the contract."

Holly tossed her superior an "are you kidding" glance, but he remained straight-faced. Something almost friendly shimmered in his eyes. The effect troubled her.

"Community service. I've heard about that. It doesn't sound so bad." His face brightening, Jeff sat back.

"And you're a first offender, right?" Holly added, piling on.

"You don't want a criminal record, do you?" Whitehouse asked. "Cooperate, and we may be able to keep this quiet. Otherwise..." He arched one eyebrow and tipped back his head.

"Jesus, no. I don't want to lose a chance at a scholarship. I want to go to the University of Michigan, and the U.S. is pretty tough on drugs."

Whitehouse stubbed his thick finger on the paper. "That's our deal, and it's a fair one. Tell us what happened."

Mrs. Faris whimpered, "Tell them, Jeffie. You've always been a good boy. This has to be some terrible mistake."

Jeff rubbed a hand over the blond stubble on his scalp. His neck was smooth and strong with the lustre of youth. "All right already. Here's what went down."

Whitehouse spoke slowly and evenly. "And don't leave one...thing...out. Even going into the bushes to take a leak."

Cracking his knuckles in a jumpy fashion, Jeff began by admitting that he had a goal of "getting it on" with Angie. He'd made bets with other boys at the school. She'd been friendly enough with him during the weekend. He'd turned on the charm with compliments no girl could resist. When he told her he was writing a poem for her, she'd almost agreed to date him again, but dating wasn't what he had in mind.

"I took some blankets, see, to this out-of-the-way place in

the woods. Pretty soft there, lots of moss. I had a whole bottle of white rum, too. Headbanger overproof stuff. Couple of Cokes. So I was feeling pretty good. If I could just get her out there, we'd have lots of fun." He looked man-to-man at Whitehouse. "Know what I mean?"

"Go on." Whitehouse fixed his hawklike eyes on Jeff.

With an unholy grin, Jeff warmed to his seduction. His thumb and finger came close to touching as he illustrated his progress. "I was *almost* there. One more soft and easy move."

Disgusted with his glee, Holly asked, "Then why did you have to give her the meth?"

"Boy Scout motto. Always prepared. It was an extra card. I might not ever get things set up like that again. A hundred-fifty bucks was riding on old Jeffer. Plus, she was in for the time of her life." He stopped for a moment, wiping at his forehead. A sheen was breaking out on his face as if he'd done the butterfly for eight hundred yards in record time. He cast a sidelong glance at his grandmother. Her breaths were coming in spurts, like little fishes. "Does she have to hear?"

"I'm afraid so," Whitehouse said. "And don't hold back. This isn't a kindergarten birthday party."

"It was the timing, see? I offered to make s'mores for her. Nice and toasty. We were at one of the smaller campfires. Only one or two others. No one was paying any attention. I pushed the jib into the middle, put on the chocolate and Graham crackers. So sweet, she'd never notice it. It's no big deal. I tried it once."

Holly felt a sour taste rise in her throat. "And..." Whitehouse looked perfectly serene, like he'd taken a pill. He gazed at the video recorder with a fond look. Would he go over the tapes many times to celebrate his victory?

"At first she seemed cool and dreamy. I steered her off in

the direction of the little bed I'd made and sat her down. Then I remembered the rum was back in the tent. I told her to wait. She was getting steamy. I could tell by her eyes."

"Then how did you get her to the beach over at Botanical?" Whitehouse asked quickly. Holly had to approve of the trick move.

Jeff jumped up. "The beach? I never got her to the beach. How the hell could I? What kind of a game are you playing?"

"If you say so, I believe you, Jeff. Go on, then," Whitehouse said.

Jeff sat down again. "I had a few more chugs, maybe too much, 'cause things started to slow down. Lost the path for a minute. When I got back, the bitch was gone." He sat down with a thud, hands on his thick thighs, powerful pistons of energy. "After all that work."

What a lucky ass he is, Holly thought. The facts were working in his direction. Too bad that Billy was paying the price.

After the preliminary paperwork had been completed and the pair had left, Whitehouse removed the tape and labelled it. Then he tidied his papers and evened out the edges. "That was lucky. If he'd had a lawyer present, we might not have this confession."

A question remained on Holly's face. "No one from the school said he was dealing. Smart move."

"No one was *asked,* according to your notes. And bluffing's done all the time, girl, on both sides." Whitehouse shrugged. "An educated guess. And he took the bait. As for the morality of the strategy, better us than them. And if I were him, I wouldn't count on that scholarship. It's out of our hands."

In the first round at the beach, drugs hadn't been a question, but she knew better than to make excuses and sound weak. The *girl* paused and tapped a pen. "Billy's suicide attempt has me wondering. He must have known he was in the clear."

"Maybe not. It wouldn't be the first time someone fooled the machine, but be glad we're not going to trial. A defense attorney would have a field day with those tests exonerating his client. Drugs. Dark. She slipped and fell. Short of a camera on the beach, we'll never know. This one is a wrap. Huh, I'm always saying that, and you turn up something new. Stop it. That's an order." His rare attempt at a joke surprised her.

She checked her watch, counting the minutes before she'd see his back. "I promised his mother I'd check on Billy, even if she doesn't want me to. I feel responsible. It's different when you meet someone face to face in their home."

"Grow up. If every officer felt like that, the justice system would collapse." He eyed her through cobra-green slits, as if concealing a nictitating fold. "I'm not sure you're tough enough for this. Probably be a corporal all your life, not that there's anything wrong with that...for a woman."

Holly felt her blood start to simmer, then reminded herself that Whitehouse was one second from gone. Excusing herself, she turned on her boot heel and left the office. "I'll be at the General, Ann," she said over her shoulder as she went out the door.

She seethed all the way down winding Sooke Road, then over to the Island Highway and off at Helmcken Road to the parking lot of the old General. Even the small deer that cropped grass in relative safety behind a chain link fence shielding a greenbelt didn't improve her mood. The upbeat sounds of Victoria's own Nelly Furtado singing, "I don't wanna be your baby girl/ I don't wanna be your little pearl/ I just wanna be what's best for me" seemed a sound retort to Whitehouse's sexism.

In the foyer, she stopped at Tim Hortons for a coffee to steady her nerves, managing to spill some on her uniform. She dabbed at it with a serviette and was offered ice water by the cashier. This small courtesy improved her demeanour. The world seemed divided between those who thought people were basically good and those who regarded them as callous opportunists. The half-full, half-empty syndrome. Which was she? Which *should* she be? Was the choice between sucker or cynic?

She approached the main desk, where a smiling volunteer offered help. "A young man was brought in today from Port Renfrew by air ambulance. I'm not sure where to find him."

The woman punched buttons, asked blunt but efficient questions, and finally told her that Billy was in the Recovery Room. Holly got directions and, weaving in and out of the busy loom that was critical medical care, arrived in the ER lobby. Medical smells pricked her nose. Disinfectant. Soap. Ammonia.

She called a nurse over, introduced herself, and was told that Billy was still unconscious but breathing on his own. "He may have tracheal damage, but since he's relatively stable, we're not subjecting him to an invasive inspection. We can do only so much at once. Miracle workers we aren't."

"What would we do without you?" Everyone knew about the high burnout rate for front-line professionals. "May I see him? He's been part of a case I'm on."

The nurse took her through the doors to a curtained cubicle at the back. One side was open to a central control area with monitors and a technician. Billy lay on a gurney with bars to prevent falls. He was hooked up to oxygen and a couple of drips. "I've got to go," the nurse said. "Dr. Morrison will probably be back for another look. She'll answer your questions." She wiped Billy's brow with a cool cloth from a metal bowl. "He's somewhere else now, but I have my fingers crossed."

The first thing Holly noticed was an angry red line on Billy's neck, raw and weeping in places. Narrowing her eyes in concentration, she recalled an elementary concept from medical forensics class. If he'd hanged himself, the mark would have been more vertical. This was horizontal. As if someone had choked him first. She could even see finger bruises on his neck where he'd tried to ease the noose. Where was the damn rope? For all she knew, the mother had thrown it away as an evil memento. Gritting her teeth, she trashed herself for forgetting proper procedures that should have taken every possibility into account. More problems of policing remote places. A detachment in Port Renfrew might have made the difference.

Footsteps sounded, and Mrs. Jenkins rushed into the room. She must have broken all speed records to get to Victoria, since the air ambulance wouldn't have allowed her to travel with her son. Her thick braids were dishevelled, and she wore gum boots over her jeans. An old flannel shirt bore the stains and smells of canning salmon. She saw nothing but her son and went to his side, touching her forehead to his. "Billy. My god." Then she began sobbing.

Holly stepped forward. "Mrs. Jenkins, the doctor's on her way in a few minutes."

The mother jumped at the sound as if she had just realized someone was in the room. "I don't blame you for what happened. Billy told me that you were fair with him. I should have remembered that."

The situation was delicate, but the timeline had to be established. No longer was she taking anything at face value. "How did you find him? I know it's hard to go over this, but if you could..." Her gaze met the dark pools of the woman's deeply shadowed eyes.

Mrs. Jenkins pulled a tissue from her leather shoulder bag and wiped her nose, the slender nostrils red and raw. She took a deep breath and placed a hand on her heaving chest. "Mike found him. See, last night Billy told him that he'd met a man at the town docks, a tourist, who offered him three hundred dollars for a morning's fishing. Our big boat's down, and all we have is a small dory. Can't take anything but smooth weather, and seats only two, so we don't make steady money. Billy was glad for the opportunity. He's proud that he buys all his own clothes, and it was a new school year."

"Then what happened?" This was making less and less sense. Despite the nature of the marks, she had hoped for easy answers, a history of depression.

"Mike came along around noon and found Billy in...in the boathouse." She lowered her voice, stroking her son's immobile arm, light walnut marble on the white sheet. "There was a note."

Holly's expectations swung like a pendulum. When a suicide didn't leave a note, police became suspicious. That omission alone was no guarantee that foul play was involved, but suicides often had been thinking of self-destruction for month or years. Only a very sick person or someone with no regard for mourners wouldn't want to leave reasons for such a decision. "In the boathouse? What did it say? You kept it, didn't..." At the woman's stricken face, she retreated. "Forgive me. I'm asking too many questions. Please take your time."

The mother's generous lips tightened. A small mole above her mouth twitched. "Not a note, exactly. Something scratched with a nail on the plywood wall."

Holly's bullshit meter started ticking big time. "And it said?"

The woman shivered. *"Sorry.* Just one word. *Sorry.* In big letters. "* She spread her thumb and forefinger to demonstrate.

"And you're sure it wasn't scratched there earlier?" Succinct, efficient, phony?

"No, it was freshly cut. I don't know where the nail went. It's a wet boathouse. Maybe it fell into the water."

"Did you recognize his writing?"

The woman thought for a minute. "It was rough, crude. Like when you write on wood and the grain gets in the way."

Holly felt her fingers tracing round and round on her baton. "Something's wrong here. He goes out on a job to make some good money, and then...or did he go at all?"

The mother shrugged, her shoulders drooping. "I sent everyone off with a good breakfast, then I left early to help a sick friend in town. Mike was pitching in at the Tourist Bureau where his girlfriend works. So we don't know if Billy went out."

"What was he wearing?"

"Work clothes and rubber boots. His slicker was in the boathouse. Usually it's in the house. We had a small drizzle, more of a mist."

This was making less and less sense to Holly. Who put on rubber boots to hang himself? Who brought along rain clothes? "What about the boat?"

"Tied at the dock. The loaded bait box was still in it. No sign of any fish being caught. Like guts or scales."

"Look at this." Holly moved the sheet aside and pointed to Billy's neck and the telltale marks.

The woman had aged ten years since their last meeting. Her voice was on the edge of breaking. "My cousin committed suicide. Gunshot." She touched the neck with gentle fingers, as if she could heal the welts. "Oh, Billy, my boy." A moan from his lips riveted their attention, but he didn't open his eyes.

"I'm saying that the marks are more consistent with someone strangling him. From behind. Then making it look like a suicide attempt." She thought about demonstrating with her own hands but decided against it. Mrs. Jenkins was upset enough.

There was a sharp intake of breath. "You mean..." She wavered and reached for a chair. At that moment the doctor walked over. Mary Morrison, according to her nametag, had silvery blonde curls cut short. Stylish narrowed glasses were pushed back on her head. She stood over six feet with the presence of a Valkyrie.

"Relatives only for now, please." She gave Holly's uniform a quizzical look.

"Please, Doctor. What are my boy's chances?" Mrs. Jenkins placed a shaky hand on her son's moist forehead. "Could he—"

Despite her cool professionalism, Mary's Cape Breton voice assumed a warmth that spread over them like a soft quilt. "In a hanging where the person… lives, there can still be serious damage to the neck. Fractures to the cricoid and thyroid cartilages and the hyoid bone." She pointed at her own neck. "Subintimal hematomas, that's like a blood clot, in the carotid arteries. So much soft-tissue swelling. Sometimes we need to operate for clots."

"Operate? You mean the spine?" The mother asked a critical question. Brain damage aside, perhaps Billy would never walk again.

The doctor shook her head as her mouth firmed. Sometime that day, she had taken the time to apply a light coat of pink lipstick. Any powder had vanished in the sweat of the job. "In judicial hangings of the past, spinal damage killed the person. The long drop. It's calculated. In these…other cases, technical death results from strangulation."

"But my son's still in a coma. What can we expect?" Mrs. Jenkins wobbled to one side and reached for the bed table.

The doctor helped her to a chair and insisted that she drink some water from the carafe. Then she spoke slowly and clearly, without patronizing. "There are lot of myths about comas. They're not always as bad as they sound. Let me explain. Cerebral hypoxia, that's lack of oxygen to the brain, can cause neurologic problems. But poor nervous system function like we see here may *not* be a predictor of a poor outcome."

Poor outcome, Holly thought. A vegetative state. Billy was so young, so vital, so virile.

The doctor added, "There is hope. So we're going to do all we can."

"And the coma..." Holly understood the jargon, but she supposed that the mother filtered out the negative.

The doctor's slender hand waved a caution. "We judge comas on a scale of one to fifteen in three areas. For eye response, there are four grades. For verbal response, five. And for motor response, another six. "

All so cut and dried, like scoring on a test. Holly asked, though she dreaded the answer, "Where does Billy score now?"

"He's moaning, so he gets a two in that category." The doctor pressed on the nail bed of his index finger. Billy's eyes jumped open for a moment, then closed. "Eyes open in response to pain. Another two."

"That doesn't sound so good," the mother said, giving another sniff.

"But look at this. Again, I'm not really hurting him." Mary pressed again near his breastbone. One hand moved up above his clavicle. "That's a five. So he's at a nine. Nine to twelve is moderate to severe."

Holly added up the scores. Medicine had to quantify everything. Still, 'moderate' sounded hopeful. "So you're saying that if he opened his eyes voluntarily..."

The doctor smiled, more out of humanity than encouragement. "Or spoke a few words, he'd be close to what we call minor coma."

"So there's a chance he'll wake up?" Holly took a deep breath. "Soon?"

The doctor nodded very slowly as if to qualify her answer. "Yes, but—"

"I see. He may not be able to...you mean...brain damage." The mother's voice trailed off as she tallied the unseen possibilities.

As the roulette wheel turned on Billy's chances, Holly was glad she hadn't chosen a career in medicine, no matter how much satisfaction saving lives might have brought her. She couldn't stand the failures any more than she could bear watching justice subverted.

"Let's stay optimistic. We've given him an MRI, and the response is normal. No damaged areas. If we're lucky, every day will show us improvement. Though I practice conventional medicine, I never discount the power of prayer or any kind of positive energy." The doctor squeezed the mother's hand. "And keep talking to him. Bring in his favourite music. Stimulate his skin with different textures."

As the doctor left, Holly found a blanket and a more comfortable armchair for Mrs. Jenkins. She also brought her hot sugared tea from downstairs. Then she gave the woman a business card. "I know you're not going to leave his side. When he wakes," she stressed the word *when,* "anything he says might be very important. Call me."

Back at the detachment, Holly filled Chipper in on the developments concerning Billy. "We've never followed up on whether anyone saw Angie on the bike that night. If it turns out Billy was attacked, it might prove that something complicated was set in motion when she died. This phony fishing trip smells like a rotten halibut. Where's the person, and where's the money? A ghost. Go to Rennie and check the Tourist Bureau to see if anyone inquired about getting a guide. Then interview people who live on the way to Botanical Beach. As I recall, there were several cabins very close to the road."

"Most of them seemed closed up for the fall."

"That's why going back is important. Someone's on a hunting trip. Someone's visiting relatives. It's a tedious but necessary part of policework. Turning over the same rocks. Sometimes something new pops up."

Chipper wiggled his fingers. "Call me the salamander whisperer."

Eleven

It was a gloomy Saturday, and the arrival of the paper at 5:15 a.m. always smacked Holly in the face as lights flashed into the driveway like a Hollywood premiere. Rain pattered on the skylights. October was supposed to begin the monsoons, but this was ridiculous. It had poured every day for the last three weeks, closing in on a record.

An hour later, she collected a coffee in the kitchen and peeked around the corner. "Tell me the weather report. No, I'm not that much of a masochist."

"Paper says RATH." Translation: "Rain, at times heavy." In his dressing gown, Norman read in his recliner from the *Times Colonist* as she came down the stairs to the tiled solarium. With the bright sun in summer, the room was warm and inviting, but another month, and it would turn into a deep freeze without the propane wall stove. Norman refused to light it until January. "Poor kid. Is this what you told me about?" He held out a section of the paper to her.

Wrapped in a cozy afghan, Holly sat on the blue leather sofa, sipped her coffee and read the article. "A Port Renfrew teenager is still in critical condition after being found hanging by a rope in his family's boathouse. Doctors say that there is an excellent chance of his recovery. The next three days will make the difference. Police are looking for a person of interest who apparently left the scene just before the teen was found by a friend."

"A person of interest. Silly jargon. Even I know what that means," Norman said. "Does the law have to tread that lightly?"

"I guess we're not allowed to use the word *suspect* any more. When did that happen?"

"Says here the young man may recover. That's good."

Holly remembered giving only bare-boned but optimistic facts to the reporter who had called the detachment. Were she right about the attack, the *person of interest* would know that he had not succeeded and that an unmasking might come with Billy's awakening. Then again, Billy might not have seen his attacker. "Odds are in his favour. He's getting the best help." She made herself a note to call the hospital.

Late nights for her and early beds for him had made them ships in the night recently. As the aroma of maple-smoked bacon filled the solarium, she watched him turn pages, always finishing with the personals column. A slender thread of faith led him to believe that he might find a message from Bonnie or someone who knew her. Every three months, he placed an ad asking for information, an indulgence foreign to his frugal nature. She'd seen it once or twice, nothing more than a simple notice: "If anyone knows the whereabouts of Bonnie Martin of Sooke, B.C., please contact 250-643-1496. Reward for information." As far as she knew, no one had ever answered. He would have told her, wouldn't he?

She still felt awkward about hiding her recent trip to Camosun. He'd always been forthcoming. "We'll work it out" had been his motto, whether or not such resolution was possible. The word "Dad" was forming on her lips when something caught her eye.

He lifted a plastic bag from the floor and removed a strange apparatus of hooks and belts. "I wanted to show you this."

She examined the oddity. "What the heck is it? Are you

going in for aerial window cleaning? Becoming a trapeze artist?"

"A seat belt for Shogun from PetSmart. So he'll be safe. I may take him to my office. With that intelligent mind, he shouldn't be left alone all day. It's cruel. And maybe we'll go see those agility trials on the peninsula."

"Good idea. Dogs riding untied in pickup beds drive me up the wall. Don't people care that in an accident their animal could become an unguided missile?" She paused. Through the patio doors and across the deck down to the street, the same seagull arrived every morning to pick worms from the road. Smart bird. His own supermarket. Then she steeled herself for the inevitable. "I visited Larry Gall."

"You what? My god, Holly, I didn't want you to humour the poor deluded fellow. That's the last thing he needs. Joining into his fantasy. People who go into the social sciences to supposedly help others need to cure themselves first."

He sounded as close to angry as he ever got. Judging from his conservative, almost prim façade, people felt he could never do violence, but she suspected that they hadn't seen the side of him that was red in tooth and claw. Once a spurned boyfriend of hers had been spreading lies about her. She knew he was behind the ugly rumours, but there was no evidence to take to authorities. In tears, she had told her father. That night Norman confronted the boy leaving his job at a pizza shop. The harassment stopped. In fact, the boy did an about face every time he saw her. "What did you say to Rick?" she had asked, puzzled. Calmly, he pulled on his pipe, blew out concentric rings of cherry blend tobacco. "That if he ever bothered you again, I'd kill him."

She looked at her father's mug. "Refill?"

Coming back with two full mugs, she sat and looked at him. They were a reserved pair, not much kissing and hugging, but love underpinning all. "I'm sorry. I know you didn't want me to go, but..."

A heavy sadness settled onto his face, still pink from shaving. "Not a day goes by that I—"

She touched his hand, counting more age spots. What had he been like in his teens? Had he ever enjoyed a wild and abandoned moment? His passion for popular culture seemed his only amusement. "If we really want to know..." she began, then stuttered to a stop.

He swallowed hard and blinked. "Where she went, where she might...might be." His voice was rich and quiet, one of his assets.

"No matter what we might find, isn't it better to know than to wonder? I hate the word *closure*, but there's something to it," she said.

Why salt his wounds with the news about the planned divorce? Yet something in the back of her mind wondered if someone wouldn't interpret that imminent blow as a motive for murder. She had to tell herself that he hadn't suspected that Bonnie was planning to leave him. He'd fasten to the best memories, Holly's baby steps, first day at school, the rare laugh shared, the kind word, not the increasing arguments. "Remember her silver amulet, that raven?"

He turned as if recalling an old friend. "Of course. She was never without it."

"Gall says he gave it to her." She flashed a look at him, though she wanted to spare his pride.

His thin shoulder drooped as if lashed. The weight of grief cast a pall of mourning over his voice. She couldn't pursue this punishment much longer. "And your mother never took it off. Even when..." His voice faded out.

Holly had no stomach for the intimate details, scenes in their former bedroom, now hers. Physicians shouldn't minister to their own families. Emotions obstructed objectivity. What about a police officer? "Did you see it before she...disappeared? The week she went up island?"

He looked far past the patio doors, out across the water. The strait was enveloped in fog, only the odd ghostly light, perhaps a trick of the eye. From far away, a fog horn moaned a lugubrious warning. "Like it was part of her. I wondered where it came from, her family perhaps. Raven figures in many Native American cultures, but I never asked." He gave a self-deprecatory snort. "Why didn't I pay more attention? People need that."

She finished the last gulp of coffee, bitter as memories best left unearthed. "This is awkward, but let's try. The first cut is the deepest."

Pain was in his sea-blue eyes as he looked at her, absentmindedly rubbing his reading glasses. "Not knowing is the worst part. It torments the imagination."

Then the clouds parted for a brief encounter. She found herself momentarily blinded by the fierce sunlight suddenly streaming through the wall-to-ceiling windows. She plunged ahead to clear fog from their minds. If only it were that easy. "Gall says Mom was planning to ask you for a divorce. That they were planning to be married."

Only his set jaw revealed that he was holding himself in check. In the long silence, Shogun trotted over, first with his rubber hoop, then with his tug rope, then with Baby, a stuffed Dalmatian, nuzzling into Norman's hand. Ignored, the dog padded off and slouched down on his bed. Finally, Norman nodded slowly. "She mentioned nothing, but the signs were clear...even for a cockeyed optimist. I thought we'd work it out. We always had. Twenty-four years is a long time, nearly our silver anniversary. I hoped she'd mellow, stop chasing these useless causes and settle down."

Useless? Because in the human drama someone always needed help? "Can you tell me anything else about that last week."

A deep sigh came from him. "She closed one of our savings accounts."

"What?" Holly cursed herself for not abandoning her exams and coming home immediately. If she'd been on the spot, she might have noticed something. Was that absurd? She hadn't been a trained officer. But Norman had insisted that she carry on with her studies, that her mother would return. Then weeks and months had passed.

He waved his hand in a half-hearted gesture. "It wasn't that much. Maybe ten thousand dollars. Not like the RRSPs. Those resource funds my father left me."

This mention of money sent electricity down her core. Suddenly the substance of it demanded answers to obvious questions. "Why did she need money? She wasn't in debt, was she?"

Norman steepled his fingers, making order as he always did. "She didn't care much about money, making it, that is. I don't remember the time she had new clothes or the kind of silly outfits women seem to want. Instead of a purse, she lugged things around in an old canvas tote bag with an embroidered German shepherd. A birthday present from you, as I recall. She spent money helping others. Gas, that guzzling Bronco, motels en route. Mostly time away from a job where she could have pulled in a salary. Everyone thinks lawyers are rich. Only the unethical ones are. That's what she said." He gave a bittersweet chuckle. "Your mother had a sense of humour."

Holly remembered her mother in jeans and sweatshirts. She didn't even own pajamas; she wore T-shirts instead. "Ten thousand sounds like a stake for a fast exit. Nothing long term. Even Mexico isn't that cheap." But she'd never leave *me*, Holly thought.

She regretted her quick words. He looked wounded as a kicked pup. "If your mother had ever asked for a separation, or god forbid, a divorce, she was welcome to it. All I ever wanted was for her to be happy. If I hadn't been so blind, I would have realized from the start that I wasn't the man for her. She was just so damn wonderful, and I felt lucky. Then the years passed. I got involved in securing tenure. Remember how the university made those cuts? Thought I was going to be laid off. Mortgage rates jumped to nearly nineteen per cent. I took her for granted. In some ways, that's worse than cheating. Such a stupid man I was."

Then the phone rang. "Just a second, Dad." In the middle of their first frank conversation about Bonnie, she would have preferred to ignore this summons. Was it news about Billy?

"I wasn't sure if you had heard. Janice Mercer has disappeared," Ann said. "In our own community. Vancouver, Calgary, Toronto maybe, but not here."

Holly recalled the interview with Janice. A strange girl, serious and studious to the point of being a prig. "I interviewed her at Botanical. Tell me more."

"I went in to do some cross-filing when a fax arrived. The Sooke detachment alerted us in case she's been hitchhiking west. She never came home from school yesterday. No call, nothing. She doesn't have any close friends. A couple kids saw her start off walking home alone. The parents are beating themselves up for not getting her a cell phone."

"Is there an amber alert?" A lot of good that would do without the hardware. The only flashing signs she had seen were on the Island Highway alerting drivers to the condition of the Malahat to the north or to ferry delays at the end of Pat Bay Highway.

"No go. That requires the child to be seen leaving with an

adult, often a family member. As in abductions in spousal estrangement."

"True. And it's Sooke's case, but we'll do what we can. Contact Andrea, Sean and the rest of our volunteers. Tell them to keep an eye out. Is there a picture?"

"Just sent over. I'll run off copies and get them out to businesses out here. Could be a tourist noticed something."

Holly rang off with an increased appreciation for Ann's gifts. If not for the accident, she would have made a top-notch commander, the perfect combination of instinct and skills.

Twelve

Chipper had taken the initiative and decided to do the Port Renfrew interviews on his own time on the weekend. He could hardly escape from his mother that morning as she pressed forward breakfast treats. Sliced mangos and bananas, scrambled eggs, parathas, even a sweet ladoo made of chick pea flour, sugar, ghee, cashews and almonds. Normally he didn't take the food to work. Once he'd kept a chicken tandoori lunch in the cruiser and earned a stinging comment from a drunk in the rear seat. "What's that Paki shit?" the man asked. "It stinks." He'd thought of the care his mother had taken to marinate the meat in garam masala, but he kept quiet, biting down his indignation.

His father, Gopal, a genial but small man with a resemblance to the Mahatma, was off to open the store downstairs. "Extra work on the weekend. I am very proud of you, son. It will not be long before you can take your staff-sergeant's exam, yes?" He dressed in slacks and a cardigan, unlike Isha Singh, who loved her saris. Finding a source of cloth had been difficult before a new fabric shop opened in Victoria.

"A few more years, Dad. I'm not even a corporal yet." After turning off the CBC news, Isha began to clean the table, a hint that both her men should be on their way. Chipper finished a last piece of kulcha stuffed with potato and onion and baked. He washed down the morsel with a mango lassi.

Isha, pleasantly plump, her lustrous black hair in a bun, wearing full white pants and a loose top for the house, added in the lilting tones he tried to repress in his own voice, "And we have a perfect girl for you. Father met the family last week. Just arrived from Jullundur. You remember that Auntie Bithika lives in Ludhiana, not far. Why, you might have met over there as babies when we visited." She plucked a few pieces of lint from his shoulder and straightened his tie.

Chipper sighed, feeling like the fatted calf. "I don't want to get married yet. And no way an arranged marriage. We're in Canada, not the Punjab. I've always lived here."

His mother wagged her pudgy finger as she packed parathas for him to snack on. "And the divorce rate. Fifty per cent in North America. In arranged marriages, the failures are only three per cent. Three! What is that telling you? You cannot deny facts."

Deciding not to anger her by asking if the story had run in the *Delhi News,* Chipper made his exit as his father opened the shop door below and set out the lottery advertising boards. For the longer trip, Chipper took the family car, an older Ford Focus wagon with a ding on the fender but a good sound system.

On the way west, he relaxed with a CD of Rasa from the *Shelter* album. The eerie tones of "Narada Muni" transported him to exotic places. Electric bass, sarangi, the elusive Swedish nyckelharpa, all combined to center the body and soothe the soul. That prayers to Shiva could sound so erotic didn't surprise him, given the history of sexuality in Indian art. His parents listened less and less to traditional music, but their tastes ended with Ravi Shankar.

Another day of rain pelted against the pitted windshield as he threaded the bottleneck through Glen Lake and Luxton. It was depressing, nothing like the sunny plains of Saskatchewan where he had first been posted. There the farmer would have welcomed rain, but that's why wheat grew there and ferns grew here. The wipers slacked back and forth at high speed. Through Sooke and Otter Point, where Holly lived, he eased to a conservative fifty instead of sixty as the pavement sluiced over. He didn't recall any serious flooding spots in the vicinity, but there was no sense risking a hydroplane in this dinky toy. The bulky police car was a guzzler but had a better safety record.

Once in Port Renfrew, he stopped first at the Tourist Bureau. "No, sir," said the young native woman, given the dates of this mysterious visitor. "We closed down that day. Propane leak. Place was locked up until we could get someone to work on the heater. And Mr. Jenkins doesn't put up any business cards on our bulletin board. Just the sign at his house and word of mouth."

Thirsty from the sweet and salty breakfast, he stopped for tea at a small restaurant, surprised that they carried herbal varieties so far west of the city. The server was Bengali himself and struck up a conversation. Placing his hands together in admiration, the man said, "And you are allowed to be wearing the traditional five pieces, then. Isn't this a wonderful country?"

Feeling like he was on exhibit, Chipper explained that he was rechecking information from a drowning incident. Dressed in an immaculate white serving uniform, the man wiped the counter and clucked in dismay. "Terrible, it was. Such publicity. Never a drowning here since I have been working. What will tourists think? A bad business, that."

"Do you know anyone who lives on the road to Botanical?"

"Many places are for sale now that the real estate boom is on, and let me tell you, the prices are not cheap. People from Victoria are buying camps or acreage to enjoy our beaches." He furrowed his brow and counted on his knobby fingers. "There are about ten places. But most are not full-time. Your best bet is to try Mr. Butch Miller. He lives around the last corner just before the beach. There will be a shack that has fallen down, a pile of shingles and wood now, then his house."

Chipper stopped at every house he saw, but it was evident that they were closed for the season and had been for weeks. Grass grew in the lanes, and windows were shuttered. Many were set far back from the road with concealing shrubbery.

In front of a small, low cabin whose roof slanted to the back, Miller was rocking on the porch. Chipper looked up as a goat walked up from the rear, munching serenely, its white beard wagging. The flat top of the roof was thick with grass. "I should charge admission, eh?" Miller asked. "Got the idea at Coombs, that tourist place up island."

When Chipper introduced himself, the man asked him to sit, paddling his fleshy lip in deep thought. A fat red cat with two ragged ears lolled at the end of the porch. Chipper described the situation.

"Let's see, now. September 20, you say?" As he hesitated, Chipper thought how unlikely it was that anyone retired and without a business agenda could recall where he had been nearly a month ago.

He went inside and brought back a Royal Bank calendar, leafing back. "Full moon?"

Chipper's mother always took note of that because she liked to plant her window-box herb garden according to the phases. And he remembered the interviews with the boys, who had mentioned the light on the beach. "I think so."

"Oh, yes. A glorious moon that night. And a bicycle? I saw someone go by around nine that night. Never came back. Not while I was there."

"And were you there until..."

"Naw, went inside to read Zane Grey. I work through his

221

books once a year. *Riders of the Purple Sage.* That's crackerjack. Not like the junk today." He wormed a finger into his ear and seemed to purr at the sensation.

Chipper let him take his time. No sense hurrying the man. He might be a hermit, but he was a friendly one, instead of armed with a shotgun. He nodded and smiled as the old fellow ruminated.

"Do recollect I heard some vehicle go by, though. An hour later, came back. Read till past midnight and never heard another peep. It's quiet here. You notice the little things."

"What kind of vehicle?"

"You got this old boy thinking now. Not a motorcycle. None of them quiet. Not a quad. Maybe a truck. But the size..." He paused and coughed into his sleeve. "Did see the ass end of it going out. Two little red lights set far apart. An older vehicle. Squarish. A van, could be."

Not long after, munching on the last paratha, Chipper assembled his notes in the car. What had he learned? That Angie had come alone? That someone else in an older car or van had followed? Maybe his information would help glue together a very puzzling picture. Altogether, he was pleased with his interview techniques. Old folks liked to take their time and enjoy a moment in the spotlight. He was learning.

*   *   *

As she did every few hours, Ann placed her hands on her hips and leaned backwards to stretch. She remembered the happy years of jogging and tennis, interspersed with the odd, discounted backache as little by little the discs had worn away. Genetics, or that summer she'd hauled lumber, stained and nailed it for her mother's wrap-around deck and porch? Never did bend her knees properly. She was in too much of a hurry and thought she was invincible. Then the accident. The coup de grâce, the specialist said. And worse yet, though hip and knee replacements were a snap, nothing could be done for backs, in Canada at least, unless you were in danger of paralysis. The no-brainer miracle fusions of the past had been discontinued because surgeons noted that the neighbouring discs began surrendering to the increased stress.

Sean hustled in with a handful of posters bearing Janice's picture. He took off his long-billed ball cap and stood at attention in front of her desk. "I put one on all the hydro poles near where people park to look at the ocean. Now I'll take more to the B and Bs." He showed her a small notebook with a list of items checked off.

Ann managed a large smile and a pat on the shoulder. "Great, Sean. You're a big help. I see a promotion in your future." She pulled out a package of red licorice whips from her desk. "Here's a reward."

He pumped his fist in the air and left, whirling a whip in the air. Then it became very quiet in the office, only a steady drip from the eaves. With Janice's poster in hand, she pondered the fact that two girls from a small high school had met danger within a few weeks. One was dead, another missing. And Billy's suicide attempt. Holly had mentioned the suspicious marks. Ann agreed. Too many coincidences.

She doubted that Chipper would find any new information in Port Renfrew. Absent witnesses, stale memories. What if she'd been there to investigate the drowning? Had everyone on the fatal night received a thorough vetting? What about the staff? Even in the sanctified halls of learning, people lied and got away with it. She had read that the Dean of Admissions at MIT had fabricated degrees nearly thirty years ago. And the Dean was a woman. Equal opportunity strikes again.

She searched the files for the copies of the reports on the drowning. Hadn't Holly mentioned doing routine background checks on the faculty? She didn't remember hearing any results, not that she got all the information when it arrived. Finally the papers came to hand. Three staff had been at the beach. She discounted the Bass woman. One disturbed astronaut aside, females did not kidnap other females. That left Coach Terry Grove and Paul Gable.

Within minutes, she had the secretary of Notre Dame on the phone. Helen Douglas was an old friend. They had attended concerts together, until Ann's back problem prevented her from sitting for long periods. "Grove? He's been here for over ten years. First post. Not a whisper of anything out of the ordinary. Of course he has his star athletes. Girls love good-looking male teachers. But he's devoted to his family and new baby. Little rascal arrived last week. I went to the shower."

"What about Paul Gable?"

Helen disappeared for a moment, then returned. "It's only his second year. Transferred from a diocese on the mainland, where he taught for fifteen years according to our records. The job as Vice Principal here was his first big promotion. Why are you asking?"

"Helen, you know I can't reveal that. But I'm trusting you to keep this information to yourself. Consider yourself an unofficial agent of the law. I'm very serious." She spoke in hushed tones with the perfect note of confidence. "Now if you have that contact number handy..."

Minutes later, Ann smiled as she read the area code. Then she dialed the last school where Gable had worked, St. Edward's in Prince George.

"Excuse me. What's this all about?" a stern voice asked. And then, "Brittany Wilcox. You sit right there until you're called.

And give me that cell phone. You know school rules." With an elaborate sigh, the woman returned to the conversation.

Ann felt a slight headache teasing her temples. She had introduced herself officially and had every right to background information. Why the hesitation? Did they want to call the detachment to verify the number? Rather than set off alarm bells, she decided to play it safe. "It's routine. He applied to be one of our auxiliary volunteers. Since he may overhear privileged information, we always do a thorough check."

The woman's tones warmed. "That's fine, then. Paul was one of our best teachers. We were sad to see him go. He started here right after university."

"Is there anyone else I could talk to? Someone who's been at the school for a long time?"

A humph rattled the line. "I am Sister Judith, and I have been here for thirty-five years."

Ann listened to the imperious voice. She could picture the Sister, mainstay of the school. Grizzle-hair in a bun, if not still wearing a habit after Vatican Two, a below-the-knee black skirt. Protective as a Rottweiler and cheaper to feed. Devoted to the administration and the reputation of St. Edward's but unable due to politics to be a principal.

Her extra decade on the planet had taught Ann to take little at face value, something a fresh-minted corporal like Holly needed to learn. She was getting used to her new boss, but the naïvete and lack of experience dismayed her. Her personal address book found its way into her hand. Nick taught high school in the nearby town of Vanderhoof. He was an avid mystery reader, particularly fond of Peter Robinson. His success with a senior-level crime fiction course converted even die-hard non-readers. Wouldn't her son enjoy a bit of sleuthing?

She left a detailed message on his answering machine and

crossed her fingers. This was Thanksgiving weekend, the second Monday in October. Perhaps he was away on a vacation or with a girlfriend. After the collapse of her career, would becoming a grandmother age or rejuvenate her?

Then she took out her mat from the closet and did leg lifts and piriformis stretches. Back in the chair, she looked at the pamphlet from the pharmacy. Cold and hot yoga, whatever the difference, was being offered at the Evergreen Centre in downtown Sooke. Twenty dollars for three sessions. What did she have to lose?

Thirteen

Holly faced a marathon of dirty dishes after a five-star dinner with her father and a neighbour. While walking Shogun, Norman had made friends with a retired librarian up the hill at Randy's Place. Her name was Madeleine Hamza. A multicultural cocktail, Swiss by way of Sweden, divorced from a mysterious Egyptian engineer, she was on the far side of the fifties, and owned four dogs, including a border collie. Norman had insisted she bring the last, a shy dog named Sushi, who was cavorting with Shogun on the front lawn as they sat outside on the deck. The eternal rain had declared a truce, and the evening was warm and inviting with a hint of autumnal woodstove smoke. The only jarring note was the CD of Spike Jones playing "Cocktails for Two" with all the bells and whistles. "In some secluded rendezvous" CLANG CLANG CLANG CLANG. Holly raised an eyebrow at her father, who shrugged in defeat, went inside and replaced it with early Frank Sinatra.

Madeleine said in a charming Euroblend accent which held Norman a willing captive, "I took the dogs up the Galloping Goose today. They have closed the Potholes Park in the north section. A problem with the water lines. Someone is still camping there, though. Bentley the corgi who runs the household chased over towards the river and took his time coming back."

"A bit late for camping. Must like to rough it," Holly said. She'd loved running on the Goose in her teens. It followed an old train route to Leechtown, a defunct and deserted gold-mining centre north of Sooke. Named for a jouncing gas-powered passenger and mail car from the 1920s, the converted trail ran for fifty-five kilometres from Victoria and was one of the area's prized possessions, open to horses, dogs, bikes and people, but nothing motorized.

Madeleine's th's emerged like z's. "They have a camper van, so I expect they have some comforts. Those Volkswagens were made to last. The people's wagon. For myself, I prefer Volvos."

Norman nodded approval at her history knowledge. "Those vans are ubiquitous around here. It's like an elephant graveyard. The island does a huge business in spare parts for classic vehicles."

In another quixotic display of atmospherics, the sun vanished like the wave of a magician's handkerchief. Across the strait, dark clouds gathered on the Washington shore. It was much foggier over there, due to the height of the Olympic Mountains. "Very dirty and dangerous weather coming," Madeline said with a shiver, pulling her shawl around her shoulders. "I have seen such storms in the Alps."

Norman cut himself another piece of pumpkin chiffon pie from the Otter Point Bakery, Madeleine's offering. "Surely not so early in the year. Still, with global warming and all that soot from China, who knows? Old timers still talk of Typhoon Freda in the Sixties. You can still see the monster trees that went down in those 150K winds."

Madeleine nudged him. "But you were just a baby then."

Suppressing a squirm, Holly felt somehow that she was intruding on their date. It was pleasant to see her father interact and even banter with a contemporary. All she remembered of her parents those last years had been her mother's temper vs. her father's stubbornness. The phone rang as the espresso machine began steaming. "Pardon me," Holly said with some relief, and went inside the patio door and up to the kitchen, perching on a stool by the counter.

To her astonishment, it was Ann. "Sorry to call you at home, but you're not going to believe this. Nick found out that Paul Gable was transferred here from St. Edward's in Prince George after sexual assault accusations." Ann sounded neither apologetic nor insistent about her self-assigned inquiries. It was simply the right thing to do.

Holly pricked up her ears and began tallying the circumstantial evidence. Perhaps here was the missing link. She'd believed the boys and wondered why Billy had become a target only days later. Angie as a drug-induced accident might pass muster, but not the staged suicide. As an administrator, Gable would find it easy to liaise casually with the staff at Edward Milne and identify a certain young man who lived in tiny Port Renfrew. "Accusations from a female student, I presume?" Most men who molested children were heterosexual.

"You guessed it. The whole thing was hushed up big time. Gable's father-in-law was the mayor. Mr. Chamber of Commerce. Owned a couple of city blocks of businesses. See where I'm going?"

"How did they get away with it?" Holly leaned forward, elbows on the counter.

"Small town, smaller minds." Ann laughed from the belly. It sounded good on her. "The same way any conspiracy works. Some people need to make sure. Others don't want to know because it would destroy their well-padded lives. In this case, the girl was dismissed as neurotic. Finally the family moved to another province. There was no proof other than her word, and Gable had top marks as a teacher."

"How very sad. And Gable's transfer?"

"A precaution to protect a dirty little secret. Nick's new girlfriend has a brother in Prince George. He's a school psychologist on contract, and he believed the girl. Found himself out of a job when June arrived. No union protection." She gave a low growl. "Since then he's located several more teens with the same story about Gable, but they won't go public. Afraid of gossip. Can't say I blame them. It takes a lot of guts for a youngster to admit to being a sexual victim."

Holly thought of the centuries of abuse coverups in the church, its members far more protected than lay teachers. "Ann, that was terrific work. You may have broken open the case."

"What now?" The voice seemed eager, galvanized. Would giving Ann tasks other than record keeping transform the detachment into a fighting unit? But it was early times. Relationships were like seedlings. They had to be tended carefully at each step and repotted only when ready. She winced at her ridiculous analogy.

"Corporal, are you there?"

Holly stood and checked her watch. Seven thirty. Like her, most people would be finishing dinner. She wondered why Ann had been free tonight. Her mother lived in a nursing home in Sooke, Chipper had said, and Ann visited several times a week. "In light of Janice's disappearance, I'm confronting Gable with this new information, holiday or not."

"Isn't that Sooke's jurisdiction?" Ann was a stickler for rules.

"But it's my...our case. Let's see what we find at the house."

"We'll need a search warrant to check his computer. There could be videos, too."

"Still too soon for that. Surprise is the best interview technique. It's obvious that he's not the man he seems." A hypocrite was the lowest figure in her cosmos of hell. "I can't wait for his reaction when I mention that girl in Prince George. And if he was innocent, why take the transfer?"

"Do you think he's connected with the disappearance of Janice Mercer? Would he go that far? In your reports, she's barely mentioned. Angie's tentmate, that's all."

Holly searched her memory. This wasn't something she could read in a notebook. Why hadn't she seen underneath Janice's goody-goody exterior? How she had gazed with fond adoration at Gable during the memorial service. Like the coach, he had his own admirers. The unloved and lost, the truly vulnerable. "I'm not sure. If he's at home, where could she be?"

There was a pause. Holly could see Madeleine and her dad peering at her through the glass doors, wondering why she had been gone so long. It was time for coffee and that bottle of Cointreau her father nursed. Ann spoke again. "May I come?"

"But your mom. I hate to take you away from—"

"It's fine. We had an early dinner here around five, then I drove her back to the home. She's more comfortable there now that she knows the routine."

Clearly Ann's back was better, or adrenaline was overriding her pain. If Holly refused to let her ride along, the hard-won progress between them might not only stop but retreat. She chose her words carefully. "We owe this discovery to you. Why not?"

As she hung up, Holly chafed to remember the pathetic and meandering nature of the early investigation. When the wrong loose ends had been tied up, a bored and easily-satisfied Whitehouse had returned to his more high-power cases. Now she felt as charged as the sheet lightning crashing a hundred miles away to the south. Her crew and her investigation, and thanks to Ann, she was running with the bit in her mouth. After mumbling apologies, she dressed hurriedly and left the house in her car.

Holly picked up Ann in front of a three-storey condo behind Sooke Elementary School. Quirky and semi-modern with strange arches on the roof, these small condos overlooking the harbour were ideal for a single person. They drove west again a few miles past the latest waterfront development. A gigantic conclave of boxy vacation condominiums had been recently completed. Quarter shares went for $170K. Would the idea fly? If not, someone was out hundreds of millions of dollars.

They turned left into Whiffen Spit. At the end of the main street was the Sooke Harbour House, one of Canada's leading fine-dining resorts. The geographical spit itself, a curvilinear toenail of land where Sooke River entered the ocean, had a host of walkers who enjoyed its gentle terrain and scenic views. Doggie poop bags were provided at the iron-work entrance gate.

In the residential area of the spit, with communal beach access at the far end of a parking turnaround, Paul Gable had a West-Coast-style Craftsman home on Narissa Street with river-rock-studded pillars and wood trim. Tall firs, evergreen hedges and expensive bushes dotted the landscape in this elite part of town. In the driveway sat a Subaru Forester wagon, the rear open and full of boxes and bags. The double stained-glass front door was ajar, and a very tall straw-haired woman charged out with a suitcase in one hand and a cage with a green macaw in the other. The parrot screeched as the sunflower seeds in its tin bowl scattered to the ground. The bone-coloured beak could crack walnuts. "Pretty birdie. Kiss, kiss."

"Jasper! Knock it off!" The woman put down the cage and looked to her left and right. "I know he's been loud. Which one of the damn neighbours called in? I don't have time for this crap now."

Despite the seriousness of the moment, Holly and Ann barely suppressed laughs at the circus. Holly spoke first, introducing them. "It's not about that, ma'am. We're looking for Paul Gable. Is he your husband?"

"Not for long. And you can call me Elanie." In a studied, calming gesture, she smoothed her long silken hair with both hands, letting it cascade down her neck commercial-style. Her face was equine. Large white teeth reinforced the image, and she blinked behind unnaturally violet contact lenses. "I watch *Psychic Detective,* and I'm wondering if you're clairvoyant, because I was about to call you." She peered with circumspection at Holly's Prelude. "Great car. But isn't that a strange vehicle for the police?

Holly pulled out her identification to satisfy the woman. She wondered why Gable hadn't made an entrance yet. Where was the VW van? In the garage? It seemed better strategy to allow Mrs. Gable to speak first before she was prejudiced by the reason they'd come. "Is something wrong?" The woman didn't look as if she'd been assaulted in a domestic argument. She wore a trim leisure suit in gold and black and pristine Mephistos.

Elanie's creamy porcelain face flushed as red as the late rhodos that bejewelled the golf-green lawn. Somehow she managed to retain her slightly surprised expression, possible with the help of Botox. "It's what I found on his computer. This is the end. I hope he does time for this, the bastard. What a sick puke. Pardon my French."

"What did you find? Does he know...your suspicions?" Unspoken thoughts about flight passed from Holly to Ann.

Elanie waved her left hand, sparkling gems on four fingers. Making a fist would be painful if not impossible. "I don't use his stupid Mac, but my laptop developed a virus over the weekend. Too much spam." She glanced at the bird, who was making a strange squawk. "Jasper was coughing. It's a bad time to call a vet. An extra hundred if they'll even see you. So

I went on-line to do research. Have you ever tried to take a bird's temperature?" Her right hand sported a number of bandages, childlike-patterned with balloons.

"So to make a long story short, clicking everywhere in panic, I ran into Paul's history. He didn't even try to hide it, the simpleton. Don't know why I never looked before, he's always on-line, but he's been such an inconsequential man. A nobody." She shoved the birdcage into the back of the Subaru and turned to them, grinning in a frightening way. "Follow me, ladies. It's showtime."

Inside, a Tara staircase topped by a large crystal chandelier led upstairs. The carpeting was off-white, a nightmare for pet owners. Elanie brought them down the hall. On the way, Holly glanced into the kitchen. European cabinets, granite counters and two islands overhung with copper pots. Not on a vice principal's salary. The wife's legacy?

The study was dark. Elanie went to the window and yanked up the Roman shades. Through the window, a giant cedar was starting to sway in the rising wind. "I never come in here. It's Paul's den, his sanctum, he calls it. Now I know why." At the computer, she called up site after site of young girls. Many might be of age but chosen for their youthful appearance. Sixteen posing as twelve. The sites could have been anywhere, Holly thought, from Ukraine to Utah. And the servers would change every week.

"Could anyone else have been using the computer?"

She snorted. "We don't have any children. Jasper's smart, but not that gifted."

Ann was studying the floor-to-ceiling bookcases, full of university textbooks and automotive manuals. The only file cabinet was locked when she inserted a pencil to test the drawers.

Elanie snapped around, tossing her hands in the air. "I

don't know where the key is. He told me he locks it to protect his father's rare coin collection. Even in this neighbourhood, we've had a few break-ins."

"So where is Paul now?" Holly asked.

"Hell if I know. I got back Friday from a trip to Vancouver. Shopping for a winter wardrobe. No sign of him, not that he leaves love notes. The van's gone. Damn dog, too. I assumed he was camping somewhere."

"Where does he usually stay?" Holly and Ann exchanged glances. The storm was going to complicate matters.

"Anywhere he can park for free. There are spots all along the coast. More inland. He carries water, propane, food. Enough for weeks. You won't catch me eating canned beans and rehydrated stew. Life's too short."

Then Holly's cell phone rang. It was Chipper. "Not you, too," Holly said. "Doesn't my staff ever take weekends off?"

He told her what he had learned from Butch Miller. Holly gave no more than perfunctory answers, then hung up and turned to Elanie. "Doesn't your husband have an old VW van? When we met after that drowning at Botanical, I—"

The woman gave a mocking laugh and inspected her Dragon Lady nails with some perturbation. "He's too young to be a hippie. Wishes he'd been a teenager in the Seventies. You know the kind. Listens to CCR, Dylan, that shit. God, what a bore that man is. Daddy was so right."

"Can you describe the tail lights on the van?"

Elanie's rolling eyes made a rare motion in the frozen face. "Are you kidding? No, I see you're not. Oh, little round things, I think. I never ride in that rat trap." She pointed to some pictures sitting on the bookshelves where Gable could admire them from his leather recliner. "That's Joan. Can you believe he gave it a name? Joan Baez, whoever she is. Sounds Middle-Eastern."

Then she seemed to pull herself back to reality. Her nostrils flared, and she placed her hands on her narrow hips. "I've given you the tour. This is absurd. If you didn't come about Jasper, why *are* you here?"

Holly explained their suspicions. "This new information looks especially bad for the system that transferred him. I doubt Notre Dame knew his history."

Her dark pupils burning with fury, Elanie nearly spat on the carpet. "History. That's a good one. That man lied to me from day one. I thought he had family money, but it turned out to be wishful thinking. Sure, his father was a lawyer, but his real profession was drinking and off-track betting. Paul was supposed to come into two million when the old man died. A pile of debts was all that was left. Even the tightest pre-nup can't anticipate that."

Ann asked, "And the girl who said he assaulted her?"

The woman gave a casual cock of the head. "She made it up, the little tramp. He'd never have the nerve. Look, don't do, is his motto. Not that this computer porn proves anything, but what an embarrassment. When this comes out, I'll be a hundred years away, not sitting in court with a frozen stand-by-your-man smile."

Ann unfolded one of the posters she'd carried. "Could Janice Mercer be with him? We haven't much time."

An ugly laugh resounded, enough to turn the strongest stomach. "Poor lost lambs. That's what Paul called them. Is she with him? For her sake, I hope not."

Holly turned to Ann. "We'd better secure the scene. Report this to Sooke and have them send a constable. Then we'll get rolling on finding Gable." Sooke would fax a request for a search warrant to the Justice Centre in Vancouver. Gone were the days of cumbersome and time-consuming trips across the water for paper transfers. An hour or less was common now.

Elanie moved to the window and pointed to the darkening sky. "Do I have to wait around? I don't like the look of the weather. My sister in Qualicum Beach is expecting me, and that's a long drive."

Told to stay put, Elanie went upstairs in a huff. The parrot began singing "Mr. Tambourine Man".

Fourteen

Paul Gable had not arrived at Notre Dame the next day by nine, nor had he called in. In addition to concern over Janice, Dave Mack, the principal, had another mystifying problem. Someone without authority had used the auto shop on the weekend. "Must have had keys, but none are checked out. I made a police report as a formality. As for prints, thirty boys come and go there each week."

Something twanged in Holly's mind as they spoke on the phone. "What part of the shop are we talking about?"

"This is very unusual. Not really vandalism. Looks like someone painted a car or a truck. Rags, the sprayer, a rough job." He paused. "Now why would anyone break the law to do that?"

"What colour paint?" Holly asked.

"Ed, he's the shop teacher, says all they had around was dark green."

Anything would look better than white with yellow flowers. Holly reasoned that the "news" about Billy's possible recovery from the coma had spooked Gable. If the boy had had even one brief glance of his attacker, the game was over. But where would Gable go?

Elanie Gable had decamped late the night before, bird in tow. Constable Minot from Sooke had secured the house until the search warrant arrived. Then a team from West Shore began to check every nook and cranny. The computer would

238

be removed for analysis. An all-points bulletin had been issued for Paul Gable and his van, using both paint descriptions. Holly knew that it took only a few hours to hop a ferry and cross to Vancouver, Seattle, or the wilderness of Olympic National Park in Washington State. He had the camper, and he was prepared. They would have to ask all the boats for their passenger lists. Ann was already liaising with Sooke on that detail.

Meanwhile, in the dim morning light as the winds rose and the rain kept falling, everyone was talking about the approaching storm. Late fall brought the excitement of a meteorological phenomenon known euphemistically as the Pineapple Express. Sounding like a Polynesian cocktail, but with a quantum punch, this sound and fury originated in the Pacific. It brought drenching rains along with high winds. As she sat sipping a coffee and nibbling at a buttery *schneke* in the Little Vienna Bakery, talking to Constable Craig from the Sooke detachment, Holly could hear mutterings from the over-seventy set.

"Damn forecasts about as predictable as a ouija board."

"My weather rock's never wrong." Rounds of chuckles followed.

"What you see is what you get. Still, this is only October. Way too early for the worst storms."

Another man took off his Mariners cap and scratched his ear. "Got me worried, watching them trees sway. My neighbour has some humungous firs. Must be a good two hundred feet. What if they..."

His voice petered out as Holly's attention was caught by a man in a scooter, shrouded in sheets of plastic to protect from the elements, tootling down the sidewalk and shifting to the street when necessary. Constable Craig shook his head and gave a what-can-you-do gesture. A man in Victoria had been killed when his scooter fell on him. The machines gave the elderly mobility, but technology had sprinted past the laws.

Sheets of rain were sluicing the streets, and the wind had picked up, blowing fallen leaves into tornado cones and scattering paper debris. Holly watched an elderly woman head for the post office. In a gust, her umbrella turned inside out. Banging it on the sidewalk, the woman gave up and thrust it into a trash can. She yanked up her hood, straightened her thin shoulders, and marched on in military fashion. Sookers were tough birds.

Her father had no classes today, but from her seat by the windows, she saw his Smart Car scoot by, Shogun sitting erect in the passenger seat. He was headed to Saanich to watch agility trials. When she'd cautioned him about the oncoming storm, he'd assured her, "The trials are inside a barn on the fairgrounds. If the weather's worse later, we'll get a motel in Victoria, and I'll be all set for classes Tuesday if a flood closes our road. I'll leave a message on the machine. 'What, me worry?', as Alfred E. says."

Later, Holly sat in the detachment as Ann monitored the Weather Channel on-line. An ominous red alert kept flashing across the page. "Heavy winds and rain expected on the west shore from Port Renfrew. Will move down the south shore to Victoria by the late afternoon. Possible winds of a hundred and twenty kilometres per hour. Potential destruction of property and danger to people exists. Do not travel unless absolutely necessary."

"This sounds serious," Ann said, pouring herself a coffee. "This area isn't prepared for a major storm. We may not have much snow, but firs and hydro lines are a fatal marriage."

Holly fiddled with the radio while Chipper left to check on an accident in Jordan River. A logging truck with a full load of pulpwood had tipped on a wicked curve, blocking the road.

No injuries reported. That was a bonus, but it illustrated how easily the one major artery could collapse. What did those logistics mean for a major evacuation? Everyone would be as stranded as the troops at Dunkirk, but waiting for a flotilla of small boats that dared not leave port.

By only ten thirty it was evident that this was "not your father's storm". The sky was black, as if night had fallen. Trees were cha-cha-ing back and forth, loose branches falling and brooming along the road like tumbleweeds. Cars with owners stupid enough to be on the move were travelling at half the limit. They heard a crash, and the cottage shuddered. Lights flickered. Ann put on her yellow slicker and went outside, returning a minute later, drenched in water and rubbing her streaming eyes.

"Nothing to worry about. A branch from that bigleaf maple fell. No damage to the shingles as far as I can see." From her shoulder, she pulled a white leathery substance laced with green, showing it to Holly. "What the hell's this stuff?"

Holly laughed. "Lungwort. A lichen that loves those maples."

"It *does* look like a lung. How'd you know?"

"Botany major. About a lifetime ago." She checked her watch and groaned. "This is only the start. I hope my dad's safe in Saanich by now."

As the lights stuttered again, Holly turned to Ann. "Turn off the computers. Make sure we don't lose any data."

"Already done." Ann blotted her face with a paper towel. "With about a million lines of hydro, you're going to get an outage every now and then. I've got a wood fireplace at home, plenty of water and food, Coleman stove and lanterns."

"Same with my father. How's the situation with our friendly generator?"

"Plenty of gas. Reg showed me how to run it. Too bad we don't have a woodstove."

Then the lights went off and stayed off. Ann, who seemed to be gaining strength as the situation worsened, went out to the small shed. Minutes later, Holly heard the dull roar of the machine. Back on went the lights and the pumps for water and plumbing. Heat was another matter. No generator had the juice for that. "Nice work," she said on Ann's return. "Give me a lesson when this is all over."

The phone startled them. The first crisis? Holly answered, only to find Mrs. Nordman on the line. "Are you all right?" she asked. May Nordman was ninety, one of the area's pioneers. Her house had been built in 1910 and was surrounded by modern bungalows sliced from the acreage of the former Nordman farm. Chances were good that her neighbours stood ready for the old girl.

"Oh, yes, dear. I won't tie up your lines. I called to find out how *you* were doing. There's a fresh batch of hermits on the wood cookstove. If you're in the area, drop by. And dear..."

Holly mouthed her name across to Ann, who rolled her eyes and nodded. "Yes, Mrs. N?"

"You're not talking to any spring chicken. I've been through these century storms before. There's a difference with this one."

"What's that?"

"It's the rain the last month following years of summer droughts. That's the part that's not normal. Old firs have strong roots. But they're weak from drought, and now the rain has loosened them. My grandfather Jorma warned me. Triple threat, he called it. When they go, it won't be just the branches, but the whole goldurned tree. And trees are not solitary. They're like a family. When one dies, the rest suffer. You mark my words. That's why our farmhouse and barn are clear for three hundred feet. But some of those others..." She gave a tsk before hanging up.

A fatal embrace for a tree hugger. Holly felt a shudder as something big went down behind the house. The grounds trembled. No power. Perhaps the phone lines were hanging on by a thread. She took another bitter sip of coffee, trying to convince herself that she was overreacting. Nothing that bad was going to happen. But those damn ugly and vulnerable overhead wires were a remnant of the nineteenth century in the twenty-first.

Then the phone rang again. She could hear confusion and static before a few words made their way. "It's Dad. How's my little girl?"

Calling her at work wasn't like him. "We're fine, but where are *you* now? The storm—"

"I know..."

ZZZZZ. Zap. She tried to piece together his fragmented conversation, shook the phone as if to wring sense from it.

"I braked...deer. Ran off the..."

A deep male voice spoke in the background. The words weren't clear, but the tone was urgent. "I have to go. They're taking me to the General."

"They? The paramedics?" She shivered with frustration. Like a frantic animal seeking shelter, wind was shrieking around the house, rattling the shutters. Still, if he were able to talk...

"Not to worry. Bumped my chin on the steering wheel and bit my lip. They say I might feel some whiplash tomorrow. What a car! It crashed just like in the video. The cage held. Shogun is okay, too. That's why I'm calling. Can you come and get him?"

"What?" She was torn between family responsibilities and duties, but the timing and placement wasn't all bad. The accident had happened at West Coast Tire, just east of Sooke.

In and out in twenty minutes. All but emergency traffic should be off the roads by now. Sensible people knew that this was the time to hole up, not try to "make it" home the last few dangerous kilometres, but the odd idiot would prevail.

Chipper pulled in from the accident call. Half-soaked, he hung up his gear and patted down his turban with a towel. "This is wild! I'd better call Sooke and get an update on emergency plans, or did you guys already do that?"

Holly and Ann both joined in a duet of ironic laughter. "What plans? Like the Disaster Evacuation Sites outside Costco in Langford? We're prisoners of our roads. If they go, we're shot out of luck."

She told them what had happened. "I'm taking the Prelude, since this is personal business. I shouldn't be long."

Outside, things were worse than she'd thought. The road was streaming with rain, and a small mudslide was starting to ooze down the hill behind her. It wouldn't reach the asphalt, but it was a sign of the dangerous destabilizing of the terrain. The front-wheel drive Prelude, with its expensive suspension system, held the road to account. It was more maneuverable than the police car, a sports model with paws.

In minutes she crossed the Sooke town line. Happily, she hadn't seen one vehicle along the way. Fir branches littered the road as if the holidays had arrived early, echoing the theme of the Charm 'n Sea B and B up the hill. "Where it's Christmas all year round," the sign promised. In the phosphorescent waning light, huge trees groaned and swayed, holding on root by ragged root as winds ripped down the strait. All boats, even the largest cargo ships, would be safe in harbour. The waters were white with spume and foam, lashing over the road with fifty-foot plumes when the margin narrowed at the beaches. Anyone living directly on the ocean would have gone inland now. High tide or not, windows would be shuttered or boarded. No one built docks except in the most protected coves. Nothing would stop the violence of wind and water. It defined the terms "shock" and "awe".

Blinking at the new sensation, she passed through a town silent of technology. Not a light was on. The sign from People's Drug Mart had fallen onto the sidewalk, leaving plastic shards in its wake. The stoplight at the main corner at Wiskers and Waggs threatened to plummet with every spastic lurch. Water poured down the streets and flooded the sewers, but to her satisfaction, she saw no people. She drove carefully so as not to drench her brakes. "Road may flood" signs looked strange to those who visited in the summer droughts, but locals knew the danger. A loose dog, a Marmaduke mutt, loped across the road and disappeared behind a gas station. She hoped he would find shelter. What about Sooke's homeless, most of whom were known by name? They "lived" under plastic sheeting and tarps in the woods behind the A and W, coming out to forage for returnable bottles and cans and eat at the Salvation Army nearby. Surely the Sally Ann would have issued an invitation to share its roof, as long as it had one.

The twists and turns past town had to be taken slowly, especially between rock cuts. At last she saw another vehicle. One rusty blue Sentra had run harmlessly into a ditch. She pulled over and went outside to check, sodden in seconds. No one.

Then she heard the Doppler sounds of a fire engine coming from Victoria, a sign of life in a fearful landscape. Why weren't the local units responding? Her cell phone rang. "It's Ann. Where are you?"

"Just arriving at West Coast Tire. I'm turning around and heading back in a minute."

"Forget that plan. West Coast Road's closed at Grant due to falling trees. The same for Otter Point. Thousands are down, and it just takes one monster to drop the lines."

"Both? Those are our only arteries." She felt an iron clamp latch onto her temples. What the hell should she do now?

"Just before it happened, Chipper was ordered to Sooke. They're focusing on the most heavily populated areas and calling in all officers to respond as needed. The mayor's declaring a state of emergency, whatever that actually means. Individuals merely out of power or stuck on their property are not a priority unless they're hurt."

Holly swallowed a lump in her throat. "Unless they're hurt? Anyone all the way to Port Renfrew is beyond medical care, even if cell phones did work. Strokes, heart attacks, forget it. No helicopter can land in this. Survival of the fittest."

Holly heard a rueful sigh from Ann. "I know. I can't get out, so I'll continue to man the radio. The land lines are down. Surprise, surprise. Before they went, I managed to get hold of a neighbour to feed Bump."

Her cat. Now Shogun. Animals were running the show. A little humour might help. "No cable TV then. Break out the solitaire deck." Ann would be without her usual combination of liquor and pills to see her through the evening. How far could a life-threatening situation juice the adrenaline? The thought occurred to her that Ann might have a supply in her locker. "Sure you're okay?"

"I'm good. And I wouldn't be shocked if Mrs. Nordman sends her son with a pie on the ATV. You be careful, too. This post is small enough."

As long as she stayed in the dark and deep, Holly risked being crushed by a tree, but she thanked Ann for the caution. The woman sounded genuinely concerned. Holly felt a wave of warmth and gratitude rise in her chest. Around the next curve, at the tire store, she could see the tangled remains of the

Smart Car shoved like garbage against a mossy knoll to wait for a wrecker. It had done Trojan duty, but the price of environmental stewardship was steep. A flashlight moved inside the building, and she heard rapping on the window and a muffled bark despite the storm's raging tempest. The door opened, and Shogun stitched out, jumping on her and whining like a long-lost sibling. "Thanks for babysitting," she said to a chubby man in overalls with "Ed" on his nametag. To her amusement, he was sipping from a quart of over-proof beer.

"Emergency provisions?"

"Lady, I ain't going nowhere, nohow. There could be looting."

She had to grin as rain poured down her face and licked at her mouth. "What, tires?"

"You got no idea. Some bad apples are probably cruising around looking for a chance to pick up a thousand bucks of wheels for their 1970 Scottsdale." He took another sip, then burped and excused himself. "That's a great dog. How mucha want for him?"

"He belongs to my father. How was the old fellow?"

"Him? Bragging his head off about that midget car. Got a Crown Vic myself."

She took off west with Shogun down Sooke Road, following a derelict truck that looked like the culprits Ed had described. But it turned off onto Harbourview Drive. She passed Ayum Creek, where locals often parked their vehicles with For Sale signs. Except for the world's oldest Jeep and a shaky truck camper covered in green mildew, it was deserted.

So the plan was to mass all personnel at the Sooke detachment on Church Street. She might end up doing any number of jobs. Accident response. Helping with ambulances. Making sandwiches if someone had hit the grocery stores before they closed. The grid would be off by now as a general caution. No hydro repair personnel would be out in this storm. They were heroes, but they weren't suicidal. Getting wet or cold never bothered them. Getting fried or crushed did.

Shogun sat in the rear seat without his harness, now an intricate part of the metal Christmas-tree ornament which was the Smart Car. Once at the detachment, she planned to leave him in the Prelude for the next few hours. As she passed a hobby farm, she saw someone leading a pack of llamas to safety in a barn. Safety was relative. Huge cedar trees loomed over the building. Cedars were especially dangerous. Not only did they hide rot inside, but they twisted on the way down. It was hard to guess where they'd fall, pirouetting like the late PM.

In the immediate crisis, she had shoved Paul Gable and Janice Mercer to a distant burner. The welfare of two people in the face of this Armageddon seemed a secondary problem. Where was the man? Did he have Janice with him? Was he even on the island? She approached the bridge over Sooke River at the turn to the road to the famous Potholes. These geologic wonders, gorge after gorge of carved basalt, along with the part of the Goose that wound its way nearby, were huge tourist draws. In summer, the jewelled necklace of quiet pools beckoned swimmers to its cool, clean water. And there was camping in the north of the park on acres of forested sites.

Her foot trembled on the gas pedal, and the car shuddered to a stop as she pulled over. Hadn't her father's friend Madeleine mentioned a VW camper hidden in the woods near this spot? Holly examined her options, drumming her fingers on the wheel. The CD player thumped out k.d. lang's "High Time for a Detour". Then she made her only choice. She called Ann on her cell and described her suspicions. "Remember how Gable's wife said that he went camping? I'm going up to the Potholes to check for the van. Twenty minutes max."

"Bad idea. It's solid trees up there. Big mothers. What if you get trapped? If he's around, he's not getting out of the area. But chances are, if he saw the weather coming, he left a long time ago."

"What about Janice? I have to satisfy myself. Remember the school body shop and that missing paint."

"At least let me check to see if there's an update. Maybe the kid's home. Damn it, Holly, don't you realize—"

Holly clapped the phone shut. It was five o'clock. Some feeble light remained amid the dark torrents of water and raging sky. As she turned up the road, she passed Wink's restaurant and convenience store. Beyond was the soccer field, the safest place in town. Broad and open with an osprey nest at the top of one tall floodlight. There was one windy perch to wait out a storm, she thought with a grim laugh. Then the trees got larger. Some were three hundred years old, up to five feet at the base, nothing like the first-growth eight-foot-wide round at the Sooke Museum, but jaw-dropping all the same. Douglas firs were the tallest on the island. They could live for thirteen-hundred years and reach one hundred metres. With even greater lifespans, some cedars were twenty feet at the butt. Wonderful to behold, but an entire forest when they fell, bringing tons of debris. What had her father said when he had hired a service to cut the last two killer firs on their property? "I want to go to the trees, not see the trees come to my living room."

On one side of the road, the sagging hydro wires tossed like spaghetti. By now, either the power was off or every street should have an officer posted. At a corner near a trailer park, a loose tin roof on a shed clattered. Shingles from some hapless property fluttered across the road like a deck of cards. She felt Shogun's warm velvet muzzle creep over the side of the seat, nudge the belt aside, and rest on her shoulder, an oddly endearing and self-taught gesture.

She passed Charters Creek, then Todd Creek, with their legendary trestles upstream, prized by photographers. These tributaries were prime salmon territory, and the fish were finishing their runs. Water was flooding over the bridge boards, and one plank seemed dislodged. Maintenance had been minimal lately with budget cuts at the Capital Regional District, which managed the park. As she got out of the car to gauge the stability, she gagged at the smell of rotting salmon carcasses. Come back to spawn, the female laid her eggs and the male covered them with milt. The nest, or "redd", was hidden under gravel. Exhausted and mere shadows of their rainbow selves, the faded fish waited in the quiet shallows to die. From her peripheral vision, she spotted movement in the bush. A juvenile black bear was feasting on the remains, eating only the heads. Seeing her, it rose to its feet and chick-chick-chickered. Nearly soundless through the din, the bear's message was clear in its body language. Mine. Keep away. Shogun was pawing at the window, frantic to come to her "rescue".

She got back in, trying to shake the stink off her clothes. At least the road was deserted. Everyone was wise enough to hunker down in their homes, praying that the trees they should have cut wouldn't crush them.

At last she reached the main parking entrance, including a cement-block bathroom, an information kiosk, and a collection box for fees. The mountainous and rocky terrain belied the fact that in the Thirties and Forties the area had been a farm where turkey and prize-winning Jersey cattle had been raised. Deertrails, the home of the Weilers, had passed into the hands of a developer in the Eighties and had attracted interest from architects and investors worldwide. What a challenge to incorporate a massive stone lodge and recreational complex on top of this steep cliff. Wealthy tourists would have paid hundreds a night to stay here. Though built in her lifetime and a source of wonder every time she passed, this Camelot's builder had the vision of Arthur but not the resources, and a fire had ravaged the initial efforts. Its timbers burned, and only the rusted beams of its steel structure intact, two massive chimneys lifted into the air, fireplaces large enough to roast oxen. To the right, the river danced and broiled in steep cataracts. Stairways led to scenic views. To prevent vandalism and injuries, the place was fenced with chainlink. One pet owner had fallen to his death when his dog ventured too close.

The storm howled on, venting its rage down the narrowing canyon. It was verging on dark, the purpling shadows making inspection difficult. Madeleine had been walking farther up, where the Goose intersects before kilometre 49. Holly made her way through more deserted parking lots and reached the empty camping area. Down she drove through the hills, squinting against the pouring rain that blurred the windshield, despite the manic blades. More than once, she stopped to let the windows clear with the defroster. Shogun was fogging the cab with his breath. She imagined he was hungry, missing his lunch. Her stomach growled with companionable protest, and she felt lightheaded as she gripped the wheel. This was no time to think of food, yet the body needed fuel. She rummaged in her glove compartment for a stale granola bar. Shogun licked the shards, nabbing a raisin, which she'd heard were toxic to dogs. About to turn back, she thought she saw something far off, white against the muted green and browns of the landscape.

"Jesus. I wonder," she muttered to herself, feeling the sugar surge kick in. Was it a mirage? Were her eyes too tired to focus? One side of the road was eroding with flood water, and she drove at a banana slug's pace. Finally she stopped at a cement barrier, picked up a hefty Maglite, and opened the car door. A solid wall of water, SWOW as her father called it, poured in and soaked her from hat to boots. Shogun whined at her departure, and stuck his head over the headrest. She recalled that he hadn't been let out for a pee. Moving the seat forward, she said, "Get out. Quick one only. No fooling around."

Instantly he lifted his leg to decorate her tire. She walked a few paces toward the white object as her focus sharpened. The hat brim couldn't protect her from horizontal rain, and she wiped her eyes. Suddenly the dog's ruff hairs went up. Before she could grab him, he rushed forward. "Shogun, no!" She stumbled after him, falling and thumping her knee.

Nose to the ground like a bloodhound, the dog moved around bushes and charged toward the river, its torrents raging over the crash of the storm. Then she saw the dark green van emerge from the background like Arnold in *Predator*. Other than the white curtains, the van was perfectly camouflaged amid the trees.

Head dipped in the classic herding pose, shepherd's lantern tail flipping from side to side, Shogun began circling the van. Holly moved to the rear door. Pepper spray? In this holocaust, she might as well aim at herself. But overkill was dangerous. She flipped open her holster and drew her Taser, feeling its smooth power ease into her hand, a true equalizer, but not to be used lightly. She flashed her light at the paint. It looked fresh. There was always the chance this wasn't Gable, but the percentages were moving in her favour. A bumper sticker read "Free Tibet", along with a bright blue and yellow national flag. "Hello," she yelled, rapping at the rear door. "Police. Are you all right?" Whoever was in there, even Gable, must be frightened to death. But did he have a weapon? She could see nothing through the curtain, only a vague bluish light. As seconds ticked by and her heartbeat tripled, a fierce barking arose. Tiny paws scuffled on the back windows. Chucky?

Then the door flew open, flinging the Taser to god knows where. With a roar, Gable leaped out, hatchet in hand, a deadly caricature. He struck at her, but she parried with the Maglite and fell back, bruising her hip on a picnic bench. When the Yorkie rushed out like a rabid squirrel, Shogun gave a mortal howl that began with a roo and proceeded to a guttural barking that matched his name. Chucky laid back his ears and squealed under attack as they whirled circles around each other. In the melee, Gable moved toward her, menacing the hatchet. His face, rough with days of beard, looked pale green in the light. "Bitch," he growled. "Why didn't you just leave me alone? I didn't do anything. I didn't."

Staggering to her feet, her hip and knee throbbing, Holly fingered open her holster and pointed the gun at Gable. "Stop, Paul. Everything's over. I don't want anyone hurt." When he swung the axe toward her, she gave a warning shot in the air. "Don't make me do this."

Moving his hand to the edge of the axe head, Gable took off on a path toward the river, Chucky at his heels, a dust mop with fangs. The man wore a leaf-coloured camo outfit but only socks, as his hesitant steps and the occasional yelp proved. He wouldn't get far dressed like that, Holly reasoned, so she stopped to think out the situation that the storm had complicated. She needed to call for backup, but cell phones didn't work in these hills. She had no choice but to capture and handcuff him, then get out while they could. Or wasn't that an option any more? In his state of mind, he had nothing to lose. She didn't even have the police car to contain him.

She gripped Shogun by his collar. Then a whimper made her turn to the van. In the cramped space, Janice Mercer shivered, her pudding face wide with terror. She wore no glasses, and her skin was sallow, her hair greasy hanks. Holly reached in and tossed her a blanket from the floor. "Stay here! I'll be back," she called, shutting the door. On second thought, how could the girl go anywhere?

Time was a whisper before the accompanying terrors of complete darkness where the worst would be imagined. The wind howled, and trees creaked in all directions like an arthritic symphony. One by one as the gusts attacked, their heavy branches surrendered and fell to the sodden ground. Where would Gable go? It was hours back to town, and he was on foot. With luck, he could travel a few kilometres to the houses on Sooke River Road, menace the inhabitants, even steal a car. Was the road east to Victoria closed by now? Then she froze, her "what if" reasoning kicking in. Suppose he doubled back and grabbed the Prelude? She'd left the keys inside.

Holly followed Shogun, who had found a job and was on the trail of the two, his ears pricked, flicking from time to time in the rain. Though he wasn't by nature a tracking dog and was often fooled by the twists and turns of the circuitous paths, he kept ahead of Holly. Her hair was plastered to her head, and her clothes soaked, but she was boiling from exertion. Salty sweat seeping into her eyes made them sting. She searched the area for signs of Gable, losing sight of Shogun in the distance. Ahead she could see the towers of Camelot. They were back at the ruins, beside the cliff at its steepest, most dangerous point.

Then she heard a dogfight, as feral and primitive as in prehistoric times when all canines were wolves. Shogun was a friend to all the world, but this ankle biter he didn't care for. It had attacked his mistress. Suppose Gable hit him with the axe, a natural reaction when he was running for his life? She struggled on and at last came to the fenced edge of the site, her breath coming in short puffs, her lungs aching. She wiped rain from her face and followed the sounds to her absolute horror. On one precarious ledge beyond a gap in two posts, nearly inaccessible to humans, Chucky and Shogun were battling it out, spitting and raging at each other, their fangs white and sharp. Gable was hauling huge gulps of air. His shoulders drooped as he turned an odd stare at her, dead inside but one small spark ignited by his devotion to the animal. "Call off your dog! That's not a fair fight."

"You've got to be kidding." Her heart raced to see Shogun scrabbling for purchase on the edge, a volley of small stones scattering over the cliff. With space at a premium, the tiny terrier had a size advantage. "Shogun, here!" Gesturing with her left hand, she clutched her gun and kept it aimed as she balanced at the precipice. Gable might be playing for a break or revealing a weak underbelly as he watched his dog's perilous last stand. Mesmerized by the spectacle, she shook herself back to reality. People, not dogs must be the priority. They were close enough that she could hit him in an arm or leg. Still, they were hours from medical help. He might die from blood loss. The possibilities made her sick with indecision. He was a monster. Guilty of kidnapping, possible molestation, not to forget attempted murder in Billy's case and, she was sure, the death of Angie. The list went on, folding back into itself. This was not a deal-making television show. Why hadn't she figured it out before? Too hesitant to stand up to Whitehouse? Thank god Ann had made the breakthrough. And Chipper, too, finding out about the van. They were a team, but would they ever work together again?

Miraculously skirting Gable with the delicate taps of a ballerina as he made his nimble way along the cliff, Shogun returned to her. Tail up in aggression, he kept glancing around at Gable and that "stick" in his hand as if wondering if he should forgive all sins if the man tossed his favourite toy. Groaning in despair, Gable put down the axe, crouched onto the ledge and began inching toward Chucky. The dog was shivering, his tiny body tensed in the cold. Drenched, he looked no more than a pound of Big Mac makings. His marble eyes rolled in his head, and his tiny black nostrils ran with foam. "Good boy. Come to Daddy." Gable seemed poised for a desperate lunge.

The scene mimicked an absurdist play. Spume lashed the air as a log jam burst free and tumbled down the waterfall. Holly cupped her free hand and yelled over the noise. "Paul. Leave him. You're going to..."

Then the wee dog seemed to blow over into the torrent and Gable lurched forward in a last effort to grab him. His legs twisted, and he fell. Rushing to the edge, she watched his body bump and bang like a rag doll on its way down to the flooded river. The way he landed on his back on a giant tooth of rock, she knew he was dead. Salvation or suicide? But where was Chucky? Only a dog lover would ask.

After shaking himself from head to tail, Shogun whined and led her downhill and downstream several hundred feet, where at a bend and an eddy, the tiny dog had pulled itself free of the water and crawled onto the gravel shore. Shogun ran forward and nosed him as if they'd formed an instant entente cordiale. His spirit fled with his master, Chucky allowed himself to be lifted and carried. Tucking him into her jacket, Holly gave one last look towards the river and saw Gable's body bobbing in the wild currents, face down as it headed for the ocean...or toward whatever tree snags would entangle it. Despite the miraculous back-to-life scenarios of horror films, he would not drag himself from the water for a final round. She walked the hundred feet to the road, where progress back to the car would be faster. The heat of battle over, she began to shake with the chill.

Light was gone except for what ambience and odd reflection

remained. Without the flashlight, she'd be as helpless as a blind mole. A crash stopped her in her tracks. With a torturous groan of apology, a huge Sitka spruce fell across the road, pulling a massive cedar in its wake and leaving a rootball over twelve feet high. The pavement crumbled away under the load. Holly swore to herself. No going back to town now. With the dark and deep nature of the area, a thousand such accidents waiting to happen, that was probably the most dangerous choice.

She didn't like the location of the van, hidden under too many trees. She would fetch Janice and move the car into a more barren spot.

When she reached the old VW, Janice was cowering in the back, wrapped in the blanket. Holly crawled in with the dogs, now licking each other, with a common sense of reality and alliances far wiser than man's. Twin silver rods of a feeble electric lantern provided the only light. The van's batteries had probably drained long ago. "How are you doing, Janice?" she asked.

"Is he gone? Is he really gone?" the girl said. She pulled Chucky to her and stroked his tiny head as he nuzzled her face.

"He's not coming back. The river has him."

Janice broke into sobs, tears streaking her filthy cheeks. Holly reached forward to pat her shoulder. She wore a dirty sweater, ripped jeans, and pink plastic clogs. Holly gave the girl time to regain her fragile composure.

The van had a small bed that held barely two, a mini-fridge and stove. The rest of the space was taken up by boxes of canned goods and dried foods as well as a five-gallon container of water. The smell of damp wool and unwashed bodies filled the air.

"Did you go with him freely, Janice? Or did he make you?" Holly asked.

The girl nodded as another crash and thump outside reminded Holly of the danger of staying dry and warm in the vehicle. The van bounced as some great fir fist pounded the ground. The girl's answer had been frustratingly ambiguous, but now was not the time for an improvised interview. "Don't worry. You can tell me about it later. I know it wasn't your fault. We have to move now, get to a safer place." She had no idea if she could start the van, whether it had gas, or how it handled. The car was better.

Janice's lower lip twitched, and she shrank back against the wall, squeezing her eyes shut. "No, I'm staying. Why do we have to leave? I don't want to get wet and cold again."

Holly gripped her by the arms, tight enough to mean business. "Wet and cold's better than dead. Do you want to be crushed by a ten-ton tree? Now get out!"

A strange procession carrying blankets and sleeping bags and bottles of water hunched its way through the blackness to Holly's car. She folded down the seat so that the girl and dogs could stretch into the trunk. "It's crowded but the best we can do."

Shogun gave a low growl as he settled. Janice mewled in alarm. "Is he going to bite me?"

"Just border collie mumbles. Means nothing except that he thinks he's a superior species. You're in more danger from Chucky. Settle down. We have to find another parking spot."

Janice finally spoke with some intelligence. "There's a shelter over by the Goose. Paul, I mean Mr. Gable and I, stayed there one night."

Holly had seen that plywood shack with open windows, constructed for major rain storms. Not for this hell. "Too many trees around it." She tossed the belongings into the front seat. They could arrange everything later. If they had a later.

She started up the car, hit the brights, only to have the light reflect back. Dimming to the regular setting, she moved slowly north through the campground. If she remembered correctly from her hikes on the final part of the Goose, farther up was a gravel pit, a flat and open space. Suddenly she braked. Another tree blocked the way. "What's the matter?" Janice asked with a whine.

"A tree. I'm getting out to look."

"Don't leave! I'm scared."

"I'll be right outside." She returned to the rain and flashed her light around. A tangle of fallen red alders blocked her path, more nuisance than size. If she moved that picnic table three feet, she could drive around the barrier. She tried but couldn't lift it. The top was made of a pebbled, cement-like material.

"Janice, get out and help." She opened the door and shone her light on the girl.

"No, I can't."

"Yes, you can. I need your muscles."

No doubt pleased that she was required for the first time to do anything but intellectual work, Janice humped out and added her bulk to the chore. "We did it," she said with pride in her voice, smacking her hands together.

Back in gear, Holly finally reached the gravel pit minutes later. Used by the park for minor road repairs, it had enough clearance in all directions except for a couple of young and sinewy arbutus trees.

Holly pulled over and turned off the engine. "We're staying here. Last chance to have a pee."

"I think I'm getting my period. Cramps."

Woman's worst nightmare. "Do you have...all you need?"

"No, I thought we were leaving in a few days when everything quieted down. He said we'd stop at a store before going up north."

Holly searched her memory. "I have some tampons in the glove compartment. Let me know if you want one."

A plaintive voice answered, "I'm not allowed to use those. My mom said."

Holly stretched out her legs and shifted the steering wheel up an inch. "You may change your mind, and by the way, welcome to the twentieth century."

Tucking the flashlight under her seat, Holly found the CD that Larry Gall had given her. Despite the minimal drain on the battery, perhaps a bit of music would help. "I'm playing some music, Janice. It'll take our minds off the storm."

She slipped in the disk and lay back. The first six songs were in a foreign language. She recognized French and perhaps Portuguese, so like Spanish. One tune captivated her so much that she pulled out the light and read the liner notes. Tamara Obrovac, a Croatian, was singing "Touch the Moon". Her words linked the present with the past. "I watch the world/ Falling backwards.../The two of us like feathers/ Placed on the church tower in the night." How helpless she felt, but how soothing the sky could be. It was still up there somewhere, beyond the tempest. She remembered how her mother had pointed out the constellations when they lay on the deck one warm summer night, a barred owl's glowing eyes watching from the woods. "That's the Great Bear," she would say. "He turns a somersault as the year ages."

Like beasts in a cave, they waited out the fearsome hours. When the winds began dying like a fire-breathing dragon out of fuel, Holly tuned in ragged sound bites from 105.3 in Victoria, which aired local news programs. The region was under siege. As she sipped from a water bottle and debated the pros and cons of getting out for a pee, she realized that she had no idea where her father was.

Fifteen

Dawn couldn't come quickly enough for Holly, who dozed fitfully in her semi-reclined seat. Both dogs snored all night, and Janice cried softly from time to time, thrashing in the back. At the first glimmer of light, 5:47 according to the car clock, Holly got out to stretch her aching muscles. The wind was down, and so was everything else. She reached back for her water bottle and drank deeply, letting out Chucky and Shogun to decorate the bushes. Fast friends now, not a bark or nip, they didn't even wake the dreaming Janice.

Holly dropped trou at a blessed leisure, watching her boots carefully from sad experience, then she roused Janice. "We'll drive back as far as we can, then walk to town. My cell should kick back in once we're out of these hills."

Janice looked almost happy as she rummaged in her backpack for a brush to attack her tangled hair. She was talkative, a good sign. If she drew inside herself, she might never recover from the trauma. "How long do you have to go to school to be in the RCMP?" she asked as they started out, a motley company. Holly had to give her credit. Though short on personality, the girl didn't deserve what had happened to her. She outlined the basic training program, adding, "Many recruits start their careers at twenty-five, so you could go to university first. You might change your mind."

Her unplucked brows furrowing, Janice considered this

advice. "That's true. I was going to major in history, but now I want to help people. Maybe studying psychology?"

Holly sided with her father about the social sciences, but smiled in non-committal fashion. "It's a start."

By eight, leaving the car behind the huge Sitka spruce and scrambling over its bulk, they had reached the main parking area and sat down to rest. Janice availed herself of the bathroom. The sun was out, blessing yesterday's ruins. Then they heard a chug. Weaving between obstacles, Chipper was driving down the littered road on a monster quad. He hailed them with a vigorous wave. "Ann sent me. She was worried and figured you got stuck out here. How do you like this toy?" he asked. "It's the only way to get around with the trees down." With a cocky smile, he gunned the engine to enjoy the noise.

Chipper explained that Sooke had been cut off from Victoria until an hour ago. "That road's finally open in one lane, but nobody's going west. Telus has helicoptered a satellite feed for the phones in Port Renfrew. It could be weeks before they're connected." He gave the girl an inquiring look. "Isn't this—"

"Not the time." She gave her head a warning shake. "Janice, you remember Constable Singh, don't you?"

Holly sat on the long padded seat behind Chipper and Janice perched on the carrier frame with Chucky in her backpack. As they putted down the road with Shogun at the pace of a steady ox, the devastation of the storm revealed itself with a vengeance. Power wires were down everywhere. "Look out!" she called to Chipper, who drove merrily over them.

"Everything's off, guaranteed. 250,000 homes and businesses are out of juice on this end of the island. And Stanley Park's a nightmare." The legendary oceanside paradise with its fabled walkways was one of Vancouver's feature attractions. Apparently the storm had raged along the south coast, crossed the Georgia Strait, and slammed into the Pacific Northwest.

"Where to, boss? What's the plan?"

"God knows somebody better have one." She laughed and squeezed his shoulder. "Janice needs to get home first. That's a priority."

"Where do you live?" she asked the girl.

"Dover Street."

"Perfect. It's on the way."

There wasn't a hundred feet of road without a tree across the lines. Sometimes it had snapped the pole. Other times it bounced like a trampoline. Mechanical snarls met their ears in a chorus. Everywhere they looked, men and women in gumboots were out with chainsaws and pickups, clearing the road. An army of volunteers. Many had worked in the timber industry. Others wanted the wood. The most desperate hoped to reach their homes.

Janice's house was a white bungalow with a scenic pond and rock terraces. In front of the house, a compact car had been crushed by a fir. A tall man with a chainsaw had just finished lopping both ends off, leaving the vehicle with a six-foot log bonnet. Insurance documentation. The man wiped his brow and turned. "Janice! Sweetheart!" he called, and a smile lit his face. "Where have you been all this time? I thought we might not ever..." His voice trailed off as he struggled for control.

Janice leaped off the quad and ran to his arms. Chucky followed, yapping at the interloper taking her affections. The girl picked up the animal and hugged him until his tongue stuck out. "Is it okay if I keep him, Daddy? He was my friend...the whole time."

"Sure, honey. If it's all right with your mom. Get right inside now. She's sick with worry." Wiping a tear from his cheek, he considered the dog's ample endowment. "Those will have to go. It'll make him less...excitable."

When the girl had gone inside to clean up, Holly gave Jack Mercer a quick and clean update on Janice's situation, and explained that Janice would be required to come to the Sooke station for a statement. Since Gable was dead, the girl would be spared a trial. "No hurry on the interview. Priorities will go to this disaster. It's going to take days to restore even minimal operations."

"You got that right. I don't have a car any more." He waved his hand at the stricken Honda. "But I'm just so damn glad to get her back. You don't suppose she..." A worried look crossed his kindly face.

"Honestly, I don't know. I couldn't ask her to think about that in the storm. The police will put you in touch with a good counsellor."

Holly remembered that neither she nor her father had wheels any more. The Prelude was unharmed, but who knew how long it would take to clear the park roads? That was a low priority for now. Food, water and shelter were paramount. And she could use a long shower. Then as she hopped back on the quad behind Chipper, her cell phone rang.

"I finally reached you. The phone kept saying that you were out of the area. The land lines were down to Fossil Bay and the Sooke detachment."

"I'm merely starving. Where are you? I hope you didn't try to get back in the storm."

"I stayed last night in a great little hotel near Beacon Hill Park. Emily Carr died there."

"That's some recommendation. But you did pick the right time to leave Dodge."

A pause, as if he were reluctant to ask more. "And Shogun, is he—"

She condensed their adventure. "So he is a hero of sorts. Small but mighty."

After taking his hotel number, she accompanied Chipper to the Sooke detachment on Church St. Cruisers were coming and going in a warren of activity. The hum of monster generators kept the lights and computers operative. Using polypropylene rope from the quad's kit, she tied Shogun to a tree on a grassy stretch in a far corner of the parking area. A passing officer offered him several chunks of jerky, which the dog wolfed. In the aftermath of the storm, the sun had never shone as brightly. Temperatures were heading for twelve Celsius, a "ding spray" as her father would say. Then she went inside to write a preliminary report to the Staff Sergeant on Gable's fall and Janice's rescue. Given a desk, pen and papers, she gathered her thoughts about the details, despite a growling stomach begging for something to digest.

A few hours later she joined Chipper, who offered her a bag of popcorn and a soda. "I'd treat you to lunch, but there's nowhere to eat. Power won't be on until the afternoon. I got this at the gas station. Only place with hot coffee is the Otter Point Bakery. They use propane as backup for their ovens. You should see the lineup."

Holly was so hungry, she would have munched dried seaweed. She'd been ordered home for the evening, and Chipper was on rotation. Until the worst was sorted out, all out-of-town staff was billeted at the only motel, the Manuel Quimper, named for the Spanish explorer. "Tri-City's going to get my car when the park road re-opens."

Chipper finished his soda and three-pointed it into a waste can. "I know you couldn't talk in front of the girl, but isn't my bribe working? What the hell happened back there at the Potholes?"

She gave him more details. "And Angie?" he asked.

"Whatever occurred between Gable and Angie is pure speculation. Her body had very few marks. But think about this. If he'd followed her, and there had been an accident, a rogue wave perhaps, why the cover-up? I'm thinking he laid his hands on her. Perhaps he saw her with Billy." They heard a cheer erupt inside and learned that West Coast Road had been temporarily opened to one lane. Holly was given a ride to Fossil Bay by Barb Cottingham, a Sooke corporal en route to check out looting at the Kemp Lake Store. Shogun had the backseat to himself.

Things looked normal most of the way through town until they reached a turn just past Whiffen Spit Road. Within a span of a hundred feet, five huge trees had fallen. One still hung in the wires, which made her nervous. A B.C. Hydro boom truck was at work, while a single lane of traffic took turns passing under the hanging wires. Then the flagman moved them on. Another five kilometres without major damage, then they came to a place straight out of a green hell. To the left was the ocean, down a steep hill that had contained several properties. Most couldn't be seen at all. They had been covered by giants.

"Some weird microburst," Barb said. "It bounced along the coast, dipping and diving, then hit here like a tornado."

"A typhoon *and* a tornado. Add a tsumani and we'd have had a hat trick," Holly said, picking up the *Times Colonist* on the seat. It had a front-page spread on the storm's wake.

"One For The History Books," the headline read. Freda's 1962 record had not only been broken but shattered. Her top speed of 143 kmph measured off Victoria was blasted by the 157 kmph recorded at Race Rocks, a lighthouse in the middle of the Juan de Fuca. The old storm's 750 million in damage (five billion in today's dollars) was sure to be surpassed.

"No one killed here, though," Holly said. "Unreal."

"Four people died in Washington State. One woman drowned when her basement flooded. Guess we got off easy." They eased past the turn for the store. "I'll take you to the detachment first, then come back."

Holly sat in astonishment as the miles increased. Just before the turn to Otter Point Road, they pulled over at another place of such monumental devastation that her jaw dropped. Betty Tully's pristine Seaward estate looked like an atom bomb had fallen. Her house had escaped damage, but the three other buildings on the property lay under tons of debris from the fall of massive Sitka spruces well-established at the time of Confederation. Betty, a retired professor with a mane of classy white hair, walked up in the traditional red coat which she wore on her daily constitutionals.

"Thanks for stopping," she told the women. "Everyone's been so kind. Food has been coming in by the carload, and I have several offers of places to stay until this gets cleaned up."

"It seems ridiculous to ask if you're all right," Holly said.

Betty's head was high, and though her eyes were tired, her cheeks were dry of tears.

"You have to stop crying sometime," she said. "It was a tough way to make the front page of the *Globe.*"

Carrying a chainsaw with a twenty-inch blade, a workman in worn overalls came over. "That spruce that took your beach house, we're bucking it up now, and the wood will build you another one."

Betty pointed towards the ocean, calming at last after the storm. "Seaward will rise again."

Barb and Holly pulled back into traffic. "The spirit of Sooke. Pioneer traditions live on."

When they reached the detachment, Holly was glad to see the Impala and Suburban safe to the side. Errant shingles had blown off the roof, and a blue tarp had been outfitted for the moment. Roofers would be busy for months, booking trips to Hawaii on their profits.

Inside, Ann was dozing, head down on the desk. She looked up as the door closed. "Did you get any sleep?" Holly asked.

"About as much as usual." She yawned then did a double take at Shogun. "Handsome man."

Holly brought her up to speed. Ann's face couldn't hide her approval at Paul Gable's fate. "Good news arrived just after you left," she said. "Billy regained consciousness and identified Gable as the man who hired him for that phony fishing trip. Came up behind him in the boathouse and strangled him to make it look like he'd committed suicide after Angie's death."

"And he's going to recover?"

"All systems go. He's lucky that his friend found him."

"Barb Cottingham's out front. She'll take you home. I'll catch a few winks on the couch, take a shower, and stay here tonight. It'll be no fun at home with the power off."

Ann grinned. "Mrs. Nordman came through. There's a pie, fresh rolls, their own goat cheese, and...half a bottle of blackberry wine. Enjoy."

Epilogue

In the glowing twilight, Holly and her father gazed from their dining table across the strait to where skitters of snow dusted the high peaks of the Olympic Mountains. Their quiet street concealed the fact that they'd been out of power for five days. No damage was apparent, but only a few hundred feet at the turnaround, a huge tree had sliced the lines. The logs had been reduced to four-foot lengths. Every day after, pieces had been cut into rounds to fill a pickup. Now only a pile of sawdust remained, and neighbours had refilled their wood bins.

"What's for dinner?" she asked, dodging the lantern which hung from the chandelier. Another glowed on the counter. Beeswax candles would take them to bed hours earlier than usual. Without the water or septic pumps, they were also without flush toilets or baths. But the inconvenience of finding a place which took dogs was more formidable.

"Emergency rations, but still consistent for my Fifties theme. Instant mashies, package of gravy, cans of turkey and green beans. Cheap and cheerful." The bruise on his chin was turning yellow-green, and his lip sported a scab, no stitches required. It gave him "character", he said.

"At least it's hot," she said, readying the paper plates while he stirred pots on the two-burner camp stove. "What I hate is that it gets dark so soon. And powdered milk in my coffee. Yuck." On her forehead she wore a headlamp Norman had brought from the Victoria Mountain Equipment Co-op. It was more convenient than carrying a flashlight.

"Imagine how your ancestors lived. This is pure luxury." Her father left to toss another chunk of wood into the stove, then returned to pour them both a glass of his latest vintage. "And I have Joan Crawford lined up on the portable DVD player. *The Damned Don't Cry.*"

"Perfect title." Every Christmas she gave him another collection from the Golden Age.

"And one good thing's for sure," he said, rubbing Shogun's silky head.

"What's that?" Her father was becoming an optimist?

"Firewood is going to be very very cheap. For the next *ten* years. I'll need the savings to pay off the car." In the drive sat a new Smart For Two.

She laughed. "Leave it to you to find the financial silver lining."

Phone lines had been restored. He dialed B.C. Hydro again and keyed in their number at the prompt, listening carefully and wiggling a hopeful eyebrow. "Any time now." The taped message carried a "Power will be restored in your area in..." It had started as a week. "Hours, they say," he assured her.

"Calling every ten minutes isn't going to help." Norman was borderline obsessive-compulsive, but the classroom and kitchen profited by his character trait.

"So is your case cleared up? Everything dotted and crossed?"

Paul Gable's body had washed up two days after the storm on Weir's Beach in Metchosin. The few full-timers left in the RV park had found a grim surprise as they strolled the seaweed-strewn sands one morning. A doctor's exam had revealed that Janice was still a virgin, but authorities might never know exactly what had happened that night in the campgrounds. Gable had seen Janice walking and offered her a ride on the day he'd decided to flee. She had been the only one who had shown sympathy for him, and they had formed a *folie de deux,* the psychologist said, which biased the girl's memory. Gable told her that he had witnessed Angie having sex with a boy and confronted her later at the beach, only to have her fall during a struggle. Pulled off the uneven rock shelves by a wave in the dark, she'd been lost to all rescue attempts. Holly didn't believe it for a minute, nor did Janice's calling Angie a "bitch" and a "slut" testify to her objectivity. Gable had probably assaulted Angie himself, frustrated by her rebuff. Whatever the case, he'd tried to distract the investigators by staging Billy's suicide. That spoke volumes.

Her father rubbed his sore chin. "Sometimes life is like that, full of unanswered questions. Do you think that we'll ever find out what happened to your mother? The raven pendant. Is it a beginning or an end?"

Holly didn't know how to answer. Some cold cases stayed cold. Others were solved even decades later under the most amazing of circumstances, especially with modern forensics. One man had been convicted on DNA from dog coats collected by officers posing as groomers offering a free pet wash to anyone on the street. The long-lost remains of American's most famous atheist and her son had been found. Could Jimmy Hoffa be far behind? She gifted her father with the present which always brightened his day, an ice cream sundae of a hug topped by her warmest smile. "Your personal sheriff's back in town."

Shogun stretched and yawned. Then the lights flickered on.

Acknowledgements:

Thanks are due to the Sooke and West Shore RCMP detachments on Vancouver Island, especially Barb Cottingham. And to Jackie and Bryan Meads, our neighbours on Otter Point Place, who helped us weather the century storm with such generosity and kindness. Much appreciation goes to Antje Wagenbach, whose curiosity makes her an excellent copy editor.

Photo by Jan Warren

Lou Allin was born in Toronto but raised in Ohio when her father followed the film business to Cleveland.

Armed with a Ph.D. in English Renaissance literature, Lou headed north, ending up at Cambrian College in Sudbury, Ontario, where she taught writing and public speaking for twenty-eight years.

Her first Belle Palmer mystery, *Northern Winters Are Murder,* was published in 2000, followed by *Blackflies are Murder, Bush Poodles Are Murder, Murder Eh?* and *Memories Are Murder. Blackflies Are Murder* was shortlisted for an Arthur Ellis Award in the category of Best Novel.

Lou has moved from the bush to the beach: the village of Sooke on Vancouver Island, the inspiration for the Holly Martin mysteries.

Lou welcomes mail and can be reached at louallin@shaw.ca. Her website is www.louallin.com